A Change Is Gonna Come

A Change Is Gonna Come

Jacquelin Thomas

BET Publications, LLC
http://www.bet.com

NEW SPIRIT BOOKS are published by

BET Publications, LLC
c/o BET BOOKS
One BET Plaza
1900 W Place NE
Washington, DC 20018-1211

Copyright © 2003 by Jacquelin Thomas

All Kensington Titles, Imprints, and Distributed Lines are available at special quantity discounts for bulk purchases for sales promotions, premiums, fund-raising, and educational or institutional use. Special book excerpts or customized printings can also be created to fit specific needs. For details, write or phone the office of the Kensington special sales manager: Kensington Publishing Corp., 850 Third Avenue, New York, NY 10022, attn: Special Sales Department, Phone: 1-800-221-2647.

BET Books is a trademark of Black Entertainment Television, Inc. NEW SPIRIT and the NEW SPIRIT logo are trademarks of BET Books and the BET BOOKS logo is a registered trademark.

ISBN 1-58314-255-X

First Printing: April 2003
10 9 8 7 6 5 4 3 2 1

Printed in the United States of America

SERENITY PRAYER

God, grant me the serenity
To accept the things I cannot change,
Courage to change the things I can,
And wisdom to know the difference.

Living one day at a time;
Enjoying one moment at a time;
Accepting hardships as the pathway to peace;
Taking, as He did, this sinful world
As it is, not as I would have it.

Trusting that He will make all things right
If I surrender to His will
That I may be reasonably happy in this life
And supremely happy with Him
Forever in the next.

Amen

—Reinhold Niebuhr

1
____

"Thank you, most heavenly Father, for this day . . ." Cordelia whispered in prayer.

When she finished praying, she opened her Bible and read for thirty minutes, as was her custom each day. This morning her studies took her to Psalm Seventy-three.

Cordelia took a few minutes more to meditate on the scriptures. In them Asaph expressed the pain and impatience one could feel when life seemed unfair. He had given significant insight on living triumphantly while being forced to wait on God.

"Thank you, Jesus," Cordelia murmured as she rose to her feet. The clock struck seven. She put away her Bible and strolled over to the huge walk-in closet in her bedroom. Her clothes had been selected the night before, so all Cordelia had to do was shower and slip into them.

To her surprise her daughter was already up and dressed by the time Cordelia came downstairs. She paused in the doorway for a moment to gaze at her, trying to gauge the mood of the teenager. Lately Devon had become more temperamental than usual and was prone to cry at the drop of a hat. She couldn't re-

giving an effect of unconcern or indifference

member her ever being so emotional. It didn't take much to set Devon off these days. "Good morning," she greeted as she walked past her daughter.

"Morning," the teen muttered nonchalantly, without looking up from the magazine she was reading.

Cordelia retrieved a coffee mug out of the cabinet overhead. Her eyes traveled over to Devon, studying her daughter's outfit. As much as she wanted to avoid an argument, she couldn't keep quiet. "What have you got on, child? That shirt doesn't even cover your stomach." Noticing the slight bulge of her daughter's belly, she acknowledged that Devon had been gaining weight lately.

Before she could comment, Devon replied, "All the girls dress like this. They don't say anything at school as long as you wear something over it." Holding up another shirt, she added, "I'm gonna wear this over it anyway."

Cordelia wasn't satisfied. "Can't you find another shirt to wear over those jeans, Devon? I know this is the first day of spring but it's still a little chilly outside." She couldn't understand why her daughter was always trying to show off her body. Although she wasn't trying to be hurtful, Cordelia added, "You're going to have to do some exercising instead of all that sleeping. You've put on a lot of weight." Her daughter's weight gain had been gradual but . . . She took a deep breath and spoke the words she dreaded saying. "Are you pregnant, Devon?"

Her daughter looked at her as if she'd grown another head. "Why would you ask me something like that? I don't think I put on that much weight."

The thought had been nagging at her for weeks now but she'd been afraid to ask. Cordelia prayed she was wrong. "You didn't answer my question."

"You have to be doing something to get pregnant, Mama." Devon slipped on the oversize purple shirt she'd been holding a few moments earlier. "Is this better?"

There was something in Devon's response, but Cordelia decided against pursuing it. If her daughter was pregnant, Cordelia would know it. But she couldn't dismiss those two nights her daughter had sneaked out of the house. Devon repeatedly denied that she'd had sex with Tonio. She said that she and Tonio had not been alone. That there had been a group of them—friends just hanging out. Maybe seeing all those pregnant teens at the office and at the church was making Cordelia paranoid.

Devon cut into her thoughts. "I made coffee. Want some?"

"I'll take a cup." Cordelia eyed her oftentimes-willful daughter with pride. Devon had grown up to be a very beautiful young lady, tall like her father but curvaceous like the women on Cordelia's side of the family. She frowned when Gerald came to mind. Although they had been divorced two years, Cordelia and her ex-husband could hardly be civil to each other. After all the things he'd done to her in the past, Gerald didn't deserve a single thought from her, as far as she was concerned.

Cordelia accepted the steaming cup of coffee from Devon. "Thanks, honey."

She took a sip. "Mmm . . . this is good. You should make the coffee every morning."

Devon laughed. "I don't think so. . . ." She finished off her toast.

Placing her mug down on the counter, Cordelia asked, "Have you talked to your father lately?" She wanted to kick herself for asking about Gerald, but she couldn't get him out of her mind. The last thing she wanted was to give Devon the slightest impression that she was interested.

Shaking her head no, Devon answered, "Not for a while. He's been traveling a lot lately. He's thinking about moving to Florida with Uncle Mike."

"Really?" Cordelia was astonished. It never occurred to her that Gerald would ever consider leaving North Carolina. He loved it here as much as she did. At least he used to, she to seek laboriously for information

amended. Cordelia decided it was best not to delve any deeper to find out why it bothered her so much. He lived in Raleigh now and barely ever came to Bridgeport unless it was to pick up Devon.

Downing the last of her orange juice, Devon stated, "I've got to get out of here. Kate's riding with me to school this morning. I'll see you later."

"Have a blessed day, sweetie," Cordelia called out.

"Same to you, Mama." She ran out the back door into the garage. Gerald had gone against her wishes and purchased a car for Devon, but thank God she had acted responsibly thus far with it.

Devon didn't kiss her good-bye anymore, Cordelia noticed. It bothered her some but she pushed it out of her mind. She was grateful that they had been able to get through the morning without an argument.

Smiling, Cordelia buttered a piece of toast. Beyond her kitchen window, flowers painted in hues of red, pink, purple, and yellow surrounding lush green trees were given a healthy glow by the early-morning sunshine.

"Thank you, Lord, for such a beautiful day," she whispered. To her, each day was a precious gift and a work of art. It was a shame that more people didn't take a few minutes each day just to admire God's handiwork. Each day was different—no two would ever be the same.

It was a blissful March morning in Bridgeport, North Carolina. The city boasted more than a hundred late-eighteenth- and early-nineteenth-century structures set along streets that still retained pre-Revolutionary names.

The Fourth of July barbecue, antique car shows, and the weekly arts and crafts festivals were just a few of the events held in the small town. A lover of historical homes, Cordelia had immediately fallen in love with the picturesque city when she attended Bridgeport University.

She had to admit that had it not been for her being so head

over heels in love with Gerald Berkeley, Cordelia wouldn't have even considered leaving Saint Simons Island, Georgia, and applying to Bridgeport. He'd gotten a football scholarship and she couldn't stand being separated from him.

They had been so in love . . . or so she had thought. Gerald was anything but the perfect husband. In fact, he always had memory lapses when it came to marriage. After their divorce, Cordelia had come to the painful conclusion that Gerald had married her because she'd been pregnant with Devon. The one thing she couldn't take from Gerald was that he was essentially a good father, although she felt he spoiled Devon unmercifully.

Cordelia felt the hair on the back of her neck stand up and she shivered slightly. She couldn't escape the deep sense of foreboding haunting her.

Despite the way it started, her day changed drastically for the worse. Cordelia hadn't been in the St. Paul County Human Services building more than ten minutes before one of her clients stomped into her office.

"Miss Berkeley, I need to talk to you," she demanded loudly. "My check got cut off and I want to know why." The woman wore her attitude like a piece of jewelry.

Cordelia could feel the building of yet another tension headache and tried to massage it away by rubbing the side of her temple in a circular motion with her index and middle fingers. She was normally a patient person, but this one particular client had a way of working her nerves.

Cordelia waited for the woman to stop ranting and jerking her head from side to side before she responded in a calm voice, "Miss Winston, you were terminated because you did not come in for your scheduled appointment. I sent you a letter three weeks ago."

Rolling her eyes, she mumbled, "I didn't get no letter."

The lie was a weak one, but Cordelia wasn't in the mood to

challenge the client. Instead she pulled a case file from a nearby drawer. She removed a piece of paper and handed it to Shanika Winston. Meeting the young woman's hostile gaze, she stated, "This is a copy of the letter I sent you. Are you still living at this address?"

"Yeah," Shanika mumbled after a moment.

Noting the rapid movement of her client's eyes, Cordelia had a strong feeling that Shanika had indeed seen the recertification letter. "You never received this letter from me?"

"I didn't get no letter," she repeated. Her tone abruptly changed from belligerence to pleading. "I need my check and my food stamps, Miss Berkeley. I don't have no other help, and my children need food and clothes. I can't afford to lose my check."

Cordelia wished the throbbing behind her eyes would stop. She couldn't remember her head ever hurting this bad. Forcing her attention back to her client, she said, "I understand that, Miss Winston. That's why it's important for you to keep your appointments."

"I told you already that I didn't get no letter about an appointment."

Shanika's attitude was back. She sat there glaring at Cordelia while playing with the straps of her Coach handbag.

"First of all, you need to keep your voice down. Screaming at me won't get you anywhere."

The woman sat there sulking, her arms folded across her heaving bosom and her FUBU-clad legs crossed.

Cordelia straightened in her chair, scanning Shanika from head to toe. Her hair was cut and styled to perfection; gold rings adorned her fingers, while her long nails gleamed with fire engine–red polish. She was not about to give Shanika the impression that she had the upper hand. "And another thing, Miss Winston. Don't walk into my office again demanding anything. This is not how we do business. I work strictly by appointment unless it's my day to be on duty; then I take walkins. If you do this again, I'll have security escort you out."

Shanika refused to back down. "I need my check."

"How's the job search coming along?" Cordelia inquired.

Rolling her eyes, Shanika answered, "I been out there look-ing. I just can't find nothing. You don't know how hard it is out there. Ain't nobody trying to hire us."

"I spoke to your child-care worker yesterday. If you don't find a job within the next two weeks, you're going to lose your child-care assistance, Miss Winston."

"I'll find something," she grumbled. "But I'm not taking no minimum wage job. It has to be worth my time."

Cordelia talked for a few minutes more before reinstating her client's case. She walked Shanika out and then returned to her workstation. She'd barely sat down before the phone started ringing.

It was probably another one of her clients calling to com-plain about something. She picked up the receiver. "Cordelia Berkeley speaking."

It was the counselor from Devon's school.

"Absent? Devon hasn't been absent this year." Her headache was worsening. "Two days? This is ridiculous." Cordelia glanced at the clock. Her vision blurred for a second, causing her to squint. "I'll be there shortly. We're going to meet with Devon and find out what's going on." She waved absently to one of her coworkers passing by.

Sighing, Cordelia hung up the phone and opened her ap-pointment book. She would have to ask Bonnie to cover her next two appointments in order to make the conference at school. "I'm going to wring your neck, Devon. . . ."

"Hey, Dee. How are you?"

She glanced up, instantly covering up her frustration with a smile. "Morning, Sabrina. You just getting here?"

"Yeah. Almost overslept, but I made it."

"I'm leaving for a couple of hours but will be back after that," she told the administrative assistant. "Could you let Kayla know for me?"

"Sure. I'm on my way out to the reception area anyway."

Just as Cordelia was about to leave, her phone rang again. This time she decided to just let it switch over to voice mail. She'd had enough for now. She got up and left her workstation, heading to her supervisor's office. As she walked, Cordelia fumbled through her purse in search of Tylenol or aspirin—she needed something to stop the explosion in her head.

2

_____

Bonnie Mae Abbott was an early riser and usually the first one in the office. She was also the last one to leave most times as well. This morning she'd been there since six-thirty and was on her second cup of hot tea by the time some of the other employees began to arrive.

"I brought some homemade blueberry and banana-nut muffins," she called out. "They're in the break room." Bonnie had gotten up at four to make them. She enjoyed baking and often made goodies for the Family Financial Assistance unit, affectionately called the FFA unit.

She had no family of her own to speak of, at least none close to her, so instead she focused all of her attention on her friends and on her team of social workers. She'd been with St. Paul County for almost twenty years, and the FFA unit was as near to family as she would get. She inhaled the citrus scent of the orange spice tea she liked to drink in the mornings. It was her one indulgence.

Cordelia knocked on the door before entering her office. "Morning, Bonnie. I need a favor from you."

Setting down her mug down on a hand-painted coaster, she asked, "What is it?"

"I need to leave. I have a conference at Devon's school this morning."

Scanning her from head to toe, Bonnie noted how pale Cordelia's tawny complexion looked and questioned, "Are you feeling okay, Dee? You look a little peaked." That was putting it mildly. Cordelia didn't look well at all, causing Bonnie to speculate that something was definitely wrong. She leaned back in her chair and waited for Cordelia to sit down.

Closing the door behind her, Cordelia said, "Devon's been skipping school. I just don't know how she could do this to me. Ever since I took her out of that Christian school she's been losing her mind." Releasing a soft sigh, she sat down facing Bonnie. "I don't know what I'm going to do with her."

"She's a good kid, Dee," Bonnie reassured her. "If skipping school is all you have to worry about, then consider yourself lucky."

"I know you're right," she agreed. "Just lately, Devon seems to have changed so drastically. She's not the same little girl I used to know. She stays locked up in her room and she sleeps all of the time. Maybe Gerald should have a talk with her. He seems to be the only one who can get through to her. I really don't know what's going on with her." Cordelia shook her head in confusion. "If you could just cover my appointments for me, I'd appreciate it. My book is on my desk."

"Sure. I'll be more than happy to do it." Bonnie wished there were more she could say—she'd never been a mother, so there was really no way she could truly understand exactly what Cordelia was going through. But she had watched Devon grow up and knew she wasn't a child with severe behavioral problems. "I think she's just going through a phase."

Awarding Bonnie a smile, she said, "I hope that's all it is. Thanks. I shouldn't be gone more than a couple of hours."

"That's fine." Once again Bonnie searched inwardly for words of wisdom, but none were forthcoming. Deep down she felt that Cordelia didn't spend enough time with Devon, and that was a big part of their problem. Most of Cordelia's time was spent involved in various church activities or with her job.

Concerned, Bonnie watched her friend walk out of her office. Cordelia hadn't seemed herself for the past week or so, and she'd been constantly complaining of a headache lately. Bonnie had even suggested on two separate occasions that Cordelia see a doctor, but she stubbornly refused. She suspected the headaches resulted from the increasing tension between Devon and Cordelia. It didn't help that Gerald and Cordelia were barely on speaking terms and hardly ever agreed when it came to Devon.

She suspected her friend still loved her ex deep down but would never admit it in a million years. Cordelia had become extremely bitter after the divorce, and with just cause, Bonnie assumed. But losing a partner was never easy—in fact, it was a lonely existence.

Bonnie understood exactly what that felt like. She hadn't lost her husband to divorce, however. Edgar had died four years ago, but to her it still felt like yesterday. His death left Bonnie feeling like her life had ended with his. Although she'd wanted children desperately, she had never conceived, and now that her husband was gone there was no one left.

She was fifty years old and alone in the world. Her parents were both dead, and what family she had left still lived up north and along the West Coast. Edgar's family had never cared much for her, and now, since his death, refused to even acknowledge her.

Tearing herself from unhappy memories, Bonnie called the receptionist to see if Cordelia's client had arrived. Pushing away from her desk, she got up and straightened her black skirt. She ran a hand through her short, graying black hair and pinned her ID badge on the crisp, white cotton blouse she wore before walking to the reception area. As long as Bonnie could surround herself with work every day, loneliness would not plague her with its presence.

3

The last place Sabrina wanted to be today was here at the FFA office. Even the new St. Johns pant suit she was wearing did nothing to brighten her mood. She'd had a huge fight with her boyfriend last night and was in a sour mood as a result of it. Taking her own sweet time, she made her way over to the reception area.

"Hey, Kayla," she greeted her dryly. Sabrina glanced around the cluttered work area and wondered how Kayla could work with all this mess around. She fingered a stack of mail, looking for nothing in particular. She just wanted to be nosy. The worker productivity reports were due, and Sabrina was curious to see how they had fared. Kayla's voice halted her hand. "Looking for something?"

"No, not really," Sabrina lied, because she knew Kayla was a snitch. "I almost forgot, Bonnie is going to cover Dee's next two appointments. She had to leave for a while."

"I know. Bonnie just came over to pick up the client." The receptionist glanced up at her. "Girl, what's wrong with you?"

"Just had a bad night, that's all." She picked up a stack of papers. "Are these already entered into the system?"

Kayla nodded. "They're done."

Sabrina glanced toward the door. A smile tugged at the corners of her mouth. Maybe her day was already getting better. The woman who had just walked in was none other than her former high-and-mighty-acting neighbor. Waving, she said, "How you doing, Pam?"

The woman smiled back. "I'm fine."

She left the desk, opened the glass door, and strolled over to where the young woman had taken a seat. Her arms folded across her chest, she inclined her head and asked, "Can I help you with something?"

Pam stated, "Girl, I hope y'all can help me. I need to get some assistance." Patting her swollen belly, she added, "Bobby's not doing what he's supposed to do and I can't work right now."

The man hasn't done right since you've known him, so you should've known better than to have another baby, Sabrina wanted to say, but wisely held her tongue. She couldn't understand why half of these women running up here to the county for help didn't try to better themselves. Half of them had several children by different fathers and were still having babies. Didn't they know anything about birth control? More important, why did they waste their time with no-good bums like Bobby? If someone actually paid for breeding children, Bobby would be rich. It was rumored that he already had six or seven children all over North Carolina.

Now that her curiosity had been satisfied, Sabrina dropped all pretense of being concerned. Pointing toward the receptionist, she said, "She'll give you some paperwork to fill out, and the duty worker will see you." She made her way around the counter and dropped down in the vacant chair beside the receptionist.

Just then another woman walked in. Sabrina blinked rapidly

and held her breath as a frisson of fear ran down her spine. The woman stood in the middle of the FFA unit reception area giving Sabrina a deadly look.

"You know her?" Kayla whispered.

"No," Sabrina lied. She pretended to sort the morning mail while hoping and praying Bonita would go away without making a scene. She had never met the woman face-to-face, although Sabrina had seen her from a distance on several occasions. She stood a good six feet tall and was in excellent physical shape. She worked as a trainer at the local fitness center.

Sabrina, on the other hand, was just under five feet tall, and barely weighed one hundred and five pounds. She gave thanks for the bulletproof glass window and wall separating them. She'd heard the woman was crazy and would fight at the drop of a hat. Sabrina kept her eyes down, refusing to meet Bonita's fiery gaze.

What seemed like an eternity to Sabrina passed before the woman turned and left the reception area without so much as a word.

"I thought I was going to have to call security up here. What was that about? You don't know her? She sure acted like she knew you."

Ignoring Kayla's questions, Sabrina got up and left swiftly, taking the back exit for fear of running into Bonita. In the safety of her workstation, she released a long sigh and turned on her computer. Her hands were trembling so much that it took three attempts before she could finally key in her password. The phone rang; Sabrina let it roll over to voice mail. She just couldn't talk to anyone right now.

Sabrina slowly began to calm down. She couldn't believe Leon's ex-girlfriend had the nerve to show up on her job like that. She picked up the phone to call him but changed her mind. After the big fight they'd had last night, she didn't feel like talking to him right now.

They were supposed to go away to Myrtle Beach this weekend, but he backed out on her. He'd been doing that a lot lately,
and it was seriously getting on her nerves. Now his ex was
showing up on her job. Sabrina had grilled Leon over and over
about his relationship with Bonita before they had started dating. He swore to her that it was long over.

She started to feel much better as she considered the fact that
while Bonita had come to the office, she never once uttered a
word. Apparently she'd lost her courage, Sabrina thought
smugly.

Her phone rang again. Recognizing the number on the caller
ID, Sabrina picked up the receiver. "LaTisha, I'm so glad you
called, girlfriend. You won't believe who had the nerve to come
up here to my job."

"Girl, who?"

"Bonita Hamilton."

"No, she didn't. I know you lying."

"Yeah, girl. The huzzy came up here and just stared at me.
She didn't say anything—she just stared. You know if she'd said
one word to me, I would've had to get ugly up in here," Sabrina
boasted.

"I know that's right. You would've had to kick her tall ass
all over St. Paul County."

Sabrina broke into nervous laughter while she fumbled with
her necklace. Deep down she was truly grateful that things
hadn't gone that far. She definitely wasn't one for fighting. Not
wanting to ponder another minute on Bonita's strange visit, she
changed the subject. "Oh, guess who's up here trying to get assistance?" The fact that her job required confidentiality didn't
faze her one bit, because Sabrina loved to gossip.

"Who?"

She lowered her voice to a whisper. "My old neighbor from
Green Street Apartments. You know. The uppity one. Miss
Pamela Score."

"Naaaw . . ."

"Yeah, girl. Pam's here applying for a check and food stamps. Heifer shouldn't have quit her job and gotten pregnant with this last baby. Probably thought Bobby was gonna settle down and marry her." Shaking her head in dismay, Sabrina continued, "These girls don't ever learn. I'm twenty-six and I have yet to have my first baby. I want to enjoy my life for a while. But I'm especially not gonna have a baby for a man who can barely support himself—much less me." She spotted Bonnie coming her way. Talking quickly, she said, "I've got to go, LaTisha. I'll call you back." She hung up and pretended to be going through her Franklin Planner.

Bonnie stopped by her desk. "Good morning, Miss Mayhew. Did the action notices go out already?"

"They went out on Wednesday." Smiling, Sabrina added, "I've got it under control, Bonnie."

"Good. I know Claire's been asking about them. How about the monthly report?"

"Done," Sabrina announced proudly. "I finished it yesterday before I left work. I was just about to print out copies and distribute them to everyone." They talked for a few minutes more before Bonnie finally moved on.

Sabrina waited for another ten minutes, then checked to make sure Bonnie and Claire were nowhere in sight. Sabrina signed on to the Internet to check her Web-based e-mail account and to view what was on sale at the Spiegel site. She found a pair of navy shoes at an unbelievable price. Sabrina jumped out of her seat and peeked into the corner workstation beside hers. "Hey, Tangie . . ."

It was empty. She noted the time and wondered briefly where Tangie was. Her coworker was not usually late coming into the office. Probably had a hot date that ran late, Sabrina mused. Tangie was thirty years old—four years older than her—and one of her closest friends. They spent a lot of time together during working hours and away from the office. As close as they were, however, Sabrina knew that Tangie kept secrets from her.

Whenever Tangie went on vacation, she would have Sabrina come in and water her plants. During those times, she snooped through her closets and drawers, curious to know more about her friend. Tangie guarded much of her personal life as if it were Fort Knox. She knew her friend was freaky, however. Tangie had an eye-popping collection of sexy lingerie and sex toys.

She caught sight of Bonnie coming her way and quickly shut down Internet Explorer. Although she was not on Bonnie's team and did not report to her, Sabrina still respected her as a supervisor. She snatched up a stack of papers and headed to the mailroom. She passed one of the social workers with a young pregnant client and shook her head in disgust. These young girls would never learn.

She heard Bonnie call her name and turned. "Need something?"

"Did Claire tell you that we have a management meeting? I'm on my way there now."

Sabrina searched her memory. "She may have mentioned it, but I don't remember. It's not in my planner." She gave Bonnie a grateful smile. "Thanks."

On her way back to her workstation, Sabrina peeked into Tangie's office. She still hadn't arrived. *Girlfriend must have had quite some night.* Grinning, Sabrina sat down at her desk to resume her surfing on the Internet. Bonnie and Claire should be in their meeting for about an hour. It gave her a chance to do some shopping on-line.

4

"Last night was unforgettable, baby."

"It was for me too," Tangie murmured against his lips. The lie stuck in her throat, threatening to gag her. She kissed him a second time before stepping out of his embrace. She'd had her eye on Michael King for a while, so last night should have been a dream come true for her. However, it hadn't been nearly as exciting as she'd expected. He, of course, probably thought he was the cat's meow.

He kissed her again, forcing his tongue into her mouth. When she felt his hands move downward, Tangie broke the kiss and gently pushed away from him. "I've got to get ready for work. Sorry." Her apology was an empty one. This would be the last time Michael would ever touch her.

" 'Bye, Tangie. We should do this again. Soon."

Although she gave him a seductive wink, she muttered under her breath, "Not in this lifetime." He had been a huge disappointment, and she was no longer interested.

Blowing her a kiss, Michael made his way to the door.

She could tell from his arrogant swagger that Michael

thought he ruled the world. He had a nice body—one that offered up promises he couldn't possibly keep. Tangie was tempted to take out an ad warning other women. Michael didn't have a clue how to please a woman.

From her window, she watched him get into his car and drive away. Turning away, Tangie stole a peek at her watch and bolted up the stairs, cursing Michael the entire way to her bedroom. She was late for work, so she rushed through a shower and dressed quickly.

Using her fingers, Tangie brushed back an errant curl and tucked it behind her ear. She rearranged a couple of bobby pins in the bun at her nape, and then put on her makeup. Giving herself a final once-over, she picked up her keys and purse and headed back downstairs.

As she walked to her car, Tangie was acutely aware of the throbbing ache between her legs. It was a sore reminder of how she'd spent her morning. She and Michael had spent most of the night having terrible sex, and again just an hour earlier. Tangie had hoped things would get better. They hadn't. After faking her pleasure, she rushed him out of bed, using her job as an excuse.

Using her cell phone, she called Bonnie's direct line. "Hey, it's me, Tangie. I had some car trouble this morning but I should be there in about fifteen minutes. Could you have my client start the paperwork?"

"Sure. I'll let Kayla know. I'll see you when you get here."

"Thanks, Bonnie."

Tangie arrived twelve minutes later. Her client had already completed her paperwork. She slipped on her glasses before going to the reception area to get her. Extending her hand, she said, "Hello, I'm Miss Thompson."

The teenager and her mother followed Tangie to her workstation.

Tangie straightened the navy double-breasted blazer of the suit she was wearing. She waited for her clients to be seated before she sat down. After straightening her knee-length pleated skirt, she crossed her legs gracefully. "Do you have everything filled out?"

"Yes, ma'am." The teen handed her a stack of papers.

Going over the paperwork, Tangie paused at an unanswered question. "You left this blank. The one naming the baby's father."

The teenager glanced nervously over at her mother, who asked, "Is that important?"

"Yes. We need to know the father's name."

"My daughter isn't sure," the woman replied in a low voice.

"I see."

Moving her chair closer to Tangie, she said, "That's one of the things I'd like for you to talk to her about. My daughter needs to understand that what she's doing is wrong. Lord knows she won't listen to a word I say. Maybe she'll listen to you. Having sex is bad enough, but sleeping with every Tom, Dick, and Harry . . ." She shook her head sadly. "She already got one child, and now she pregnant with her second and she only sixteen." Her eyes teared up. "She's a pretty girl and all the boys like her, but I keep trying to tell her that they mean her no good. I want her to grow up to be a fine lady like you."

The teenager looked horrified. Lowering her eyes, she shifted in her chair and placed her arms across her stomach as if trying to hide its distorted shape.

Tangie was silent.

"Could you talk to her, Miss Thompson?"

"Y-yes, of course," Tangie replied. She knew the right things to say and do, but she didn't exactly follow her own advice. Her conservative clothes and jewelry and her entire look were nothing but a cover. In the privacy of her own home she could be herself—a woman who loved sex. She could hardly stand going a day without it. She also enjoyed variety.

Tangie didn't really believe one man alone could ever satisfy her cravings. But it was more than that. It was obvious to her that men and women got bored with one another. Why else were they so willing to break their marital vows by committing adultery?

Tangie decided it was best to avoid the trap of marriage at all costs.

"That girl is practicing to be a ho, if you ask me," Sabrina stated as she slipped into Tangie's workstation.

"Ssssh. Girl, you'd better stop talking so loud around here. Some of these women will kill you without so much as a second thought." Tangie rose to her feet and peeked outside of her office, looking around attentively to see if Sabrina had been overheard. "You'd better watch out," she warned.

Sabrina lowered her voice and muttered, "Truth is the truth." She sat down in a chair near the window and crossed her legs. "So what's up?"

Gazing at her friend, Tangie questioned, "Are you eavesdropping on my clients?"

"No," Sabrina answered a little defensively. "You need to tell them to stop talking so loud, Tangie. I can hear everything they say without trying." Leaning forward and lowering her voice to a whisper, she said, "I can hear everything that goes on in Carolyn's office too. Girl, I don't know how she gets any work done—she's always on the phone with her husband. You should hear some of those conversations."

"That's okay," Tangie murmured with a smile. "I think I'll pass." Leaning back in her chair, she said, "Sabrina, you're too nosy, girlfriend. One day it's going to get you into some big trouble."

"All I'm doing is telling the truth. I can't help it if people can't take the real deal. That's their problem—not mine."

Tangie waved her hand in dismissal. "All right. When somebody comes up here to knock you out, don't call me, because I'm not going to get involved."

Folding her arms across her chest, Sabrina abruptly changed the subject. "You sure were late this morning. I was about to get worried."

Pretending to be scanning the duty calendar, Tangie responded, "I had some car trouble."

"Uh-huh," Sabrina uttered. "What's wrong with your car?"

"Nothing now. It needed spark plugs or something. A friend of mine is a mechanic and he fixed it." That much was true, only the work had been done last Friday instead of this morning. Feeling her temper rise, Tangie turned to Sabrina. "I know you don't call yourself grilling me."

"I just figured that you told Bonnie that excuse as a cover."

Tangie eyed Sabrina. "A cover? For what?"

"For the fact that maybe you overslept. I don't know. Maybe you were detained by a man."

"And if I were? What of it?" Tangie tried to keep from sounding defensive.

Sabrina broke into a mischievous grin. "If that were the case, it must have been quite a night. You're never late for work, so he must have been something."

Tangie stroked her hair in resignation. "Whatever." She was not about to give the queen of gossip something to talk about. Picking up a yellow highlighter, she glanced over at Sabrina. "I didn't see Dee when I walked by her office. Did she call in today?"

Sabrina shook her head. "She had to leave right before you got here this morning. Something was up, but I didn't have a chance to find out what it was."

Laughing, Tangie teased, "And I know how bad that bothers you. Not being in the center of things."

"Funny . . ." Sabrina's voice died as she rose to her feet. "I'd better get back to work. I don't want Mother Bonnie and Claire breathing down my neck."

Claire was Sabrina's team leader and they clashed often. "Where are we having lunch today?"

"Let's go to Lowell's," Sabrina suggested. "We haven't been there in a while. I have a taste for liver and onions."

"Sounds good to me. I could go for some baked spaghetti." Tangie rose to her feet and walked the short distance to the file cabinet in the corner.

"What time are you leaving for Myrtle Beach?"

"I'm not going," Sabrina answered. "Leon claims that he has to take care of some business this weekend."

"But you've been looking forward to this trip for weeks. Why don't you go on without him, Sabrina? Leon always seems to back out for one reason or another."

"We had a big fight over this last night. I was still hot about it this morning."

"It sounds like you've calmed down since then."

"I have." Sabrina broke into a grin. "Leon sent me roses. You should come look at them. They're huge, and he didn't forget my favorites."

Tangie turned to face her. "Leon sent you white roses. Wow, he must really be feeling guilty."

"I don't care what he's feeling. I love the roses, so I'm going to give him another chance. He's going to come over tomorrow night for dinner."

Tangie looked surprised. "You're cooking?"

"Yeah."

"Wow. What in the world has Leon done to you? You don't cook for nobody. Especially if they just sent you flowers. I figure they'd have to include a diamond or two."

Sabrina laughed. "It's his birthday, so I thought I'd do something special for him."

Thumbing the cases one by one, Tangie stated, "I don't think Leon treats you the way you deserve to be treated. He acts as if you have nothing better to do than sit around and wait on him."

"You don't have to worry about me, girlfriend. I have everything under control. Leon can't get no further than I let him. I give him leeway because he's paying my bills right now."

Having found her file, Tangie returned to her chair. "That's good to hear." She let the subject drop, because Sabrina was extremely sensitive whenever it came to Leon. Although she constantly denied it, Tangie suspected Sabrina was in love with him.

"I'll talk to you in a while. I need to get some work done. Claire's been on my back lately. I think she and her man are having problems, 'cause she's been a real witch these days."

"Okay. Talk to you later."

Grateful to be alone, Tangie returned calls to everyone who'd left a voice mail, then went through her tickler file and made a to-do list. She adored Sabrina but found her friend to be distracting at times. There were days she hardly got any work done because of Sabrina.

When she was done, Tangie pulled a couple of cases to be terminated and prepared to send out letters. She heard music coming from Sabrina's office and grimaced. She couldn't understand how she could work with all that hip-hop in the background.

Adjusting her glasses, Tangie leaned back in her seat and stared out the window past her potted plants. Paying no attention to the outdoor scenery, she allowed her thoughts to center on the night spent with Michael. In all fairness, the sex had been okay but definitely not earth-shattering. She'd taken a big chance bringing him home with her, but Tangie hadn't wanted to deny her curiosity any longer.

Normally she never bothered with the local men. Tangie protected her reputation fiercely. Bridgeport was a small town, and some of the residents loved to gossip. Her mother had given them a whole lot to talk about, Tangie thought with disgust. Lula Thompson had been born and raised in Bridgeport. Growing up, she'd had a reputation for being fast—no one was surprised when Lula turned up pregnant at fifteen.

Tangie's father was a married man who'd taken his family and moved away as soon as he found out Lula was pregnant. Raising a child tainted with illegitimacy wasn't enough for her mother, though. She'd been involved with one married man after another, leaving Tangie to be raised by her grandmother. Married men were the only ones who seemed to interest her. Lula's current lover was Ben Harris, a prominent citizen who owned several car dealerships. He and his family lived in a custom-built estate home outside of Bridgeport.

Tangie and her mother were barely on speaking terms over the way she carried herself. She detested the way Lula openly paraded herself as Mr. Harris's mistress. It was obvious she had no respect for herself or her daughter. Tangie didn't dislike Ben Harris, but she wasn't overly fond of him either. She knew he was responsible for her college education and vowed to repay him one day. Tangie would not allow herself to be tied to that philanderer in any way. Married men who cheated on their wives disgusted her. Tangie hated them, and she hated her mother. Lula could drop dead right then and it wouldn't bother her. The only emotion she could possibly summon up would be relief.

5

Cordelia sat in the principal's office at Bridgeport High School. Every now and then her eyes would meet the sympathetic gazes of the principal and the counselor while they waited for Devon to join them.

More and more she regretted ever agreeing to let her daughter leave Bridgeport Christian Academy to finish her last three years in public school. Their problems had started a couple of years ago when Devon changed schools, she reasoned. Absently, Cordelia fingered the diamond-and-sapphire encrusted cross dangling from a gold chain around her neck. Her right hand went numb. It wasn't bad, similar to other times in the last few days. She rubbed her hand and put the incident out of her mind.

Devon sauntered into the office a few minutes later. She gave her mother an insolent look as she sat down but didn't utter a single word of greeting to anyone.

Cordelia let this show of rudeness slide and sat quietly as the principal explained the reason for the meeting. Devon shifted in her chair all the while, looking bored.

I Sold

Staring pointedly at her daughter, Cordelia demanded, "You want to tell me what's going on with you?"

"Nothing's going on," answered Devon, casting her eyes downward.

Cordelia waited for her daughter to say more. When she didn't, she prompted, "And?"

This time Devon stared straight at her. "And what?"

"You have nothing more to say?" In her mind, Cordelia couldn't believe the child she gave birth to had the audacity to be sitting here and looking at her like this, talking to her in this manner. She stared back until Devon had the good sense to look away. "I'm still waiting for an answer, and I'd better get one soon."

Devon couldn't miss the silent threat that hung frozen in the air. "A friend and I went over to her house and hung out. We just didn't feel like being at school." Her bottom lip trembled slightly. "She's going through something right now."

"Who is this friend?" Cordelia wanted to know. "Is it Kate?"

"You don't know her," Devon replied, a little too quickly.

"Who is she?" she asked again.

"Terri."

"Terri Maynard?" the counselor asked.

Devon nodded. "I'm sorry, but I can't tell you anything that's going on. I promised her I wouldn't tell anybody. She just needed a friend, Mama, and I was trying to be one. You do it all the time for the women at church."

Devon's comment threw her for a moment. What did one thing have to do with the other? she wondered to herself. When she spoke Cordelia said, "You can't just decide that you're suddenly not going to school, Devon. I'm glad you're being a friend to this girl, but this is not the way to do it." Her headache started to worsen.

The other shock came when the counselor announced that Devon's grades were slipping.

"Why am I just hearing about this?" Cordelia asked. No one from the school had ever contacted her. This never would've happened if she'd stayed at Bridgeport Christian Academy.

"We sent notes home with Devon. They were returned with your . . ." The counselor's voice died. "I mean . . . they were returned signed. We assumed you reviewed and signed them."

Devon suddenly seemed to shrink in her chair. The air of arrogance surrounding her dissipated. Cordelia gazed at her daughter.

"I didn't want to get in trouble."

Disgruntled, Cordelia uttered, "Maybe I should have you transferred back to Bridgeport Christian—"

"I don't want to go back there," Devon interjected quickly. "It won't happen again, Mama. I'm gonna pull my grades up— I've already talked to my teachers about it. I won't skip school anymore. I was just trying to help out a friend in trouble."

Cordelia considered her daughter's comments as she listened to what the principal and the counselor had to say. Devon was let off with two days of detention and a threat of suspension the next time.

Afterward, Devon escorted her mother out. They walked side by side, not saying a word to each other.

Cordelia broke the silence. "I can't understand why you'd embarrass me like this."

"I wasn't trying to embarrass you. Terri just needed a friend real bad. She's really going through something."

"I don't have a problem with your being a friend to someone. I just don't understand why you couldn't tell me what was happening."

"You wouldn't have let me stay out of school."

"Probably not, but we will never know for sure, will we?"

Devon's look showed her disbelief. "I'm pretty sure you wouldn't have," she insisted. "I can't see that happening. Not with the way you feel about school."

"Why couldn't you just come to me? Am I that difficult to

talk to?" Cordelia wanted to know. She hated the fact that she and her daughter seemed to be drifting farther and farther apart. They used to be so close, and Devon would tell her everything.

"Terri didn't want to talk to anybody else right now."

"Is she pregnant?"

Devon looked surprised.

"Well, is she?" Cordelia prompted.

Her daughter nodded.

"I thought so. Devon, she doesn't need to talk to you—Terri needs to talk to her mother."

"I told her that, and she's going to do it tonight."

"Good." Cordelia checked her watch. "I'd better get back to the office. Now I want you to come straight home after school, Devon."

"Yes, ma'am."

"I'm not kidding. I expect you to call me as soon as you get there."

Her request was met with a loud sigh.

"You brought this on yourself," Cordelia stated. "You obviously can't be trusted."

"I make one mistake and I can't be trusted for life?" Devon snarled. "I don't think that's fair."

"You'd better watch your tone with me, young lady," Cordelia warned in a low voice. "And you need to learn to count. You've made several mistakes in recent weeks—not just one."

Devon sucked air through her teeth in response.

Cordelia practically stood toe to toe with her. Gazing hard into her eyes, she inquired, "Excuse me? Have you forgotten yourself? Girl, I'll knock you into next year. Don't you dare suck your teeth at me."

Retreating a step backward, Devon uttered, "I didn't do nothing."

"You'd better watch yourself." Cordelia warned as she turned to leave. She paused at the edge of the curb, saying, "I'll see you when I get home tonight."

Trying to ignore her blinding pain and growing numbness, Cordelia climbed into her car. For a brief moment she considered going home to lie down, but changed her mind and headed in the direction of St. Paul County Human Services. She would go home on her lunch hour and lie down. Cordelia prayed she would feel better by the time she got off work. She didn't want to miss Bible study tonight.

6

When Bonnie left her office to make copies of a case, she found that Cordelia had returned and was sitting at her desk massaging her temple. "You sure you're okay, Dee?" she inquired.

Squinting because of double vision, Cordelia answered, "I think I might have a migraine. I took some Tylenol earlier but it hasn't helped. Devon's being difficult doesn't make it any better either. Bonnie, it's that attitude of hers. She gets herself into trouble and then wants to give me attitude when I get on her case about it."

"Why don't you take an early lunch and go home for a couple of hours? Maybe lying down for a few minutes would help."

"I hope so, because I have a lot of work to do."

"Things go well over at the school?"

Cordelia gave her a brief recap.

Sabrina stuck her head inside the workstation. "Hey, y'all, we're having lunch at Lowell's. Are y'all coming?"

Cordelia shook her head no. "I was just telling Bonnie that I have a terrible headache, so I'm just going to go home and lie down."

"Oh." She paused for a moment. "Well, okay. I hope you feel better."

Sabrina was then off and running.

Shaking her head, Cordelia uttered, "That girl always seems to be in a hurry except when it comes to work. She's good at what she does—just seems to take her own sweet time doing it."

Bonnie broke into a short laugh. "She's something else."

Cordelia agreed. "She's a sweetie. Just can't keep her mouth shut."

"She probably doesn't have any business of her own. Maybe that's why she's in everybody else's." As soon as Bonnie said the words, she couldn't help but wonder if people said the same thing about her. It wasn't being nosy on her part. She genuinely cared for her coworkers and would do anything for them.

Changing the subject, Cordelia stated, "I should've followed my first mind and kept Devon at Bridgeport Christian. My spirit was never in agreement with her going to public school."

"Do you really think that would have made a difference?" Bonnie wanted to know. She didn't think so, personally. She felt that at times Cordelia was much too hard on her daughter. She was an overprotective mother who kept her child on a very short leash.

"She didn't change until she left," Cordelia was saying. "It's the people she's running around with, Bonnie. Most of them don't even see a church on Sunday, or any other day for that matter." She began to massage her temple. "Devon doesn't even want to go to church anymore. What can she be thinking?"

"I think she's just being a normal teenager," Bonnie countered. "A lot of them are rebellious at this stage."

"I expect better of her, I guess. Devon grew up in the church. There wasn't a Sunday we didn't attend. I read the Bible to her until she was old enough to read on her own. My daughter knows right from wrong. She has a relationship with God."

"She's still human, Dee. We all make mistakes and bad choices. Even Christians."

"Like I said, I expect so much more from her." Closing her eyes, Cordelia murmured, "I wish I could get rid of this headache."

"Why don't you go home for the rest of the day?" Bonnie suggested.

Cordelia shook her head. "No, I'm going to try to finish out the day. I don't have any more appointments, but I need to send out some letters."

Bonnie picked up a case file and stuck it under her arm. "You're through with this, right?" When Cordelia nodded, she said, "If you need some help, I'll be more than glad to take on some of the work."

"Thanks. I'll let you know."

Rising to her feet, Bonnie left Cordelia's office and went back to her own. She wished desperately that she could help Devon and Cordelia. Her friend was going to have to ease up some. Bonnie had faith that all would work out for the best. She sent up a quick prayer for insurance.

"Most gracious Father, help Dee to understand and discern the needs of her daughter. Free her so that she can embrace Devon without clutching too tightly. Support her without suffocating and help her to correct her daughter when she's wrong without crushing her spirit. Help them to find the way You desire a parent and child to be. Amen."

Two hours later Bonnie met Sabrina and Tangie for lunch. They were seated quickly in a booth at Lowell's restaurant. Bonnie admired the designer suit Sabrina wore and wondered how she was able to maintain her lavish lifestyle. She knew most of the men Sabrina dated had money. Were they paying

her expenses? She shouldn't be surprised, she reasoned. Sabrina
was a beautiful girl. Her face was dark and delicate. She had
high cheekbones and a regal nose. Everything she wore comple-
mented her dark chocolate complexion.

Tangie was the opposite of Sabrina, and also attractive. She
was tall and voluptuous, with a smooth caramel complexion.
She had a heart-shaped face with slanted eyes and a small nose.
Between the two of them, they had captured the attention of all
the males in the restaurant. Bonnie glanced down at her own
ample body and frowned. She hated the way she looked. Her
own coppery complexion was uneven—lighter in some areas
than others. She had come to terms with the fact that she wasn't
an attractive woman.

"Dee still not feeling well?" Tangie questioned while scanning the menu.

Unfolding her napkin and placing it across her lap, Bonnie
answered, grateful to center her thoughts on someone else.
"Her headache won't go away. She went home to rest for a
while."

"She's had that headache for a few days now," Tangie announced. "Dee should make an appointment to see a doctor.
She doesn't look too well."

Wearing a look of boredom, the waitress arrived to take
their order. They listened as she rattled off the specials before
giving her their selections.

Tangie commented, "She sure didn't seem very friendly."

"I think she's the one who had the baby with that football
player," Sabrina replied.

"Why is she working here?" asked Tangie.

"He's saying the baby isn't his. He wants to have a paternity
test done before he'll claim the child."

Bonnie glanced over at the subject of their conversation. The
young woman looked troubled. She prayed all would work out
for her. Turning her attention back to Sabrina, she questioned,
"How do you know all this?"

"I know people. Plus it's been all over the newspaper." Sabrina's voice died when their waitress returned ten minutes later with their salads and a basket of rolls.

Bonnie gave a short prayer of thanks before they started to eat.

"Why did Dee have to leave this morning?" Sabrina inquired. "Did she go to the doctor?"

Bonnie shook her head. "No."

Sabrina was clearly expecting more of an explanation but when none was forthcoming, she turned to Tangie. "So what are you doing for the weekend?" She sliced off a piece of tomato and stuck it into her mouth.

"I'm not sure what I'm going to do right now," Tangie answered. "I might drive down to Raleigh for the weekend."

"You're forever running to Raleigh. You must have a man stashed away somewhere there." Sabrina buttered a roll before taking a bite out of it. "What about you, Bonnie? Doing anything special?"

"I don't have any real plans outside of my volunteer work. It's just me and Scotty." Bonnie met Sabrina's gaze, silently daring her to comment. Everyone knew that she spent most of her free time alone with her dog when she wasn't volunteering or attending church. "Maybe I'll attend a women's retreat sponsored by the pastor's wife."

Ignoring the look, Sabrina said, "You and Dee . . . all y'all do is go to church for one thing or another. If that's all you have to do to get into heaven, y'all got it made, I guess." She sliced off another piece of tomato.

Bonnie laughed. "It's certainly takes a lot more than that."

"I go to church," Sabrina announced. "But I don't think I have to be sitting on the front pew every Sunday just to get into heaven. I'll get there by my good deeds."

Tangie and Bonnie exchanged glances before bursting into laughter.

The waitress arrived with their food. She moved swiftly, placing a plate in front of each of them.

"Thank you," Bonnie murmured.

Looking from one to the other, Sabrina questioned, "Why did y'all start laughing earlier. What's so funny?"

"Nothing, girl," Tangie responded. "Just eat your food."

Mixing her gravy into her rice, Sabrina continued: "The Bible says something about faith without works is dead. Going to church every time the doors are open don't mean a thing." She stuck a piece of liver in her mouth and chewed.

"You're right on that point," Bonnie agreed. "The church is where we get our teaching and our support. It's a haven for the needy, the wounded in spirit—anyone wanting to get to know God and His word."

Tangie took a sip of her tea. "My grandmother and Lula didn't put much emphasis on God. I don't think that they were nonbelievers—they just didn't believe in going to church."

"Are you still going to that church on Pine Street?" Bonnie asked.

Tangie shook her head no. "I wasn't getting anything out of it. The minister didn't do nothing but bore me to death. Once he started asking me about Lula—that was the end of the road for me."

"I keep telling Tangie that she should come to church with me," Sabrina said. "The congregation is huge—too many to be in your business."

"They probably already know or have heard of Lula and her exploits. Besides, your church is for the rich and famous. I don't belong there," Tangie stated.

"You're welcome to visit mine as well."

"Bonnie, are there any blacks in your church besides you? I always see a bunch of white folks outside."

"Sabrina . . ." Tangie gave her friend a playful nudge. "I can't believe you asked that."

"How else will I find out anything? I don't think I was being rude or anything. I just figured since she was married to that white man, she went to an all-white church." She met Bonnie's gaze. "Did I offend you?"

"No, it's okay," Bonnie responded. "We have a mixed congregation at my church."

Waving her hand excitedly, Sabrina asked, "Hey, did y'all hear about Mandy? Her husband was caught with her sister last week. And you're not going to believe this. They were in her bed. Can you imagine that?"

Tangie's mouth dropped open. "Where did you hear that?"

"I heard Mandy talking to her mother about it on the phone."

Bonnie gave Sabrina a strong look of disapproval. She'd warned her repeatedly about running off at the mouth.

"Why are you looking at me like that? I didn't do anything. She was talking loud and I overheard her conversation. You know how loud she talks."

"I don't think she'd appreciate your spreading her business around, Sabrina."

"I only told you and Tangie," she huffed. "Y'all act like all I do is gossip."

"You do," Tangie countered with a short laugh. "We love you though."

Sabrina had the nerve to look offended, causing Bonnie to burst into laughter.

Folding her arms across her chest, she huffed, "I guess this is Pick on Sabrina Day."

"Sabrina, we're not picking on you," Tangie explained. "Friends should be able to tell each other the truth, shouldn't they?"

She gave a stiff nod. Bonnie knew Sabrina was seething on the inside. She hated to be criticized. She could dish it out but couldn't take it. She also enjoyed being the center of attention. Sabrina was a very self-absorbed person.

"Well, you *do* have a strong tendency to gossip. Sometimes that can lead to problems. That's all I'm trying to say."

Waving off Tangie's words, Sabrina stated, "I don't start rumors. I simply state what I've seen or heard. People should be more careful if they don't want their business in the street. Humph. Rumors always start from the source."

Bonnie and Tangie exchanged a look of resignation.

Sabrina continued to grumble. "The way I see it, Mandy shouldn't have been discussing her personal life in the workplace."

"She's never going to get it," Tangie uttered. "Let's just drop it and change the subject."

Sabrina was not going to let Tangie have the last word. "Besides, y'all don't need to worry about it since I'm not talking about y'all."

Wiping her mouth with a napkin, Bonnie inquired, "Does it even matter that you signed a statement of confidentiality?"

Sabrina rolled her eyes heavenward but did not respond.

Bonnie hated this side of Sabrina. She was a gossip and very critical of others. She was also very selfish. Sabrina never did anything unless it benefited her in some way.

Although it seemed hopeless, Bonnie tried to counsel Sabrina. She didn't want to see her friend lose her job or get into some sort of confrontation because of not keeping her mouth shut. Sabrina refused to listen, but now limited her gossip to her coworkers and not the clients—at least within Bonnie's hearing range.

They paid for their meals and left the restaurant.

Sabrina pouted all the way back to the office, while Bonnie was grateful for her silence.

7

Cordelia left work and drove straight to Bible study. She got out of the car and slipped quietly inside the church. She took a seat in the third row.

"Tonight we are going to talk about how Christians react to suffering, taken from the twelfth chapter of Hebrew," Pastor Grant announced.

Cordelia opened her Bible, quickly finding the book of Hebrew. She was proud of the fact that she knew all sixty-six books of the Bible, and in order. She could even quote scripture as well.

". . . we either despise it," Pastor Grant was saying, "that is, treat it too lightly, as did Esau his birthright in verses five through sixteen; or we faint under it—that is, treat it too seriously; or we are exercised by it—that is, receive instruction from it. This is the reaction desired by God."

Writing as swiftly as she could, Cordelia took lots of notes.

Someone asked, "Why does such a loving God permit his children to suffer?"

Cordelia was interested in knowing the answer to that question as well, so she stopped writing to pay full attention to Pastor Grant's response.

"A number of reasons can be found in the scriptures," Pastor Grant stated. "One reason is to produce fruit. If we allow suffering to accomplish its purpose, it can bring forth patience, knowledge, and maturity; another reason is to glorify God; and another is to teach us dependence on God. This is brought out by both Christ and the apostle Paul when you read the fifteenth chapter of John, and in Second Corinthians, the twelfth chapter. . . ."

Cordelia started to write again, making notes on what had been said so far. Soon her mind began to wander; Cordelia felt light-headed and unfocused. She started to become restless. As the class drew to a close, Pastor Grant assigned scriptures for them to read before the next class.

Normally she would have stayed to chat with a few of the members, but the headache was still there. Cordelia nodded and waved at everyone before taking her leave.

When she arrived home, she found Devon was in her room sleeping. *That girl don't do nothing but sleep,* she fumed to herself.

She was about to close the door when something on her daughter's shirt caught her eye in the dimly lit room. She eased forward for a closer inspection and turned on a bedside lamp.

There was a stain covering her left breast and another one on the right breast. Her breasts were leaking.

Oh, dear Lord. Cordelia's heartbeat raced and her temples throbbed. She felt herself sway and tried to support her body by leaning against the oak dresser. *Breasts leaking, Devon's weight gain and all the sleeping . . .* Cordelia's heart started to pound faster.

"Devon!"

Disoriented, the teen shot up straight as an arrow. It took her a moment to gather her wits about her. "Mama . . . I didn't know you were home."

"I want the truth." Cordelia wasn't sure how she managed to get the words out.

Devon swung her legs over the side of the bed. "What did I do now?"

Cordelia pointed to her chest. "You tell me."

Looking down, a look of confusion crossed her daughter's face, immediately replaced by fear. "Mama, I don't know what's hap—"

"Are you pregnant, Devon?" Cordelia interjected. Deep down she already knew the answer, and the pain of the truth was excruciating. Her eyes welled with tears and it suddenly became hard to breathe.

Devon was silent, choosing not to respond.

Swallowing hard, Cordelia stated, "I know you heard me."

Still no answer.

"Tell me!" she shouted in anger. "Girl, I already know the answer. You did the deed—why can't you act like a woman now and own up to it? You were woman enough to get pregnant."

"Mama . . ."

Curling her fist, Cordelia pursed her lips. "How could you do this to me, Devon? How could you ruin my name like this? I can only imagine what people are going to say." She put a trembling hand to her chest when her church members came to mind. "How can I ever hold up my head in church again?" Giving Devon a hard look, she asked, "Tonio is the father, isn't he?"

After a moment, Devon nodded. "Yes, ma'am."

She'd suspected as much. Cordelia couldn't stand Tonio and had tried to discourage her daughter from forming any type of relationship with him. He was the cause of most of their arguments lately. "I'll have to call his parents." She certainly wasn't looking forward to that.

Devon looked horrified. "Why?"

If her head had not been throbbing so much, Cordelia probably would have tried to slap some sense into her daughter. Staring at her stomach, she uttered, "Surely you already know the answer to that question."

"His dad is going to kill him—"

"I wouldn't be worried about Tonio if I were you, Devon," Cordelia interrupted. "You need to worry about your future and how you've ruined it—not to mention the situation you've placed me in."

Devon looked thoroughly confused. "What situation?"

"Because of you my credibility is ruined. Here I am advising young girls that they should wait until marriage before having sexual relations and you turn up pregnant."

"People will know you had nothing to do with it."

"That's not the point, Devon, and you know it. How can I counsel other girls when I can't even manage my own child?" Cordelia's eyes filled with tears. "Didn't you listen to anything I told you? You told me that you weren't having sex. And what about protection? I've talked to you about diseases."

"We . . . we used a condom, Mama. It—" Devon stopped short when her mother glared at her, and cast her eyes downward.

"You shouldn't have been having sex at all," Cordelia reminded her. "As the saying goes, what's done in the dark will soon come to light. That's why you got pregnant." Her eyes traveled to Devin's stomach. "When were you going to tell me?"

Shrugging, she answered, "I don't know. I wanted to say something but I was scared you'd kick me out."

"I just asked you if you were pregnant this morning. You stared me in the face and lied."

Devon cast her eyes downward. "I couldn't bring myself to tell you. I didn't even know how to bring it up."

"Did you lie on Terri—this friend of yours?"

"No, ma'am. We're both pregnant. She's telling her parents tonight."

"Do you have any idea how far along you are?"

Devon shook her head. "No, ma'am. Not really."

"Children wanting to be grown..." Cordelia muttered. "Devon, when was your last cycle? Do you even know that?"

Devon winced at her mother's words. "Yes, ma'am. It was November sixteenth."

Cordelia did some mental calculations. "Your baby's due around the middle of August. That makes you around... sixteen or seventeen weeks pregnant." She turned on her heel, heading toward the door. Looking over her shoulder, she asked, "Have you seen a doctor? It's important to have good prenatal care."

"No, ma'am. All I had was the pregnancy test. Tonio wanted me to have an abortion until we found out how much they cost. Then he wanted me to ask you and Daddy for half."

Cordelia's heart started to pound faster. "You want to have an abortion?"

Devon shrugged in response.

"Excuse me? What in the world does that mean?"

"That's what Tonio wants. He—"

"Don't tell me anything about that boy," Cordelia interrupted. "I have never liked him."

"You thought he just wanted me for sex."

"And you've proven me right, haven't you?" Cordelia shot back. "So you want to have an abortion?"

Devon shook her head.

Cordelia released a sigh of relief. She had her own beliefs when it came to the issue of abortion. In spite of everything this was not the route she wanted Devon to take. A thread of fear slid down her spine. What were they going to do? Her daughter was too young to be a mother. This was all wrong.

Her head began to throb. "I can't talk to you right now. If I do, I may end up saying something I can never take back." Cordelia stormed out of the room. She felt so sick to her stomach she barely made it to the bathroom in time. She quickly lowered herself to the toilet and vomited.

When she felt stronger, she got up and brushed her teeth. Cordelia placed a wet cloth to her forehead and walked to her room. She couldn't remember ever feeling so bad.

She took her time and changed for bed.

Devon appeared at her door an hour later. "Mama, did . . . did you eat something?"

"I'm not hungry." Cordelia glanced over her shoulder. "What about you? Have you eaten?"

"I made a sandwich."

They stood in silence for a moment, watching each other warily.

Cordelia was the first to speak. "I think I'm just going straight to bed. I have a lot on my mind, as you can well imagine."

"Mama . . ." Devon began.

"What is it?" Cordelia didn't mean to snap, but she was extremely upset at the moment.

"Nothing. I'm going to clean up the kitchen and then I'm going to bed myself."

"Good night," Cordelia uttered.

Devon left the bedroom, leaving Cordelia to sob softly.

She fell to her knees. "Heavenly Father, I come before You a wounded soul. I am so thankful for all Your blessings, but I really don't understand. Oh, dear Father, I have worshiped You and I've prayed for wisdom and Your guidance. Lord, how could Devon do this to me?" Cordelia continued to pray, but for the first time found no peace in doing so. She had done everything she could to prevent something like this from happening. She had failed, she thought miserably.

Cordelia did not sleep at all. She got up around five and ventured out into the living room. She sat out there on the sofa, staring into space for almost two hours. For the first time in years, she skipped her morning devotions and prayer.

When the clock struck seven, she propelled herself off the

sofa. It was time to get dressed. She came back downstairs later and made herself a pot of coffee.

She wasn't too surprised when Gerald arrived early Saturday morning. She knew Devon would turn to her father.

Following Cordelia into the kitchen, he questioned, "What's going on, Dee? Devon was in tears when she called me last night. Are you two having problems again?"

"Why don't we sit down?" Cordelia picked up her coffee, carried it into the den, and took a seat. Gerald followed and sat down on the sofa facing her. He wasn't a coffee drinker so she didn't offer him any.

"Will you tell me what's going on? I know there must be more to this than what you've told me so far. Devon could have told me about school on the phone."

"I think your daughter should be the one to tell you about this situation."

Gerald sighed in frustration.

Cordelia picked up a magazine and began to thumb through it. She had a strong feeling that her ex was going to try to blame this on her somehow, but he couldn't. This was Devon's fault alone. Had she listened to anything she'd said, her daughter wouldn't be pregnant.

He got up and strode over to the bottom of the stairs. "Devon, will you please come down here, sweetheart?" Gerald called out. "Your mother and I would like to talk to you."

Cordelia took a sip of her coffee.

Devon joined them in the den a few minutes later. She greeted Gerald with a hug but refused to meet her mother's gaze.

The teenager had barely sat down when Cordelia said, "Your daughter has something she needs to tell you, Gerald."

He looked at his daughter expectantly. "What's going on, sweetheart?"

"Go on and tell him," Cordelia urged. "You want to be grown so much—tell him." She was still very angry with Devon and resented being put in this situation.

"Daddy," Devon began, "I . . . I'm gonna have a baby."

A range of emotions washed over his face. "Excuse me?"

"You heard her correctly," Cordelia stated. "She's pregnant."

Gerald fell back against the cushions of the sofa, his eyes closed.

Devon teared up. "I'm sorry, Daddy. I know I disappointed you."

Cordelia couldn't believe her ears. Gerald got an apology, while she was the one who would have to endure this humiliation. She was the one who would be stuck with the baby once it was born. The very thought filled her with rage.

She sat tight-lipped while Gerald counseled their daughter. What in the world did he know? Cordelia thought nastily. She couldn't get over the fact that Devon had apologized to him. Did she get an apology? She tried to think back but couldn't remember.

"Mama's gonna call Tonio's parents," Devon announced.

"I'm afraid I have to agree with her on this. You didn't do this by yourself."

She started to cry. "Tonio's not gonna want to have anything to do with me or the baby."

"That boy won't have much choice in this situation." Gerald's tone was deadly. "I blame him too."

"It's not his fault, Daddy. I wanted to have sex," Devon stated.

Cordelia almost fell out of her chair. She fought the rising swell of anger threatening to consume her. "I guess you were trying to hurt me," she stammered.

"Mama, it had nothing to do with you. I love Tonio—"

"You know nothing about love, Devon," Cordelia cut in. "What you feel for this boy is not love. I know you think it is."

Devon's eyes filled with tears. "How do you know what I feel? You don't have my feelings, Mama."

"Whether or not you love Tonio is not why we're here,

Devon." Gerald ran his hands over his face. "This is about the trouble you're in."

"I didn't mean for this to happen. I'm so sorry."

Nodding, Gerald said, "Sweetheart, why don't you leave your mother and I alone so that we can talk."

"Yes, sir."

Devon left the room as quickly as possible.

"What are we going to do?" Gerald asked when they were alone.

She was incensed at the question. "What do you mean? *We* are not going to do anything." Wagging her finger at him, Cordelia said, "This is Devon's problem."

Gerald's eyes revealed his anger. "We are not going to abandon our daughter, Dee. Yeah, she's made a big mistake, but we should be here to support her."

Shaking her head, Cordelia announced, "I'm not interested in raising another child, and I don't like being forced into doing so."

"So what do you want her to do? Have an abortion?"

"Of course not. There are maternity homes. She could go to one of them," Cordelia suggested. "My cousin sent her daughter to one. Devon might even want to consider adoption."

Gerald was shaking his head. "I'd rather she come live with me before something like that happens. I'm not going to have my grandchild raised by complete strangers."

"You weren't ready to be a husband—now all of a sudden you want to become a full-time father and grandfather?"

"I'll do whatever I have to do for my daughter. I'm not going to abandon her. I have to be honest with you—I never thought you'd treat her like this. I can't even believe you're suggesting adoption. Surely you'd want to know your own grandchild."

She winced at the thought of becoming a grandmother. "I never thought she would do this me," Cordelia shot back. "I thought Devon would use better judgment. You know that no account Tonio boy is good for nothing. He's not going to stick around for her and this child. She's just going to be another statistic."

"Devon's a smart girl. It may be a little harder but she'll manage. She can still finish school and go to college. Her life doesn't have to end because she's having a baby. Don't get me wrong; I don't like it either, but there's nothing we can do about it."

"If she was so smart then how did she end up pregnant?"

Gerald rose to his feet. "Dee, you need to calm down. Being angry is not going to solve anything. It won't change what's happened."

She glared at him. "I have a right to my anger, Gerald. Don't you try to take that from me."

"We need to find a way to get through this. All of us."

"If you want Devon to live with you, that's fine. I've always told her that she can't bring any babies here. If I let her bring this one home, then I've made myself out to be a liar. I can't have that."

"How can you turn your back on your daughter like this? You turned your back on our marriage without a second thought, but—"

"Don't go there with me," Cordelia cut in. "I wasn't the one running around all over town with other women."

He stood up suddenly. "I'm tired of you throwing that up in my face. Maybe if you'd remembered you had a husband when you found God, I wouldn't have had to cheat on you just to get some attention."

His words wounded her, but Cordelia refused to let him see how much. "What a pitiful excuse. I can't believe you're trying to blame this on the good Lord above."

"I'm not blaming Him. I blame you, Dee. You didn't have to forget your husband just to serve God. Marriage should have come somewhere near the top on your list of priorities."

"How can you sit here in my house—"

"The house I'm paying for," Gerald interjected. "And the same house that my name is still on."

Cordelia continued as if she hadn't heard a word he said. "You need to own up to your own mistakes."

"You need to follow your own advice," Gerald countered. "You can sure sit in judgment of others but you can't take it, Dee. You've always been that way."

Cordelia couldn't think of a response, so she simply rolled her eyes at him.

"I think Devon should come live with me, and I don't want to argue about it."

"You won't get an argument from me, but you know how your daughter feels about Raleigh. She may not want to leave Tonio Bradshaw."

"You just said a few minutes ago that Devon couldn't stay here with a baby. Are you trying to backpedal? Woman, I can't keep up with you."

Cordelia sighed in frustration. "I don't know why I bother talking to you. You don't listen to me."

"Why do you always have to turn everything into an argument?"

"Is that your way of saying I'm confrontational?"

"There you go again," he accused.

"I just asked a question."

"Have you spoken to Tonio's parents yet?" Gerald asked, changing the subject.

"No, I wanted to wait until you were here. I'll give them a call now." Cordelia reached for the phone.

8

Life hung around Bonnie's shoulders like deadweight.

On the weekends she hated the long hours of trying to keep busy enough to forget just how lonely she really was. On Saturdays she volunteered at the women's shelter as well as visiting some of the sick and shut-in from her church. She'd just gotten home from the hospital but now wished she'd stayed a litter longer. The house was much too silent—or was she feeling more lonesome than usual? Bonnie had never preferred her own company. She enjoyed being around other people.

Her dog, Scotty, met her at the door. He was always happy to see her.

"Hey, baby," she cooed. "Mommy's baby hungry?" If it hadn't been for her dog, Bonnie wouldn't have rushed home.

Bonnie headed straight to the kitchen after slipping off her shoes. She opened her refrigerator and retrieved a pot of meat.

A few minutes later Scotty dined on a bowl of bottled water and some lamb chops. Bonnie had grabbed a hamburger on the way home, so she wasn't hungry.

Her dog taken care of, Bonnie went about the house doing

her weekly housecleaning. She took her time dusting the photographs scattered throughout her living room and the hallway. She stared lovingly at the frames containing pictures of her late husband. He had not been what one would call handsome. Edgar Abbott was a chalky white color, on the portly side, and had a mouthful of false teeth.

"It's so hard carrying on with my life without you," she whispered. Picking up the photo with shaking hands, Bonnie pressed it to her heart. "I miss you so much."

Twenty years ago, their wedding had been a small ceremony in a tiny church just outside of town. Bonnie had worked months making her white wedding dress and writing out invitations.

Edgar's relatives had outright refused to attend the wedding. Most of her family was opposed to the interracial marriage as well, yet they had come to witness the ceremony anyway. She'd been heartbroken when she peeked into the church right before the ceremony began. His side was virtually empty outside of a few friends.

When she'd walked down the aisle, Edgar watched her with tears in his eyes. He'd truly loved her; that much she knew. His love showed in his every action, the way he talked and the very way he looked at her. That knowledge alone made some of the hurt she felt vanish. She had never known such love in all of her life. Bonnie knew she would never experience such raw emotion again. She stood there for the longest time caught up in memories of the day her life began.

As much as Bonnie tried to fight it, the day Edgar died resurfaced. It was the day her world had crashed. Without her beloved husband, she was nothing.

She finished her dusting and strolled out into the hallway. Bonnie paused for a moment, scrutinizing the area. It was dark and drab-looking even to her. Looking at the cherry-wood furniture, she was overcome with the urge to add some color. Bonnie made a mental note to go by a paint store after work on

Monday. She was going to give the halls a face-lift. Something warm and welcoming. Maybe a nice mint green or apricot color.

She finished her dusting there and moved on to the formal dining room. From there she navigated to the kitchen. After washing the few dishes that were in the sink and mopping the floor, Bonnie settled in for the evening.

With Scotty in her lap, she surfed television channels, looking for a good movie. Finding nothing on TV, Bonnie went outdoors to work on her flowers. She paid particular attention to the roses, picking a few to arrange in vases in her living room and in the dining room. Flowers always added life to a room.

When there was nothing left to be done in the yard, Bonnie went back inside and showered. She chose a simple caftan to lounge around indoors.

For a moment she considered calling Cordelia but changed her mind. Bonnie figured that she was probably resting. Especially since she hadn't been feeling well over the past few days.

Bonnie found a book she hadn't read. Taking it off the shelf, she carried it with her to the den and settled down. Scotty played at her feet, bringing a smile to her face. "Hey, sweetie," she cooed. "Mommy loves you so much." He was her child—her only child—and she spoiled him terribly.

Her eyes watered. The one thing she'd wanted all her life was to be a mother. But for some reason or another God had decided otherwise. Bonnie never understood why she was barren, but she didn't question God. Apparently He had another plan for her life.

Later that evening Bonnie reorganized her sewing box, mainly because she had nothing better to do. As she arranged spools of colorful thread in rows, she watched her collie napping near the door. He loved her.

Her eyes were heavy with unshed tears. Outside of her dog, who else loved her? It was a question she'd asked herself so many times. Did anyone really care about her, or were they simply putting up with her?

Cordelia, Tangie, and Sabrina all claimed to be her friends, but they hardly ever inquired about her feelings. They were always talking about their problems, never taking time even to ask if anything bothered her. Bonnie carried her burden quietly. She suddenly felt ashamed. This was not how a friend should feel. She wanted her friends to cry on her shoulders. Bonnie wanted to be there for them. It was her life's purpose to be needed.

Putting the sewing box back in its place, she then decided to go through the trunk of fabric she had. Bonnie picked up a swatch of silk in a purple color. "This is beautiful," she murmured. "Just enough to make a pillow."

Feeling inspired, Bonnie began to spread out fabric swatches all over the floor. "Maybe I'll make a quilt." Her initial joy started to wane. What would she do with it once it was finished? She already had more than enough quilts crafted by her own hand.

"I won't worry about that now," she decided aloud. Bonnie pulled out a roll of lace. The ecru color completed the swatches of cloth in vivid shades of purple, teal, pink, and blue.

She spent the rest of the evening sitting on the floor playing with the fabric. Bonnie would arrange them one way, then another. Scotty woke up and ambled over toward her. He sniffed one of the swatches.

"No, baby. Sit," she commanded softly. "Mommy has an idea." Clearing a spot beside her, she said, "Sit, Scotty."

He did as he was told.

It was well after midnight when Bonnie finally headed to her bedroom. She put on a pair of pajamas and climbed into the four-poster bed.

She was asleep before her head hit the pillow.

9

"Mama, I need to borrow some money," Sabrina said. "I'll pay you back next month." Holding the phone to her ear, she braced herself for the lecture she knew would come. Her eyes traveled the room, looking for something to read. Sabrina found an old issue of *Ebony* lying on the edge of the coffee table and picked it up. This one featured Halle Berry on the cover.

Thumbing through the magazine, Sabrina allowed her mother to voice her opinion, responding every now and then with, "I know that."

This went on for about five minutes before she interjected, "I loaned a friend some money and she can't pay me back right now." Sabrina was lying, but her mother didn't have a clue. She'd spent most of her money preparing for Leon's birthday, including the hundred and fifty dollars she'd lost on the nonrefundable deposit for the condo in Myrtle Beach, South Carolina.

"You need to stop giving all your money away," her mother

counseled. "Learn how to say no sometime. That's your problem, sweetie. You're much too nice for your own good."

Sabrina had grown tired of hearing the familiar spiel and
asked, "Are you going to loan me the money, Mama?"

There was a long sigh, followed by, "Just withdraw it from
the joint account, baby. I trust you."

Sabrina breathed a sigh of relief. "Thank you, Mama. I really appreciate all you've done for me. As soon as everybody
starts paying me back I'll be okay, and I won't have to keep
coming to you for help." She tossed the magazine aside.

"You know I don't mind helping you out if I can. That's
what parents are for."

Sabrina's eyes traveled the large family room in her condo.
Her mother had paid for half of the furnishings and the expensive artwork on the walls. "I guess I'm real lucky to have you.
If my friends had a mother like you, they wouldn't keep running into problems."

"You're right about that," Mamie Mayhew intoned.

Sabrina broke into a grin. She'd always known how to ma-
nipulate her mother. Their only turbulent times had come when
her stepfather was still in the picture. He and Sabrina had never
gotten along, and he tried in vain to break her hold on her
mother. When that failed, her stepfather resorted to having af-
fairs.

Sabrina followed him to a hotel one night and promptly
called her mother to report his whereabouts and whom he was
with. She then generously offered to pay for their divorce because she was glad to have that jerk out of their lives.

"Sunday is the pastor's anniversary. Are you coming to
church?"

"I was invited to another church," Sabrina lied. She'd always hated going to the little old country church with the hard
wooden benches and no air-conditioning that her mother attended. She loved the elegance and sophistication of the church
she had joined six months ago. Anyone who was anyone at-

tended New Hope Baptist Church, and that was why she had been so eager to join. "If I don't go there, I'll come."

"Okay. Just remember I won't be home because we're eating at the church."

"Are you making sweet-potato pies?" Sabrina asked hopefully. She adored her mother's cooking.

Mamie took the hint. "Want me to make you one?"

Sabrina broke into a grin. "Yes. Actually, can you make me two of them? And some potato salad? Oh, throw in some collard greens. I've been wanting some greens."

Mamie gave a short laugh. "Anything for my baby girl."

Sabrina stole a peek at the clock on the mantel above her marble fireplace. Talking quickly, she said, "Thanks, Mama. I really appreciate it."

"Sure you can't make it on Sunday?"

"I'll call you if my plans change, Mama." Sabrina didn't miss the disappointment in her mother's voice. She wasn't bothered by it though. "I'll be by the house to pick up my food Sunday evening."

"I went to see your aunt Hazel. She asked about you."

"I hope you told her I was fine." Sabrina had a feeling her mother was about to lapse into a long story. Her aunt always had major drama in her life. The woman had been married six times and maintained she still loved all her ex-husbands.

"Do you remember your uncle Benjamin? Well, Hazel's been seeing him at the Motel 6 on Highway 74. His wife followed him and found them there—"

"I'd better get off this phone," Sabrina interjected. "I'll talk to you later, okay?" Normally she would have stayed on the line to hear the rest of the story, but she still needed to get dressed. Leon was expected in about an hour. Sabrina ended the call and let out a squeal of joy as she put her plans in motion.

*   *   *

Everything was perfect.

Sabrina had worked quickly to get the condo in order for Leon's birthday celebration. She'd bought the perfect outfit by St. Johns: it was a black ruffle tie jacket and pants. She'd also found the perfect teddy for later—she intended to make this night very special for him.

Sabrina gave the condo another once-over. Leading from the doorway to the bedroom was a trail of rose petals. She took a peek over at the clock and frowned. Leon should have been here by now.

"Where are you?" she whispered to the empty room.

Sabrina pursed her lips into a line of displeasure as she stomped over to the sofa and dropped down. With the soft sounds of jazz dancing in the background, she passed the time by playing with the ribbons on Leon's present while waiting for him to arrive. She found it hard to believe that she'd spent all of her money on a watch for a man who hadn't had the decency to be prompt for his own birthday dinner. It was going to take more than roses for her to forgive him this time around. She had actually taken the time and energy to cook Leon dinner.

The hour grew late, and Sabrina got madder and madder. She'd blown out the last of the candles and was about to stomp off to bed when she heard a knock on the door. Sabrina debated whether to answer it.

She heard Leon's voice on the other side saying, "Come on, Sabrina. Baby, please don't act like this. I know you're in there. Open up."

After a moment she marched over to the door and threw it open.

"I made dinner well over two hours ago, Leon," she snapped. "I can't believe you're trying to play me." Glaring at him, Sabrina blocked his entrance.

"I had to take care of some business." Leon was standing only inches away from her. Tossing a furtive look across his

shoulder, he asked, "Can we finish this inside? I don't like people in my business."

Sabrina let her eyes roam over his body. She started at his
head and worked down to his feet, her eyes slowly rising to
meet his. "Why should I let you in my house? It's clear you
don't want to be here or you would've been here on time."

Leon was very apologetic. "I'm sorry for being late. I really
am. Now will you let me inside?"

Her jaw tight, Sabrina moved aside to let him enter the
condo. "Whatever!"

His mouth went grim and he lashed out. "Don't start tripping, Sabrina. I don't need to hear it tonight."

She slammed the door behind him. "Well, you're gonna hear
it! I don't appreciate this mess. I was invited to a party tonight
and I could have been there; I could have been in Myrtle Beach,
but nooooo . . ." Sabrina paused for effect. "Like a fool I'm
here cooking your favorite steak and garlic-parsley potatoes,
and look how you treat me. . . ." She stalked over to the sofa
and dropped down.

Leon followed her. "Sabrina, I wanted to be here; I really
did. But I had to make this meeting. Now stop tripping."

Looking up at him, she shot back, "You could have resched-
uled your so-called meeting."

"No, I couldn't. Look, Sabrina, I'm sorry."

Gesturing toward the kitchen, she stated, "Your dinner is in
the oven. I was starving so I already ate."

"This is supposed to be my birthday celebration and I have
to eat alone?"

Peeved, Sabrina nodded. "You were the one late, Leon."

He gave her a sharp look before heading to the kitchen.
Leon paused when he spied a white box on the table. Pointing,
he asked, "You bought me a birthday cake?"

"I don't half-step. Yeah, I got you a cake." Trying to think of
a way to get even with Leon, Sabrina jumped to her feet.

He grinned. "Chocolate?"

Brushing past Leon, she strode into the kitchen, where she warmed up his food. Smiling sweetly, she said, "Go on and have a seat at the table. I'll bring it to you."

"That's much better," Leon muttered.

Sabrina rolled her eyes behind his back.

A few minutes later she sat down beside him, watching him tear into the steak as though he hadn't eaten in days.

"Baby, you can really cook. This steak is bangin'."

"I guess that warrants a thank-you," Sabrina uttered with her arms folded across her chest. She shot him a penetrating stare before turning away.

Leon stuck a forkful of potatoes into his mouth. "Yeah. This is what I'm talkin' 'bout." He took another bite. "Mmmmm . . ."

Sabrina gritted her teeth in anger. She couldn't stand the way Leon hummed while he ate. The truth was that there were a lot of things about him that drove her crazy. But he was generous with his money, and that was all that mattered to her. She wasn't looking for love—just financial security. At least that was what she kept telling herself.

"Oh, yeah. I saw Bonita yesterday. You need to tell your little girlfriend not to come up to my job."

Leon stopped eating. "Bonita came to your job?"

"That's what I just said, Leon," she snapped in anger. "I don't know what's up with you and her, but you'd better straighten her out before I have to." Sabrina tried to make it sound like a threat.

"What did she say?"

Folding her arms across her chest, Sabrina replied, "Nothing. Just stood there looking stupid."

"Maybe she was looking for someone."

"Me. Duh-uh . . ."

Leon glared at her. "Knowing Bonita, if she went there to see you, she would've said something. She don't play."

"Neither do I," Sabrina huffed.

Shaking his head, he added, "Baby, I don't know. Bonita, she crazy."

To add insult to injury, Leon seemed to think more about Bonita. The evening was not getting better. "Hurry up and finish your food."

Leon glanced up from his plate. "Girl, why you being so hateful? This is my birthday. I want to have a good time tonight."

"You almost done eating?"

Leon muttered a curse.

Neither one of them spoke another word while he ate. Every now and then Leon would look over at her. Sabrina was burned to the core at his actions. She did not forget when someone wronged her.

When he finished, Sabrina took the plate back to the kitchen. She took her time washing the dishes. From the living room Leon called her name, but she ignored him. She was very disappointed in him right at the moment. Sabrina hated having any part of her plans ruined. It spoiled the entire evening for her.

Leon was stretched out on the sofa watching television when she returned. Sabrina frowned. He sure didn't have a problem making himself comfortable in her place. It didn't matter that he'd paid her mortgage for the last four months.

"Come here, baby."

She did as he asked. When Leon tried to kiss her, she pulled away.

"What's wrong with you? Why you acting like you don't want to be touched?"

"Because I don't."

"You don't mean that." Leon pulled her closer to him.

She sat there unresponsive while he planted kisses all over her face and groped her body. Feeling vindictive, Sabrina suddenly began to respond. She even allowed Leon to untie her shirt, but before he could get it completely off her, Sabrina pulled away from him.

Surprised, Leon questioned, "Where are you going, baby?"

She faked a yawn. "I'm tired, so I'm going to bed," Sabrina announced as she rose to her feet.

Leon stood up too. He moved to follow her.

Sabrina stopped in her tracks. "Where do you think you're going?"

"With you. I'm going to bed."

"Not here," she stated coldly.

"What do you mean, not here?"

"You're not going to treat me like some ho. Don't think you can come up in here anytime you want and just climb in my bed. If you want to make love to me, you need to treat me with more respect."

Leon waved her off with his right hand. "Stop tripping, Sabrina."

"Call it whatever you want, Leon. You ain't getting nothing here. So just stroll your tardy behind out my door. Next time, *be here* when you're supposed to be," she advised. Holding up the gift, she added, "This here was supposed to be your birthday present, but you're not getting it now. You don't deserve it." She paused for a heartbeat before adding, "By the way, you can leave the hundred and fifty dollars I put down on the condo on the table. I don't have money to waste. Every penny I make goes to help take care of my mother."

"I'll give you your money back—that ain't no problem. Girl, why you acting like this?"

"I demand respect."

"I can't help it if I had to take care of some business, Sabrina. I need to make sure I have all my investments straight."

"Look, I'm tired and I'm in a very bad mood, thanks to you. You ruined this night for me, Leon." Pointing the way to the door, she said, "Now I just want you to leave."

"If I leave, I won't be back," he threatened. "We're finished."

"You don't ever have to come back, Leon. It's not like I love you or anything."

Curses spewed out of Leon's mouth as he stomped toward the front door. Sabrina gave a short laugh when he slammed the door on his way out. She didn't care. Leon should've known better. Anytime he mistreated her, she placed him on lockdown: no sex until he was back in her good graces. This time it was different.

Sabrina was really hurt by his constant lack of consideration. Even after he'd canceled out on spending the weekend in Myrtle Beach, she had still wanted to make his birthday special. Especially after he'd sent her two dozen white roses.

She was not about to let him dog her out like some of the other girls running around here. And she certainly wasn't going to get stuck with a bunch of babies either. In her twenty-six years, she'd been pregnant three times but aborted them all. Sabrina wanted the whole package—a big, beautiful house, a luxury car, and financial security. She refused to settle for less. But as much as she tried to fight it, Sabrina found herself falling for Leon. She also had to admit that their relationship was headed nowhere. He wasn't the type of man who would settle down—not until he was good and ready. Sabrina was growing impatient.

He lived in the next town, which was twenty-five minutes away, and was constantly on the go. Leon didn't have a job but he owned several Laundromats, thanks to a large sum of money from a lawsuit he won due to a back injury sustained in a car accident several years ago. He was currently enrolled in business classes at the university. He had a dream of starting a nonprofit foundation for youths.

Sabrina ripped down the comforter on her bed. She muttered curses as she pulled down the black sheet and pumped up her pillows. When the bed was ready, she took off her clothes and dressed for bed. She climbed in and curled up, feeling lost in the king-size bed.

Sabrina tossed and turned for about thirty minutes before she sat up to call her mother.

"Hey, Mama. I know it's late but I wanted to call and let you know that my plans have changed for tomorrow. I'll meet you at the church."

10

Tangie was more than ready for a party. She'd had a hectic week, and on top of that Lula had been calling her at home and at the office. She left messages at both places. She was the last person Tangie wanted to have a conversation with, and she had no intention of calling her back. When would her mother ever get the message? she wondered.

She was filled with tension throughout her body, and Tangie had no idea why. It had started a few days ago—just a feeling of being overwhelmed. What she really needed right now was a strong drink and a sexy man afterward. It would take her mind off her troubles temporarily.

Standing in her walk-in closet, Tangie decided on a slinky black dress with spaghetti straps. She would wear her short, fitted red leather jacket over it, along with her knee-length leather boots with the spike heels.

Tangie wished her friend Sheryl were in town. She missed her running buddy. As close as she and Sabrina were, Tangie would never invite her along. She talked entirely too much, and Tangie didn't want her business all over St. Paul County.

She experimented with her hair, trying to decide whether to pin it up or leave it hanging past her shoulders in a cascade of curls. In the end she decided to wear it down. It gave her a sexier look.

Next Tangie applied a thin layer of makeup. Staring at her reflection, she decided she was ready. She was proud of her smooth complexion and her body. She was confident of gaining the attention of most of the men tonight. Satisfied with her look, she quickly packed an overnight bag and carried it out to the car. She enjoyed being the center of attention and having her pick of the litter.

She was on her way to Fayetteville a few minutes later. Tangie slipped in a recent CD by recording artist Mya. She hummed along as she drove along Interstate 40. An acquaintance of hers was celebrating her birthday at a club near the military base. Tangie grinned as she thought of what was to come.

Her thoughts traveled to Sabrina, and Tangie wondered if Leon had even bothered to show up for dinner. He made a habit of blowing Sabrina off. She couldn't understand at all why her friend didn't get the hint. Leon was a player and wasn't the type to settle down. A few years back he'd won a huge settlement from a lawsuit against Southern Railroad. He'd been injured, but his mother and brother had been killed in the car accident due to negligence on the company's part. Since winning the millions, Leon treated women as if they were nothing more than playthings.

Tangie was glad that she didn't allow herself to get emotionally attached to any man. Love didn't last forever, but it wasn't just that. She didn't want to end up like Lula. The way she chased after men—married men—disgusted Tangie. She was nothing more than a diversion to them, but Lula couldn't see it.

*   *   *

Tangie woke with a start early Sunday morning and sat up, looking around the hotel room. It took her a moment to remember where she was. She stole a quick peek at the sleeping man beside her. She didn't know anything about him outside of his name, but it didn't really matter anyway. After today, she had no plans to ever see him again.

Tangie slipped out of bed and stealthily made her way to the shower. Turning on the water, she stepped into the tub, enjoying the warm spray of water tickling her body. Tangie lathered her washcloth.

She jumped when the curtain suddenly opened and tried to cover her body with her hands. "You scared me. I thought you were still sleeping."

He tried to kiss her and stuck a leg into the tub.

She caught the faintest whiff of stale whiskey and turned up her nose. Backing away from him, Tangie asked, "What are you doing?"

"I missed that sexy body of yours, so I thought I'd join you in the shower."

Tangie didn't like the way he was leering at her. "No."

He looked stunned for a second. "What?"

Nervously Tangie cleared her throat. "I like to shower alone. It's just a quirk I have." She gave a slight shrug. "Sorry." Showering together wasn't part of the package. She used this time to clear her mind as she washed away the traces of filth where his hands had roamed her body.

He stared at her for a moment before saying, "No problem." He removed his leg and closed the curtain.

I'm not like her, she thought when her mother came to mind. Tangie heard a noise and called out, "You okay?"

"Yeah, I'm okay. I just hit my toe on the toilet."

Biting back a smile, she turned off the water and then reached for a towel. Wrapping it around her body, Tangie stepped out of the tub. "I'm sorry about the shower. I just have a thing about sharing my bath with anyone."

"It's okay," he uttered nonchalantly. "Could you turn the water back on?"

"Sure." Tangie did as he asked. She allowed him to kiss her, but it no longer excited her. All she felt right now was disgust for this man she barely knew. This was the first time she'd ever felt sickened by a night of pleasure, and it scared her. Sex normally helped her relax, so why was this time so different?

While he was in the shower Tangie dressed as quickly as she could, wanting to be as far away from him as possible. Just looking at him made her want to vomit. Grabbing her purse, she rushed out of the room. Tangie didn't bother waiting for the elevator. She took the stairs four levels down.

On her way home Tangie tried to turn to her favorite radio station. She hit the gospel station by accident. She listened for a moment before switching to the CD player. For some reason she felt guilty. It was probably the song, Tangie reasoned. Gospel songs were designed to make you feel that way. Besides, she heard gospel music all the time at the office. Cordelia kept it on whenever she worked.

Tangie checked her messages when she arrived home. There were two from her mother. "Why don't you leave me alone, Lula? I don't want anything to do with you." She burst into tears. "Haven't you made my life miserable enough? This is all your fault."

11

Today seemed little better than yesterday.

Cordelia found it hard to concentrate during Sunday morning services. Every time she caught sight of Devon sitting in the pew ahead of her, the crushing memories moved to the forefront. Again she silently beseeched, *How could she do this to me? Dear Lord, how could you let this happen?* Cordelia had just recently began to feel she was getting her own life in order. *I don't deserve this.*

Pastor Grant was still on the subject of suffering. He had no idea what it was all about, she thought silently. All of his children were grown and had gone on to become doctors, lawyers, and engineers. He could never understand how brokenhearted she was.

Pretty soon Devon would be showing, and everyone would know. Everyone would know that she couldn't even manage her own household. Cordelia cast a spiteful look at her daughter. Not once had Devon shown an ounce of remorse. She didn't appear the least bit bothered that she had put them in a position to be gossiped about. Cordelia had survived all the talk surrounding her cheating ex-husband, but this was different. She would be the one blamed.

Cordelia struggled to focus on Pastor Grant's sermon. This wasn't like her at all. She normally devoured the message, soaking it up like a sponge.

Every now and then she could feel Devon's eyes on her, but she refused to meet her gaze. Cordelia couldn't remember ever being this angry with her daughter.

After church Devon hid away in her room. Cordelia didn't pester her to come out because she needed some space between them. She was grateful that her daughter had decided to drive her own car to the church.

Devon had just turned seventeen. What would she do with a baby? What did she know about being a mother? Even though Cordelia and Gerald had gotten married, it had not been easy raising a child. Gerald was still in law school at the time, so much of the responsibility had fallen on her shoulders. Having her daughter had matured her, Cordelia admitted.

The headache Cordelia had been fighting had not quite gone away. The pain was not as intense as before, but it still weakened her. Just taking off her church clothes had exhausted her. She felt nauseated and decided to lie down for a while.

When she felt up to it a while later, she got up and navigated to the kitchen to cook. Cordelia fried chicken, warmed up some leftover turnip greens, and made fresh potato salad. She also made a pan of macaroni and cheese.

While she was setting the table, Devon ventured out of her room. Pulling a bottle of water from the fridge, she leaned against the counter looking nonchalant. "Dinner almost ready?"

Cordelia glared at her in response.

Turning to leave the kitchen, Devon uttered, "I won't eat if you don't want me to."

She glanced over her shoulder and said, "There's no need for theatrics."

Devon stopped in the doorway. "I didn't do anything. You

were the one looking at me like you didn't want me to touch your food."

Folding her arms across her chest, Cordelia stared at her. "Really? Why don't you show me what that looks like? I can't honestly say I'm familiar with that particular look. And since when have I ever denied you food?"

Devon twisted her face into a frown. "You know what I'm talking about. You go around acting like you don't even want me in the same room with you. You don't talk to me."

"Your mouth is cut the same as mine," Cordelia pointed out. "If you want to talk, you know where to find me. Right now I have to admit that I really don't have any words for you, Devon. I'm very disappointed in you, and I'm very hurt. It's going to take some time for me to work through this mess."

"Mama, I didn't mean for this to happen."

Cordelia released a long sigh. "I'm sure you didn't. You probably didn't think about anything but satisfying your lust." Her tone had turned ugly. This was the only way she could strike back at her daughter.

Devon's eyes filled with tears. "I can't talk to you about this. You won't even listen to me."

"No! I'm not saying anything you want to hear."

"All of my friends who've had babies—their mothers are excited and buying baby clothes."

"I'm not them."

"Why can't you be more like them? I mean, they were upset at first, but then they talked to their daughters and everything is fine."

"I'm not going to sugarcoat this for you, Devon. You screwed up big-time."

"Haven't you ever made a mistake, Mama?"

The bluntness of the question surprised her. It took a moment for Cordelia to respond. "I've made plenty of mistakes, but I've tried to learn from them." Cordelia knew that sooner or later Devon would realize that she had been conceived before her parents were married, but it was a different time, she reasoned. Besides, her mother had never talked to Cordelia about sex. In fact, it was a subject that had never been brought up.

Cordelia tried to maintain open lines of communication with her own daughter. She and Devon had talked candidly about sex. Maybe that was where she went wrong, she surmised. She took the macaroni out of the oven. "Have you researched any of the maternity homes I told you about?"

"I don't want to go to a home," Devon replied. "Daddy said I could move in with him."

Cordelia didn't glance up from the food. "I know. He told me."

The room grew silent, and Devon washed her hands in the kitchen sink. After drying them, she assisted Cordelia with the meal. This was one of the few times she didn't have her cordless phone glued to her ear.

They were soon seated at the dinner table. Cordelia recited a prayer of thanks before fixing her plate.

During the meal, Devon announced, "I don't really like Raleigh." She gave her mother a hopeful look.

"I'm not going to raise another child, Devon. I'm sorry, but I just can't do it."

"I intend to take care of my own child, Mama. I'm not asking you to do that. Believe me, I know how you feel about it. You won't have to do anyth—"

Meeting her daughter's gaze, Cordelia interrupted, "I just think it's best that you go to live with your father. It's not just the baby—you don't want to abide by any of my rules."

"This is my home." Devon's voice broke. "How can you do this to me?"

Cordelia sat there a moment watching her. "I didn't do anything to you. You did this to yourself."

"You made Daddy leave and now you're throwing me out,"

she lashed out in anger. "I don't think you ever wanted me in the first place."

"Stop being a drama queen, Devon. I told you many times that I wasn't going to have babies in my house unless they were mine, and I meant it." Cordelia stuck a forkful of macaroni into her mouth, chewing slowly.

Conversation ended and they finished their dinner in tense silence. Devon left the table as soon as she finished eating. Frustrated and disappointed, Cordelia pounded her fist against the counter.

Thank God it was Monday, Cordelia thought as she pulled into the parking lot of St. Paul County Human Services. It had been a tension-filled weekend, with Devon sulking most of the time.

It had been decided that Devon would be moving to Raleigh during spring break. She wasn't happy about it at all. Cordelia planned to call her doctor this morning to get Devon an appointment—that was all she was willing to do at this point.

She sat in the car for a moment, struggling to gather her thoughts. Cordelia felt a deep sense of loss where Devon was concerned. She was losing her daughter, and it hurt.

Cordelia had to consider that Devon would never forgive her for sending her away. "There is no other way," she whispered to herself. "I can't change my mind about this. It would make me a liar."

She felt sick all over again. Cordelia sat in the car for a few minutes more, hoping her stomach would settle.

When she felt as if she could make it without embarrassing herself, she got out of her car and walked into the building. She nodded at a few of the other employees before stepping onto the elevator. She wasn't in the mood to chat, so she kept her head down until she reached the floor she worked on.

She sat at her desk, noticing through the windows the men

and women getting out of their cars. Cordelia silently watched the men with their ties flying as they walked toward the building.

The clicking of high heels on the floor caught her attention and reminded her of tiny mechanical figures, much like the ones on a music box.

Her headache was back, and Cordelia felt like a ticking time bomb. She needed to talk to someone before she exploded. She turned midstride and headed straight to Bonnie's office.

12

Bonnie strolled into the FFA unit shortly after seven, this time bringing doughnuts from Krispy Kreme for her colleagues.

She'd struggled through the weekend but felt revitalized being back at work. She wondered if she would ever make peace with the loneliness. Working on the quilt had taken up some of her time. It didn't keep Bonnie's mind off the disappointing phone call she'd made to her cousin in Los Angeles after church yesterday.

Once a month she tried to reach out and connect with some of her family members, but the calls always left her with an empty feeling inside. Each time Bonnie would vow that it would be her last call, but when the next month rolled around, she couldn't seem to help herself. Edgar's family had flat-out told her never to call. His sister had even had her number changed.

This particular cousin was ten years younger than Bonnie. They had once been close, or so Bonnie thought, but every time she'd called, the woman would exchange a few pleasantries and then make up an excuse to end the conversation. None of

Bonnie's family members had really liked the idea of her being married to a white man. It didn't matter to Bonnie at the time. Edgar was her only chance for happiness, and she had grabbed it.

Humming to herself, Bonnie settled down at her desk and prepared to get her workday started. She had a lot to do.

A few minutes later Cordelia was rapping softly on her open door. "You have a minute to talk? I really need to confide in someone."

Bonnie waved her inside. "Sure, Dee. Come on in."

Cordelia closed the door behind her and dropped down in one of the visitor's chairs. Her demeanor gave Bonnie the impression that something was terribly wrong.

"My goodness. What's going on with you, Dee?"

Cordelia's eyes were tear-bright. "Devon's pregnant, Bonnie."

"What?" she shrieked with surprise.

"I can hardly believe it myself. She went and got herself pregnant." A tear rolled down her cheek. Cordelia swiped at it with her hand.

Bonnie handed her a tissue. "Oooh, Dee. I'm so sorry. I wish there were something I could do."

"I've talked to her over and over about this subject," Cordelia murmured tearfully. "Just a couple of weeks ago I was bragging on her—talking about how grateful I was that she hadn't . . . hadn't gotten pregnant. . . . Devon was pregnant all this time." She wiped her eyes with the tissue.

Bonnie felt so sorry for her friend. Cordelia looked heartbroken. "I'm sorry," she said softly. "Devon made a mistake, Dee. You have to remain calm and loving. She's probably feeling alone, frightened, and embarrassed about her pregnancy, but she'll get through this."

"I'm not worried about *her* getting through this mess. I don't know if *I* can do it."

"Honey, you can," Bonnie assured her. "No matter how the baby was conceived, he or she is still a gift from God."

"I'm so angry," Cordelia confessed. "I could strangle that girl. I've worked all these years for her."

"I know. I would feel the very same way if it were my daughter. But as a parent you've got to get past the anger. Devon may be feeling ashamed and unworthy of love. Show her that you love her unconditionally."

"I thought Devon was smarter than this. I really did."

"Try not to judge her too harshly, Dee. She—"

Irritated, Cordelia raised a hand to cut Bonnie off. "I'm not judging her, but God will. He will hold her responsible—not me."

"God loves her no matter what. I know it's real hard to see past your anger right now, but it'll get easier."

"You know what hurts the most? She didn't come tell me. I had to find out by accident." She massaged her temple with her left hand. "She's due in August, Bonnie."

"My goodness. How did you find out?"

"I came home Friday night after Bible study and went to check on her. She was sleeping and her breasts were leaking."

Bonnie could only imagine Cordelia's shock upon discovering that her baby girl was pregnant. She had to be devastated, but she was going to have to put aside those feelings and start listening to Devon's deepest concerns. Cordelia was going to have to be there for her daughter.

A confused expression attached itself to her face. "I just don't understand. We have always been able to talk—at least I thought so—but she didn't tell me a thing."

"I'm sure she was scared. Devon was afraid of disappointing you, Dee."

"What on earth did she think I would do?"

"I don't think she feared you—just didn't want to hurt you."

"She wouldn't have slept with that boy if she didn't want to hurt me."

"She cares for him, Dee. Most girls her age think that they

have to have sex to keep a guy, or Devon may have been looking for love."

"I told her that Tonio Bradshaw was no good."

"Have you talked to him?"

Cordelia nodded. "We had them over on Saturday. Can you
believe that his mother tried to put all the blame on Devon? His
father gave Devon a check for a thousand dollars."

"That was nice."

"It was . . ." Cordelia admitted.

"Is Tonio going to be there for her? For emotional support?"

"I don't think so." Cordelia paused a heartbeat before continuing. "Of course, Devon has all of her faith in him."

"So Devon really wants to keep the baby?" Bonnie asked
softly.

"She does. She says that abortion is not an option. Adoption
is not an option either."

"Did anything good come out of the meeting with the Bradshaws? Besides Tonio's father giving Devon the money, I mean."

Cordelia grimaced. "I wish you could have seen the snooty
expression Margaret Bradshaw wore. She acted like butter
wouldn't melt in her mouth. She had the nerve to think that
Tonio was just going to run off to college without sharing in
this responsibility. I have no respect for parents like that."

Bonnie was stunned. "You're kidding."

"I don't like this situation, but I'll tell you what: Devon isn't
going through it all by herself. Tonio is going to shoulder some
of the blame. Not his father—him. I mean that."

"I don't blame you, Dee. I would feel the same way."

"I wish you could have seen the way Margaret Bradshaw
looked at us. Like we were nothing."

"I've never met any of the Bradshaws, but I've heard a lot
about them. They're real uppity, from what I hear."

"They are," Cordelia confirmed. "Although the father was
real decent. I have to give him credit. He seemed real determined to make Tonio do right."

"That's good to hear."

"We'll see if he means it. I could tell those people think they're too good for us."

"I'm real sorry, Dee. I know you may not see it right now, but things will work out. They will."

"Thank you so much for listening. Please don't say anything to Sabrina or Tangie about this yet. I'm just not ready for everybody to know."

"I won't," she promised. Cordelia rose to her feet unsteadily. The room started to spin, causing her to reach out blindly. "This has taken . . . so much . . ." Her voice seemed to vanish.

Bonnie knew something was wrong. "Dee, what is it?"

"I . . . I feel . . ." Cordelia's voice died as she fell to the floor in a slump.

13

Sabrina and Tangie should have been working, but instead they were in Tangie's cubicle gossiping.

"What did you do this weekend?" Sabrina questioned. "Leon and I did our usual. We had another fight." She sat with a stack of files in her lap. She handed them one at a time to Tangie.

"I spent the night in Fayetteville."

Perking up, Sabrina inquired, "Oh, really. With who?"

Laughing, Tangie recorded the name listed on the file onto another sheet of paper. "I didn't say I was with someone. Even if I were, it's not your business."

Sabrina handed her another file. "Keeping secrets again?" She secretly wished Tangie would share the sordid details of her life with her. Sabrina's curiosity was getting the best of her.

"No, I wouldn't say that. I'm just not going into a whole lot of detail. I went to a party in Fayetteville and I had a real good time. That's all you need to know."

"Hmmmm, you must have something to hide."

Eyeing Sabrina, Tangie asked, "Why do you always say things like that?"

"Because you act like your love life is top secret. I feel like I have to have high-level clearance just to discuss it."

"You do," Tangie joked. "Now why are you angry with Leon? What did he do this time?"

"I planned the perfect birthday celebration for him, but it was ruined of course. He showed up two hours late, and girl, he thought he was gonna get him some sex. I showed him, though. I sent him home to a cold shower."

Tangie shook her head. "Leon is a no-good dog. I don't know why you bother with that man. You're too good for him."

"It's all about the money." Sabrina wasn't being truthful, but she didn't want to appear to be a lovesick fool. "All Leon can do for me is pay my bills. Don't get me wrong—I like him a lot. He just makes me so mad. I—" She stopped short when she heard a loud thud. "What in the world was that?"

Tangie shrugged her shoulders and said, "It sounded as if someone fell."

They both rushed to their feet and peeked outside the cubicle.

Tangie whispered, "Do you see anything?"

Sabrina looked back at her. "Just some people around Bonnie's office. Maybe one of her clients fainted or something." She dropped the files on her desk. "I'm going down there."

Tangie followed her. They hurried down the short distance to Bonnie's office.

Sabrina gasped. Cordelia lay on the floor and appeared to be unconscious. "Oh, my God," she exclaimed in shock. "What happened?"

Tangie placed a hand on Bonnie's shoulder. "What happened?"

"We were talking and she just collapsed," Bonnie replied in a trembling voice. "I've called the paramedics and they should be here shortly. Give her some air, ladies and gentlemen. Dee needs air. Go on back to your desks, please."

"Nobody is going to be able to work with Dee knocked out like this," Sabrina whispered. "We're all worried about her."

Tangie agreed. "I'm not leaving. Some people around here just want to be nosy, but Dee is our friend."

Sabrina shook her head sadly. "I can't believe this is happening to poor Dee. You know she's been having all those headaches lately. I told her she needed to see a doctor."

St. Paul County security personnel pushed forward through the growing crowd. Bonnie gave them a short overview of what had happened. One of the men instructed onlookers to go back to their own workstations, while the other knelt down to check Cordelia's pulse.

Sabrina maneuvered through the crowd until she was face-to-face with the security guard holding back the onlookers. "This is my friend," she said in a low whisper. She even managed to work up a tear. Giving him a doe-eyed look, she said, "Nothing can happen to her."

He gave her a reassuring smile.

In the distance they could hear the wailing of a siren piercing the air.

"The paramedics are here," someone announced.

Sabrina's ears pricked at the low murmur of voices surrounding her. Like an antenna, she wanted to pick up every tidbit being said.

The arrival of the EMTs halted the separate conversations going on. Sabrina watched in fascination as one EMT talked with Bonnie and another employee.

They checked her pulse, her heart rate, and her breathing. Cordelia was still unconscious and did not respond to their voices. A third EMT hooked up oxygen and placed a nonrebreather mask over Cordelia's nose.

All of the employees of the FFA unit were gathered in nearby workstations, silently watching as the paramedics worked on Cordelia. A couple of the women had tears in their eyes. Bonnie wrapped her arms around one who was openly weeping.

Satisfied that their patient was stable, the team prepared Cordelia for transport to the hospital. They gently lifted her, moving her to a rolling stretcher, and covered her with sheets and blankets. Sabrina ran over to Cordelia's workstation and returned with her friend's purse, intent on going with them.

"I'm going to the hospital with her," Bonnie announced. "I'll take her purse."

"You have so much to do here," Sabrina argued. "I don't mind going."

Bonnie shook her head. "I'd rather you stay here at the office. I'll call back as soon as I hear something."

Sabrina was fuming as she reluctantly handed over the purse.

Bonnie followed the EMTs out of the FFA unit and to the elevators. A few of the workers migrated to the reception area. Tangie and Sabrina remained behind.

Reaching for a nearby telephone, Tangie announced, "Someone should call Devon's school and let them know what's going on."

"I'll do it. Then I'll go pick her up and take her to the hospital," Sabrina volunteered. She was thrilled to be able to take part in some way. "Devon shouldn't drive. She's going to be scared and upset. Could you let Kayla know that Bonnie's going with Dee and that I'll be going to the hospital with Devon?"

"Sure, I will," replied Tangie.

Sabrina started to tremble with excitement. She didn't want anything to happen to Dee, but she was enjoying her part as the rescuer.

Sitting down at her desk, she called the high school to notify them of what had transpired. Sabrina was on Devon's emergency card, so there wasn't going to be a problem picking her up. "Please have her in the attendance office and ready. I want to get her to the hospital."

As soon as she hung up, Sabrina rose to her feet and grabbed her keys. She was on her way to the high school a short time later.

She wanted to get Devon to the hospital as quickly as she could. Mother and daughter needed each other.

14

In spite of the events earlier, Tangie managed to see all of her afternoon appointments and return most of her phone calls. She kept checking the clock because she was worried about Cordelia. Her friend was very healthy, so Tangie reasoned that it couldn't be anything serious. Maybe Cordelia had passed out because of something as simple as not eating. She made a quick call to Kayla to see if she'd heard anything.

In her nervousness, Tangie played with her pen. She heard Sabrina's voice and got up. "When did you get back?"

Sabrina checked her watch. "About twenty minutes ago. Have you heard anything?"

"No. I just got off the phone with Kayla. I thought Bonnie might have called her to give her an update."

"Girl, she's too busy trying to run things at the hospital. When I got there with Devon, she thanked me and basically ordered me back to the office."

Tangie held back her smile. "How was Devon when you took her to the hospital?"

Shrugging, Sabrina answered, "I don't know. She didn't say

much. I guess she's in shock. You should have seen Bonnie. She was—"

"You think Dee's going to be okay?" Tangie quickly interjected.

Sabrina nodded. "She's going to be fine, Tangie. Probably just a little dehydrated or something. You know how she hates to drink water, and she eats like a bird. Well, I'd better check my messages and try to do some work."

She was back in Tangie's office fifteen minutes later. "I can't work," Sabrina confessed as she dropped down in a nearby chair. "I keep thinking about Dee."

Leaning back in her chair, Tangie agreed. "I know the feeling. Maybe we should just call it a day."

"Works for me. I was here early anyway." Sabrina rose to stand. "I'll shut down my computer and grab my purse."

"I'll be ready to leave by the time you come back."

Tangie made a quick phone call. When she was through, she readied to leave.

Sabrina and Tangie walked out to their cars together.

"I thought we would've heard from Bonnie by now," Sabrina stated. "Kayla hasn't heard a word from her."

"I thought so too. I'm getting worried because she hasn't called. It must be something pretty serious if it's taking this long." Tangie stopped at her car. "Did they say anything when you took Devon to emergency?"

"They didn't have any information then. Bonnie sent me back before I could find out what was going on," she grumbled.

"I'm thinking about going to the hospital right now," Tangie announced. "Want to ride with me? We can drop your car off at my place, since I'm on the way."

Sabrina nodded. "That works for me. Afterward, why don't we stop and get something to eat? I could go for some Jersey Mike's."

Tangie opened her car door. "Okay. I guess I'll get a pastrami sandwich. I haven't had one in a while."

"That sounds good. Maybe I'll get one of those myself." Sabrina walked four cars down and climbed into her car, blasting music as soon as she switched on the ignition. She waited for Tangie to pull out, then followed her.

Just as they'd planned, Sabrina left her car at Tangie's town house and rode with her to the hospital. They found Bonnie sitting in the waiting room with Devon.

"What's going on? How's Dee?" Tangie asked as she embraced the teen.

"She's still unconscious," Devon answered. "But they think she might have had a stroke."

Tangie put a hand to her mouth. Her eyes grew wet with tears. "Nooo."

"Dee's a fighter. She'll get through this," Sabrina said. "We have to believe that."

"I can't lose my mom," Devon whispered.

Sabrina sat beside her and placed an arm around her. "Honey, your mother is the strongest woman I know. She'll pull through this. I just know it."

Devon laid her head on Sabrina's shoulder. "I'm glad you got me out of school. Thank you so much."

"You and Dee are like family to me. Don't you ever forget that."

Tangie gazed at Sabrina in amazement. Cordelia merely tolerated her—they weren't close at all.

"Why won't she wake up?" Devon cried.

Sabrina stole a peek at Bonnie, who explained, "Sweetie, your mother is in a coma."

"But she is going to wake up, isn't she? I don't want her to miss my graduation."

Bonnie smiled and nodded. "The doctors are doing all they can to make that happen. Devon, you know your mother is not going to miss your graduation or your prom. She's looked forward to those events for a long time."

"I don't know about the prom."

Removing her arm, Sabrina asked, "Why not? All girls want to go to the prom. I sure enjoyed mine."

Bonnie tried to silence her with a look, but Sabrina didn't seem to be paying attention.

"Don't tell me Dee wasn't going to let you go—"

"It isn't that," Devon cut in. "I just may not feel like going, that's all."

Tangie decided the girl needed rescuing. "Devon, if you don't want to go to the prom, it's fine. I personally don't think it's that big a deal, myself." Placing a comforting hand on her arm, Tangie added, "You don't have to worry about that right now." She sent a warning look to Sabrina.

A look of irritation washed over Sabrina's face. "The point I was trying to make is that Dee's gonna pull through," she stated.

Tangie agreed wholeheartedly.

"I can't lose her," Devon stated. "She can't die."

"Sssshh, honey. Don't talk like that," Bonnie said. "Just think good thoughts. Your mother is going to pull through."

"Has anyone called Gerald?" Tangie asked.

"I did," Devon announced. "He was in court but he should be on his way here."

"I think your father's here already. I think that's him coming through those doors now." Sabrina rose to her feet for a better look. "Yeah, it's him."

Gerald joined them a few moments later. "Hello, everybody."

Devon rushed over to him. "I'm so glad you're here, Daddy." She wrapped her arms around him tightly.

Tangie enviously watched them holding each other. She had never met her father because he'd wanted nothing to do with her. Tangie felt her eyes grow wet, and she blinked rapidly. She didn't like Gerald either because he was no better than her father. They were both adulterers. She was always polite to him out of respect for Cordelia.

They sat down, each of them caught up in their own thoughts.

When the doctor came out, Gerald and Devon crossed the room in quick strides.

Tangie heard him mention tests like an echocardiogram, a CAT scan, and an MRI. When her grandmother had had her stroke a few years back, Tangie recalled that they had performed all those same tests.

"Mrs. Berkeley has had a stroke . . ." Dr. Wilcox confirmed.

Devon burst into tears.

"Did he just say that Dee had a stroke?" Sabrina whispered.

"Dear Lord . . ." Bonnie murmured softly. "I was afraid that's what happened."

Tangie's heart raced. She still had some trouble digesting the news. She had not been completely surprised, but somehow it didn't seem real. Cordelia was still a young woman. Goodness, she was only forty-two years old. She'd always considered strokes an older person's sickness.

Sabrina tapped her on the arm. "Hey, you okay?"

She nodded. Tangie stole a peek at Bonnie. Her eyes were closed and her lips were moving. To her amazement she realized her friend was praying. Why would Bonnie pray to God when He had allowed something like this to happen? Another thought came to her: Maybe God wasn't to blame. Maybe it was simply fate. That was what her grandmother and Lula would say.

Gerald and Devon came over to them. He repeated what he'd been told by the doctor.

"It's probably best that you all go on home for now. I'll give you a call if there's any news."

"You sure you don't want us to stay with you?" Bonnie inquired.

"We'll be fine." Gerald gave a sad smile. "I know Dee appreciates you all being here for her."

Tangie rose to her feet, followed by Sabrina and Bonnie. Touching him lightly on the arm, she said, "If you need anything, please don't hesitate to call."

She knew Gerald was just as surprised as she was. She normally didn't say more than two words to him. "Thank you, Tangie."

She gave Devon a hug. "Call me, sweetie." Tangie stood off to the side as she waited on Bonnie and Sabrina to say their good-byes.

The trio didn't say much as they walked out to the parking lot. They brought Bonnie to her car first.

"We'll see you in the morning," Tangie announced.

"Good night." Bonnie hugged her, then Sabrina.

Tangie and Sabrina located her car in the next row and got in. A few minutes later they were on their way.

When Tangie drove Sabrina back to her car, Sabrina said, "I hope that we're right. About Dee getting better, you know."

"I was just thinking about that," Tangie confessed. "I'm not sure we should have told Devon all that stuff. What if we're wrong? From what I could hear, Dee had a pretty severe stroke."

"I know. Nobody wants to think that Dee might not ever regain consciousness, much less recover from the stroke. However, to tell Devon the truth might devastate her."

"But what's worse?" Tangie questioned. "Telling her that there's a chance her mother won't pull through or sugarcoating it with positive thoughts? People die from strokes. My grandmother is dead because of a stroke. Granted, it was the second one that killed her, but it was a stroke all the same."

"As preachy and holy as Dee was, I'm surprised this happened. I would've figured that if God had anybody's back, it was hers."

"I don't think it has anything to do with God. It's fate, Sabrina. I think people give God way too much credit."

"Girlfriend, don't even worry about stopping to get something to eat. Just get me back to my car."

Tangie glanced over at Sabrina. "What's wrong?"

"The way you're talking reminds me of the *Titanic*."

"*Titanic?* Girl, what are you talking about?"

"Somebody once said that not even God could sink the *Titanic*—you remember what happened?"

Tangie burst into laughter. "It hit an iceberg. That was nothing but fate."

15

Cordelia was lost in a thick black vortex edged with light. She struggled to reach the brightness and was rewarded by the sound of voices.

They were all around her. In the dark tunnel Cordelia couldn't quite make out what they were saying, but it gave her comfort to know she wasn't alone. She wanted to reach out to them but couldn't seem to lift her arms. Maybe if she could make it to the bright glow highlighting the path.

Just as she neared the light, Cordelia felt something take hold of her, holding her tight in its grip. She was being pulled back into the eddy. She tried in vain to scream for help but no sound would come out. There was something wrong, she knew. She was dying and there was nothing she could do about it.

A sudden weariness took over, forcing Cordelia to release herself to it.

Cordelia came alive for the second time that day. Once again she could hear voices all around her. When she swam for the light, she made it this time. She opened her eyes.

The brightness all around her blinded Cordelia, hurting her eyes so much that she immediately closed them in reaction.

When she felt strong enough, she opened them a second time. She was aware of some type of bandage on her head, an oxygen mask on her face, and fluid dripping into her arm from an IV.

"She's awake," someone announced.

Cordelia's eyes bounced around the room. She was disoriented and had no idea where she was or who these people were. Every now and then the room would loom into another shape. Cordelia shut her eyes in an effort to clear her vision.

The face of a young girl appeared before her. Her vision was blurry, so she couldn't see her clearly.

"Mama, can you hear me?" Her voice was sweet and she smelled of strawberries and cream.

She tried to recall the identity of this girl but her head ached so badly that it hurt to think. Cordelia opened her mouth to speak—at least she thought she did. She tried to speak. She felt a shot of panic and began to thrash her head. She wanted to shout, "Help me!" but she didn't have the strength.

"Mama?" The girl looked over her shoulder. "I think she's getting upset. I don't want to make her upset."

"Honey, give your mother a moment."

It was a man's voice that time. Who were these people? Cordelia felt the edges of darkness threatening to surround her. She fought with all the strength she had left. Her eyes traveled the room. Monitors stood nearby like sentinels, beeping rhythmically. She was in a hospital but she had no idea why.

"Dee? It's Gerald. You're going to be okay, sweetie."

Gerald? Who was this man to her?

"Can you hear me, Mama?"

Mama. This girl was her daughter, Cordelia realized. Her daughter. It was her daughter speaking. She had a daughter. The realization seemed so unfamiliar to her at the moment. What was her name? she wondered.

Cordelia tried to focus but her vision still wasn't clear. She blinked rapidly, trying to fight unconsciousness.

She felt so weak and out of control. Cordelia could hear two men talking—one was the doctor, she assumed. When she heard the word *stroke,* Cordelia became agitated.

The nurse was instantly beside her, trying to calm her. Wanting to escape, Cordelia closed her eyes and gave in to the darkness.

"Mama's out of the coma, right?"

"Looks like it, baby. But don't stop praying for deliverance over this stroke."

"I feel real bad about what happened. This is my fault, Daddy. I know it is."

Gerald wrapped his arms around his daughter. "Devon, you didn't do this—I can't let you take the blame."

"Mama was under so much stress."

"I'm sure I'm part of the blame. Every time I came around we argued. It's been happening more and more lately. She never wanted to listen to me."

"Mama doesn't like to listen to anybody. She thinks she's the expert on everything."

"We can't change her, sweetheart. Dee is who she is. There's no pretense."

"I know I'm supposed to come live with you in Raleigh, but I can't leave Mama right now. She's going to need me."

"I've been doing some thinking of my own. I'm thinking about hiring a companion for Dee—either that or I'm going to have to take time off from my job."

"You know how I feel about it—I want you to come home. Mama and I both need you."

Gerald stroked her cheek. "I'll let you know what I decide, okay?"

"Okay. But hurry up. We have a lot to do."

It wasn't long before Devon had fallen asleep. Gerald stroked her hair while she slept, her head on his chest. The teen was exhausted but still she refused to leave her mother's side. He was so proud of the way she was handling the situation.

He spied a nurse walking into Cordelia's room and resisted the urge to follow. She came out a short while later and said, "She's still sleeping."

Gerald let out a sigh of relief. He sent up a silent prayer of thanks. His biggest fear was that Cordelia would lapse back into a coma. It looked now as if she was on her way to recovery. *Thank God.*

He and Cordelia had gone through turbulent times together, but he still cared for her. There were times Gerald wished they could become friends; however, he knew better. Too much had happened, leaving Cordelia very bitter.

16

"Cordelia's had a stroke," Bonnie announced the next day at the FFA unit meeting. "Let's keep her and her family uplifted in prayer. In the meantime we're going to have to all pitch in to work her cases for her."

Although none of them voiced their complaints, Bonnie knew a few of them were already grumbling in silence. They had been short-staffed for months, and everyone was pulling more than her share. "I know it's asking a lot, but it's something we have to do."

One of the workers decided to put into words what they all wanted to say. "We already have a lot of work to do on our own cases, Bonnie. I don't think we can take on any more work."

"For y'all to have so much work to do, how is it when I walk by, I find people playing solitaire on the computers or surfing the Net?" Sabrina questioned.

A few of her coworkers glared at her.

Bonnie could hear their minds working. Who did Sabrina

think she was? Clearing her throat, Bonnie continued, "All of management will be helping out."

There were still a few deep sighs and soft grumbles.

"I'm sorry, ladies, but we have no choice. When Mandy goes on maternity leave in a couple of months, we're going to have to do the same thing all over again. We're short-staffed."

"Can't we look into hiring a temp to help out?" Tangie suggested. "There's no guarantee that Dee will be able to come back to work right away—especially after suffering a stroke. Truth is, we really need some help."

Bonnie had to admit that she hadn't considered hiring temporary help until Tangie mentioned it, but it sounded like a good solution. "I'll have to check with personnel. It's a good suggestion."

"Tangie's right. A couple of temps would help," Sabrina chimed in. "All of management will have to take on extra case loads if we don't get somebody in here."

Everyone seemed to agree. "Okay. I'll give personnel a call this afternoon," Bonnie said.

They made plans to send flowers to the hospital.

"Make sure they're bright," Sabrina said. "Dee needs something colorful and cheery to see when she opens her eyes."

"I think Sabrina's right," someone stated. "They should be nice and bright."

After the emergency meeting, Bonnie retreated to her office. Closing the door, she took a few minutes to pray for Cordelia's recovery. Her reasons were not exactly selfless. She didn't want Devon to lose her mother, but she didn't want to lose her best friend. She'd lost a lot of people throughout the years, and she was tired of it.

"You've got to be okay, Dee," she whispered. "Devon and Gerald need you. I need you. We all need you."

*   *   *

At the end of the workday, Bonnie was actually looking forward to leaving the office. She headed straight to the hospital.

Devon spotted her as soon as she entered the waiting room and stood up. "Hey, Miss Bonnie."

They embraced.

Rubbing Devon's back, she asked, "How are you doing, sweetie?"

"Okay." Stepping aside, Devon announced, "Mama's out of the coma."

Bonnie's heart skipped a beat. "That's wonderful news."

"She's sleeping right now. The doctor had all kinds of tests done to find out the extent of the damage. Daddy can tell you more about it."

"I'm so glad to hear this. Lord knows I've been praying for her recovery."

"Me too. I don't think I've ever prayed so hard in my life. Mama and I have our problems"—Devon gave a tiny smile—"mostly my fault, but I don't want to lose her."

Bonnie nodded in understanding. "Keep her lifted up in prayer."

"I hope God will listen to me, Miss Bonnie. I feel like He's been ignoring me lately."

"I don't think that's it at all," she reassured Devon. "God's not like that. God's mind is full of us, honey. We are always on His mind."

"Sometimes I wonder. . . ."

"Hello, Bonnie."

She turned around at the sound of the male voice and smiled. "Hey, Gerald. You holding up okay?"

He nodded. "I just checked on Dee. She's sleeping."

"She's not back in another coma, is she?" Devon wanted to know. "Is Mama okay, Daddy?"

Gerald wrapped an arm around her. "She's just sleeping, baby."

"She's out of danger?" When he nodded, Bonnie sent up a silent prayer of thanks.

He nodded a second time. "Thank God for that," Gerald murmured as he continued to hold Devon. "I don't know what I'd do if I lost her."

"Have you all put some food in your stomachs?"

"I had a muffin earlier, but I'm starving," Devon admitted. "I don't know if Daddy's eaten at all."

Bonnie went down to the cafeteria and picked up sandwiches and drinks for them. She returned ten minutes later. Bonnie handed a sandwich to each of them. Gerald took the sodas from her and offered one to his daughter. She smiled as she watched them eat, satisfied that she'd been able to provide a small form of relief.

"Thank you for this," Gerald uttered between bites.

"I'm glad you're eating," Bonnie observed. She was dying to see Cordelia but resisted the urge to peek in on her. Cordelia was still in intensive care, and only her family could visit her for now.

Devon finished her sandwich first. "I'm going to check on Mama."

When she disappeared around the corner, Gerald said, "I'm worried about her."

"She's going to be fine."

"Did Dee tell you about Devon's situation?" he whispered.

Bonnie nodded. "Right before she collapsed."

"All this . . ." Gerald shook his head slowly. "It can't be good for the baby."

"Has she seen a doctor?"

"No. Cordelia was supposed to make an appointment for her. I don't think she ever got the chance."

"We have the same doctor. Why don't I make the appointment?" Bonnie offered.

He looked relieved. "I'd really appreciate it."

Bonnie was more than happy to help. She stayed with

Gerald in the waiting room until Devon returned. She didn't push for conversation because she had a feeling he really didn't want to talk.

"Mama's awake," Devon announced. "The doctor's with her now."

"How does she look?" Bonnie asked.

"She looks good." Devon broke into a grin. "I think she's gonna make it."

Bonnie agreed. "I know she is. Your mother is a very strong woman. She's probably just about the strongest woman I know." She leaned closer to Devon. "I'm going to call Dr. King to make an appointment for you."

She nodded. "Mama was supposed to make one for me. Guess she didn't get the chance."

Bonnie smiled. "Sweetie, I don't mind at all. I just want you to bring a happy baby into this world."

"Thanks, Miss Bonnie. I really appreciate it," Devon started to fidget in her chair. After a while she asked, "Miss Bonnie, I need to ask you something. Would you go with me for my pre-natal visit?"

"What about Dee?"

"We don't know what's gonna happen with Mama."

Bonnie embraced her. "Have faith, sweetie."

"I try not to be scared, but sometimes I can't help myself."

"I understand. I'm like that myself. There are so many times when I get so scared, just of life itself, that I want to hide."

"I keep telling myself that this is just a bad dream and I'll wake up soon."

"Your mother loves you so much, Devon. I hope you know that."

"I love her too, Miss Bonnie. I feel so bad over the way I've treated her. I was jealous. Jealous and stupid."

"Jealous?"

Devon nodded. "She was always spending her time either at the office or at church. The youth group saw my mother more than I did. The only time she'd really talk to me was when she wanted to lecture me."

Bonnie didn't know what to say.

"I just wanted her to notice me—really notice me. Why couldn't we go on short trips together? You know, without the youth group."

"Did you ever tell her this?" Bonnie inquired.

Devon shook her head. "Didn't see much of a point. Mama probably figured she was doing God's work. Only God was important to her."

"Honey, that's not true. You are very important to Dee."

"Maybe I used to be. But she changed a lot this year. Mama wasn't the same."

Bonnie agreed but held her silence. "She loves you like crazy. You are all she talks about."

Her comment brought a smile to Devon's face.

"Miss Bonnie, Mama cares a lot for you too. She is always saying what a good friend you are."

An older couple entered the waiting area and sat down.

Bonnie greeted them, then returned her attention to Devon.

"I didn't know you were coming to the hospital, Bonnie."

She looked up to find Sabrina walking toward them. A small part of Bonnie wished that she had not come to join them. Sabrina had a knack for making her feel uncomfortable. "I wanted to check on Dee."

"Me too." Sabrina dropped down beside Devon. "How're you doing, girlfriend?"

"Fine. How about you?"

"I'm okay. Just tired."

Bonnie sat there silently listening to Sabrina and Devon chat. She observed the way Sabrina's eyes watched everyone entering the waiting room.

"What's wrong, Bonnie?" Sabrina asked. "Why are you so quiet?"

"I was just thinking about something." She smiled. "I'm going to the nurses' station for a moment. I need to have a question answered." Bonnie rose to her feet. "I'll be right back."

She wasn't gone long. Bonnie found Devon and Sabrina engrossed in conversation once more. Gerald was sitting beside his daughter, reading a book.

Bonnie stayed for another half hour before deciding to go home. She'd been able to peek in on Cordelia for just a split second. She looked as if she was sleeping peacefully. Bonnie found she really missed her.

17

Sabrina couldn't recall Cordelia ever having anything other than a cold. She squinted her eyes from the sunlight. "Why did this have to happen now?" She moaned softly. "We already have so much to do around here." Sabrina's mouth twisted. The other social workers were going to throw a fit; then Claire would put more work on her. . . .

"I hope Dee recuperates from her stroke okay," Tangie muttered as she strolled into Sabrina's office. She plopped down on one of the nearby chairs. "I still can't believe she's even had a stroke. She's the healthiest woman I know. I've always thought of people much older than us having strokes. My grandmother was eighty when she had her first one. She was eighty-six when she had the second one—that one killed her."

Pouring bottled water into her plants, Sabrina agreed. "I know what you mean. It's hard for me to believe it myself."

Tangie spoke her thoughts aloud. "I wonder if anybody has called her aunt. She lives in Durham, I think."

"Bonnie probably has," Sabrina replied. "You know she's

always in everybody's business when it comes to stuff like that. Or maybe Gerald called her."

Tangie burst into laughter, surprising Sabrina. "Girl, you need to quit. I know you're not talking about somebody being in somebody else's business."

Her perfectly arched brows furrowed, and Sabrina ground her lips tightly together but didn't respond. Instead she continued to water her ferns.

"Did Devon stay at the hospital again last night?"

Sabrina nodded. "Yeah. Gerald tried to get her to go home but she refused. She still won't leave her mother."

"You can't really blame her. They weren't what I would call close, but that's still her mom."

"Dee was too overprotective, though. She needs to loosen the apron strings some. If she doesn't, Devon's going to be buck wild when she does get out on her own."

Tangie played with a pencil. "When did you become an expert on motherhood?"

Sabrina sat back down at her desk, saying, "I didn't. Dee's not a bad mother—don't get me wrong; I'm not saying that at all. She's just real strict."

"You're right," Tangie agreed. "She would hardly let Devon do anything. But I guess that's best for some children. It's better than your mother not caring one way or another about what you did."

"First thing Devon is going to do is end up with a baby," Sabrina predicted.

"Why would you say something like that?"

"Because she's so naïve."

Tangie shook his head. "I hope you're wrong, 'cause something like that would kill Dee."

Sabrina chuckled. "You're right about that. Dee would lose her mind." Scrunching up her face, Sabrina added, "Devon's been putting on some weight. Come on, don't tell me you didn't notice it the other night at the hospital? If I didn't know any better, I'd say girlfriend is pregnant."

"I noticed but I don't think she's put on that much weight," Tangie argued. "Have you forgotten that she's a growing girl?"

"I don't know. But I have a feeling that it's more than that. She's kind of got that look about her."

Puzzled, Tangie asked, "What look?"

Grinning, Sabrina asked, "You think she really could be pregnant?"

"You've got to be kidding. Devon's not crazy."

"The more I think about it . . . hmmmm, I don't know, Tangie." Sabrina forged ahead. "Maybe that's why Dee had the stroke. You know something has been going on with her." She had a strong feeling about this. Sabrina had no intention of abandoning the idea until she knew the truth.

"Drop it, Sabrina. You know Devon is not pregnant. You shouldn't even be thinking this way. There could be something terribly wrong with Dee. Why don't you focus on that?"

She arched her brow with a slight arrogance. "Calm down, Tangie. I was just wondering aloud. Besides, if Devon really is pregnant, she won't be able to hide it. That's for sure."

"If she were pregnant, Dee would've told us. We're her friends."

"Friends don't tell friends everything. You should know that, Tangie." Sabrina couldn't resist this little jab. She could see the wonder in Tangie's eyes, showing she was curious as to what Sabrina meant by her statement. She almost had to re-mind herself to breathe as she waited for the question that was sure to come.

It never did, much to Sabrina's disappointment.

"Mama, what are you cooking?" Sabrina questioned when she entered her childhood home on Carter Street. This address, along with those of the other houses in this area, used to count among its residents, some of Bridgeport's affluent African-Americans.

Now it was just another middle-class neighborhood, Sabrina thought with disgust. She'd tried to get her mother to move into one of the newer communities. Most of the wealthy families had moved out to Bethany Estates. Even Sabrina lived in one of the Ravenscroft luxury condominiums at Bethany.

Mamie Mayhew wouldn't budge, however. She loved her house and was determined to stay there until death.

Sabrina could hear the clanging sound of pots and pans being shuffled about in the kitchen. She strolled in the direction of the sound. "Mama . . ." she called out.

"Sabrina, is that you?"

The question brought a round of laughter from her. "If I were a burglar, you'd be in trouble," Sabrina pointed out. She stood in the doorway that separated the kitchen from the dining room, her arms folded across her chest.

Mamie tossed a look over her shoulder. "Nobody else had better stroll into my house like that. I'll lay 'em out with my frying pan. I don't call it Big Black for nothing."

Giggling, Sabrina embraced her mother. "What are you cooking that smells so good?" She was careful to avoid the counter. Sabrina didn't want to risk ruining the powder-blue St. Johns chambray blazer she wore over a striped tank and black pants.

"I'm making a meat loaf and cheddar potatoes." Mamie gave her daughter a knowing smile. "You staying for dinner?"

"Sure."

Removing the meat loaf from the oven, her mother asked, "How is your friend doing? The one who had the stroke."

Shrugging, Sabrina answered, "She's going to be okay. When I last spoke to her ex-husband, they were trying to determine what all had been affected by the stroke."

Mamie shook her head sadly. "She's so young."

Sabrina agreed. She selected a banana from a bowl. "Can I eat this?"

"Sure. Now you know you don't have to ask about eating no food."

"I don't live here anymore. I don't want to be rude."

"This is still your home, Sabrina."

She peeled the banana and took a bite. "Mmmm . . . this is good." Sabrina picked up a napkin and wiped her mouth. "Mama, when are you going to make your banana bread?"

Mamie gave her an indulgent smile. "How about I make some just for you? I'll do it this weekend."

Grinning, Sabrina tossed the napkin into the trash. "Thanks, Mama. Hey, can you make some roasted garlic chicken for me too? I've been craving it."

"Girl, you act like you're pregnant. What's with all this craving certain foods?" Mamie surveyed her daughter carefully. "You need to tell me something?"

"Oooh, no. I'm not pregnant, thank God. I can promise you that."

Mamie burst into laughter. She bent to check the meat loaf. "How is that boyfriend of yours?" she asked.

"Who? Leon?"

Glancing over at Sabrina, Mamie nodded.

"We broke up." She leaned against the refrigerator door and folded her arms across her chest.

"Was he cheating on you?"

"No. At least I don't think so. We just seemed to be on different roads."

"He's stupid if he can't see what he has in you."

"I'm going to give him some space—maybe he'll come to his senses soon. If not . . ." Sabrina moved to stand beside her mother. "When is dinner going to be ready? I'm starving."

Sabrina felt like she'd stepped into heaven. The confectionery-colored living room was a pleasing blend of pink, white, and green. She'd been in this condo for two years and was very proud of it.

The condo had once served as the model in the newly built residential community, and Sabrina had fallen in love with it at first sight. She'd immediately put in her bid to buy the place as-is. After she'd waited nearly eight months, the condo had been hers.

She knew everyone wondered how she could afford to live in Bethany Estates. They didn't need to know that Sabrina's mother and her current lover paid her mortgage. Her mother pretty much supported her lifestyle financially whenever she was between men.

Her father had left Mamie in a lot of debt when he died. Luckily she'd married quickly, but Sabrina had hated her stepfather. He owned the local Ford dealership and had given Mamie a nice settlement. In addition, there was the money from the Mayhew relatives.

Sabrina wearily made her way to her bedroom, where her four-poster bed awaited. All she wanted right now was a bubble bath in her garden tub.

18

Tangie canceled her date. Cordelia's well-being dominated her thoughts. Her friend had been in the hospital for three days, most of which she'd spent drifting in and out of consciousness. Although Cordelia was often too self-righteous and preachy, Tangie truly loved her like a big sister and was worried about her.

She'd stopped by the hospital on her way home and found Gerald and Devon huddled together in a corner of the waiting room on the fifth floor. Tangie bought them dinner in the hospital cafeteria and stayed with them for about an hour before leaving.

Since arriving home she'd already called the hospital twice, but the news was the same: Cordelia was in critical condition. She would check again just before going to bed tonight, Tangie decided.

The telephone rang but she didn't answer it. She didn't feel much like talking. It was probably that gossiping Sabrina anyway. Tangie made her way to the kitchen and found an orange.

She carried it with her to the den and turned on the television. She was felling very tense and was filled with nervous energy.

"I can do this," she chanted to herself. "I can do this."

The phone rang again. Tangie still refused to answer. According to the caller ID, it was Mack, the guy she was supposed to see tonight. He'd warned her that he would call back to see if she'd changed her mind, but she wouldn't—even if it killed her. Besides, it was a Thursday night—she should probably stay in anyway, she decided. Tangie was no good at the office whenever she was up late the night before.

The throbbing between Tangie's legs refused to go away. Tonight she wanted to put someone else's needs before hers.

She crossed her legs tightly, hoping to ease some of the tension. She could do it. She could go without sex for more than a day or two. Tangie knew she could do it—she had to.

She tried to concentrate on the movie showing on television but eventually gave up the struggle. Next she tried reading, but found herself getting excited. Tangie slammed the book shut. She tried listening to music.

When that failed to take her mind off sex, Tangie called her friend Sheryl. Maybe hanging out with a friend would do the trick.

"I hope you're not busy, 'cause I want to come over. I haven't seen you in a while."

"I was just thinking 'bout you. Come on over. We can get some hot wings or something."

"I'll pick up a pizza and some wings on the way. I'll see you shortly."

Thirty minutes later, Tangie arrived at her friend's apartment.

"Sheryl, how did your trip go? I missed you." Tangie embraced her friend. She and Sheryl partied together often.

"My title of the week is wedding coordinator. I'm helping my cousin pick out a dress for her wedding."

Tangie made herself comfortable. "How fun. I love weddings. It's marriage that scares me."

"After the week I've had, I can't stand to see another bridal gown. It's not like it's one of those fancy gowns—it's just a regular dress. Bonita's not having a big wedding."

Tangie almost choked on her soda. "Who?" She dabbed at her mouth with a napkin. She couldn't possibly have heard Sheryl correctly.

"Bonita. She and Leon are gonna sneak off and get married."

Tangie couldn't contain her surprise. "No way!" She just assumed Leon and Sabrina were still seeing each other.

Sheryl nodded. "Yeah. They are finally gonna make it legal. It's about time, I say. She's been waiting on him a long time."

Picking up a slice of pizza, Tangie stated, "I thought they broke up."

"They did. Leon started sniffing around her the last couple of months, saying he was ready to settle down with her." Sheryl picked up a hot wing and took a bite.

"What about Sabrina?"

"Bonita said he told her he didn't want her. Said Sabrina was all about the money. You know your girl. She loves men with big bank accounts."

"Yeah, she does," Tangie had to admit.

"Leon told Bonita that they broke up a while back." Licking her fingers, Sheryl gazed at Tangie. "Do you know if it's true?"

"Sabrina's been talking about some other guy she's met. That's all I know." She and Sheryl had made a pact long ago to stay out of the Bonita and Sabrina mess. "Well, I wish Leon and Bonita the best of luck."

"Girl, so do I. I kind of have a wait-and-see attitude where they're concerned anyway. You know Bonita will lie and say they're engaged in a minute. She's been trying to get him to marry her forever. He must be awfully good in bed for Bonita to keep putting up with his crap." Grinning wickedly, Sheryl added, "But I guess you would know about that, wouldn't you?"

"I thought we decided to forget about that little situation. That happened a long time ago, and I'd like to keep it in the past. That was one of the biggest mistakes I've ever made." Long before Tangie knew Sabrina, she and Leon had spent an incredible night together after meeting at a party. Back then he'd been in the military and was stationed in Fayetteville, while she was finishing up her last year at Fayetteville State University.

The next day they met at his apartment for a repeat session. When Leon suggested videotaping them having sex, Tangie didn't object. Unbeknownst to her, he also had a friend hidden in the closet. In the midst of their having sex, the man came out and joined them on the bed.

Tangie had sex with both of them. Initially she enjoyed it, until Leon started calling her a whore. She cursed them both out and threatened to scream rape unless they gave her the videotape.

When she saw him again years later, he was involved with Bonita, and neither one of them ever mentioned the incident. The only evidence of that night was the tape, which she had carefully hidden in her town house. She had no idea why she kept it, because it made her feel dirty just having it in the house, but each time she attempted to throw it away, she couldn't. She wasn't a whore—just a woman who enjoyed sex.

Men could sleep with as many women as they wanted, but let a woman do it and she was labeled a tramp or much worse.

19

Cordelia was still sleeping most of the time and had some problems with her memory. All she wanted was to come out of this nightmare.

Every time she opened her eyes, medical personnel gathered around her, checking her reactions while learning the extent of her injuries.

One of the first things Cordelia noticed was that she could not move her right arm. Her right leg was very weak. She could move it up slightly, but only with a great deal of effort.

The nurse was immediately at her bedside. "Just relax, Mrs. Berkeley."

Cordelia was having trouble trying to express herself.

A man strolled into the room. Leaning over the bed, he asked, "Mrs. Berkeley, how are you feeling today?"

Cordelia could only stare.

"You've had a stroke, Mrs. Berkeley," the doctor announced. "An embolic cerebral infarction in the left hemisphere."

He went on to tell her the prognosis but Cordelia wasn't listening. His announcement was still on her mind. She'd had a stroke. Her initial thought was that she was too young.

"Thank you for coming, Pastor." Gerald shook hands with Pastor Grant. "It's good to see you."

"The church has been praying for Sister Berkeley and your family since we heard. I want you to know that we're here for you."

"A few of the members have come by the hospital, but they're still just letting family in to see Dee."

Pastor Grant nodded. "How is she doing?"

"She's getting stronger and stronger each day," Gerald replied. "But she's got a long way to go, Pastor. A long way."

"Sister Berkeley knows the Lord. She knows that He will supply her strength and give her courage."

While they were talking, a couple of women and teenagers joined them. Gerald assumed they were from the church, because Pastor Grant introduced them. He greeted them with a smile.

The teenagers spotted Devon and went to sit with her. Out of the corner of his eye Gerald glimpsed one of the young girls embracing her. Devon appeared to be crying. He was about to walk over there but Pastor Grant's next words stopped him.

"Why don't we have a word of prayer?"

Gerald nodded. "I'd like that."

One of the women requested that the teens join them. In the corner of the waiting room they made a semicircle by joining hands.

Pastor Grant began to pray. "O heavenly Father, we come before you as humble spirits. Dear God, You are our refuge and our strength. We ask that You comfort the Berkeley family in their time of suffering. Help this family with Your power and deliver Sister Berkeley from this attack on her health. You promised that You would turn our mourning into dancing, turn our sorrow into joy, and our weakness into strength. Lord, I thank You for those who try to make others well and care for those suffering and in pain. Give them wisdom in curing and gentle patience in caring. For all they have done, grant them the reward You promised those attending the sick: come, blessed of my Father, here is the kingdom made ready for you. These blessings I ask in Your name. Amen."

Gerald felt a small measure of peace after Pastor Grant's prayer. They all sat down and talked for the next half hour. When he and Devon were left alone, she laid her head against her father's chest and whispered, "It's my fault, Daddy. I did this to her." she wiped away a tear.

Gerald embraced his daughter. "Honey, you had nothing to do with this. Your mother is a strong woman, and she's a fighter. She's going to be fine. You have to believe that."

"She can't die. Mama doesn't look like she's getting any stronger."

"She's not going to die, sweetheart. She's not. The doctor says her chances for recovery are good. Your mother is not going to let something like this get her down. You know her better than that." If there was anyone so stubborn and determined, it was Cordelia. It was those same qualities that Gerald both loved and detested in her. "I need you to be strong because Dee is going to have to depend on you for a while."

Wiping her tears, Devon nodded.

Gerald pulled out his wallet. "Why don't you go to the cafeteria and get something to eat?"

"I'm not hungry."

"Honey, you have to eat. I can't have you falling out on me too."

"Do you want me to bring you something back?" she asked.

"I'll eat later." He handed her a twenty. "Go on and get yourself something."

"Thanks," Devon murmured, taking the money from her father. "I'll be right back."

"Take your time, sweetheart." Gerald watched his daughter as she made her way along the corridor of the hospital. He couldn't remember ever seeing Devon look so scared.

The truth was that he was just as scared. His grandfather had had a fatal stroke ten years ago. His mother had happened by for a visit and found him on the kitchen floor dead. Gerald figured Cordelia was going to need assistance for a while after she went home, and Devon couldn't do it alone. Cordelia's aunt was an older woman, so she wouldn't be able to help out. There was no one but him.

Gerald sank down onto one of the chairs in the waiting room, trying to figure out what would have to be done. Cordelia wouldn't like it, but he really didn't have any other choice. He was going to have to move back into the house.

20

It was Friday and the weekend was looming right before her eyes. Bonnie knew what she would be doing this evening—she was going to the hospital. Hopefully there was something she could do for Gerald and Devon. Tomorrow she would be working at the women's shelter, and after that she had a meeting at the church.

"How is Dee?"

Bonnie glanced away from her computer monitor. "About the same, Claire."

"I'm going to try to get by the hospital tonight."

"She'll appreciate that, I'm sure." She was on the verge of tears, so Bonnie quickly changed the subject. "Have you finished your report?"

"Not yet. How about you?"

Shaking her head, Bonnie answered, "I haven't even started on it. Hopefully I can get to it later today."

Sabrina joined them, saying, "Just the two women I'm looking for."

"What did you need?" Bonnie inquired with a smile. She

watched in amusement as Claire rolled her eyes heavenward. It was obvious to everyone in the FFA unit that she had a strong dislike for Sabrina even though she tried to hide it. None of the workers really cared for Sabrina.

"I have some letters I need y'all to look over," she drawled. "They're in your mailboxes. Can you look at them and get back to me as soon as possible?" Sabrina brushed manicured nails over her jacket, calling attention to the glittering diamond ring on her finger. She'd gotten it on Valentine's Day from Leon.

Bonnie recalled how upset Sabrina had gotten over the ring. She'd wanted an engagement ring instead of the sapphire-and-diamond cocktail one Leon gave her.

"We'll do what we can," Claire responded dryly. "We're still trying to finish our reports." She gave Bonnie a devilish smile before asking, "Have you finished the project I left on your desk?"

Sabrina nodded. "I sure did. Do you have anything else you want me to do?"

Claire looked as if she'd swallowed something foul. Bonnie gave Sabrina a knowing smile.

"Let me know if there are any changes."

Sabrina didn't make a move to leave, prompting Bonnie to ask, "Is there something else?"

"I called the hospital earlier and they said Dee's stable, but I couldn't find out anything more."

"I really don't think there's any more to tell, if you want to know the truth. This stroke hit Dee pretty hard."

"My money's on Dee. She is just about the strongest woman I know," Claire stated. "Her faith is enough to sustain her."

Bonnie nodded in agreement. "She's got a lot on her plate right now. . . ." Her voice died as she realized what she was saying. She quickly changed the subject. "Sabrina, did you schedule the team meeting?"

"I couldn't find a conference room available that day."

Sabrina gave her a curious glance but for once kept her mouth closed.

Claire decided to leave. "Well, I'd better get back out to my office. I need to get my report done." She made her way to the door. Before walking all the way out of the office, she tossed a glance over her shoulder and said, "I'll keep Dee in my prayers."

Sabrina made a face behind Claire's back.

"Shame on you," Bonnie admonished.

"You know she doesn't like Dee," Sabrina said with a sneer. "Claire's just being a fake. She barely opens her mouth even to speak to the woman."

"She might be concerned."

"I doubt that," Sabrina retorted. "I'm going to my desk. If you need any help with anything, call me."

Nodding, Bonnie returned her attention to the stack of papers on her desk. She had so much work to do, not to mention picking up Cordelia's caseload.

Hours later she was still at her desk, but Bonnie had finally finished her report. She stole a peek at the clock. It was fifteen past seven. She yawned.

Bonnie gathered up her things and left the building. She got in her car and drove over to the hospital.

She didn't stay as long as she wanted to because they were still allowing only family in to see Cordelia. Bonnie drove past Applebee's. She was hungry and didn't feel like cooking, so she made a U-turn and headed back to the restaurant.

Bonnie pulled into an empty space in the parking lot but didn't turn off the car. She sat glued to her seat, staring at the exterior of the restaurant. She was starving but could not force herself to venture inside.

Ten minutes passed before Bonnie gave up the idea of dining out and headed home. She'd never liked eating alone in public. It made a person look so lonely and pathetic.

21

Another day . . . another dollar.

Sabrina could have jumped for joy when it was time for lunch. She got up from her desk, grabbed her purse, and marched next door to Tangie's cubicle. She needed to get out of the office for a while. Computer problems had taken up most of her morning and now she was behind in her work.

"Ready?"

"Am I ever," Tangie answered. "With the day I'm having, I need a break."

While they walked out to Sabrina's car, Tangie told her about her last appointment.

"Girlfriend, this woman worked my last nerve."

Sabrina nodded in understanding. "I remember her. She used to be Dee's client before. . . . She's something else. Nothing ever pleases her."

As soon as they were seated, Sabrina announced, "I'm glad we decided to come here. This is a nice place," she murmured as she glanced around the restaurant. "I love all the greenery. Makes the place look exotic and tropical." She'd heard that this was one of Leon's favorite haunts. That was why Sabrina had wanted to come here in the first place. She hadn't expected to see him here today—just wanted to get a feel for the place he constantly talked about. Sabrina couldn't help but wonder why he never brought her here. Her mood shifted from mediocre to bad.

"I've heard nothing but good things about this place," Tangie said.

"The menu sounds appetizing. I already know what I'm going to have."

"I can't make up my mind. . . ."

"Well, you need to pick something. We only have an hour for lunch," Sabrina pointed out.

Tangie burst into laughter. "Somebody's grumpy. I guess I'll try the grilled-salmon Caesar salad."

Slapping the menu on the table, Sabrina said, "Thank the Lord. Girl, I'm starving. Now if we can just get that butch-looking waitress over here."

Shaking her head, Tangie hid her giggles behind her hand. "You need to quit. You get downright evil when you're hungry."

Sabrina shrugged nonchalantly.

The waitress managed to finally tear herself away from the table next to theirs.

"We're so happy you could finally join us," Sabrina snapped.

The woman shot her a look of pure venom but did not respond. Instead she recited the specials of the day, and they placed their food orders.

"How are things between you and Leon?" Tangie inquired when the waitress disappeared around a corner.

"Nothing much to tell. We're still on the outs right now, but then he and I are constantly on and off. He can't seem to understand that I'm not going to take his crap."

"I hear you, girlfriend."

"Humph! Leon pretty much knows he can't play me. I'm not

like those other women. He may have millions but he's not that good in bed. Not for me to be his fool."

"Have you heard from Bonita any more?"

Shaking her head, Sabrina replied, "No, and I don't expect to." After a moment, she added, "I don't know what Leon saw in her in the first place."

"Are you sure they're not together?"

"Girl . . . Leon knows better than to play me like that." Laying down her napkin, she amended her statement. "Tangie, to be honest with you, I don't know. They might be seeing each other now. I've paged him a few times and he hasn't returned my calls. He's old news as far as I'm concerned right now. I'm through with him."

Two weeks had passed, and deep down Sabrina missed Leon like crazy, but she would never admit it. She felt that Tangie would think less of her if she showed any sign of weakness when it came to Leon. She had to keep up this tough-girl act. Besides, she'd met a guy named Elwood Brown. He was an ex–NBA basketball player and drove a beautiful black Jaguar. He had no looks about him, but he had plenty of money.

"Why are you so quiet all of a sudden?"

Turning her attention to Tangie, Sabrina asked, "Huh?"

"What are you thinking about?"

Sabrina shook her head. "It's nothing important." Playing with her fork, she teased, "So who's the man in your life this week?"

Tangie's expression suddenly became unreadable. "What do you mean by that?"

Sabrina was caught off guard by Tangie's reaction. "Nothing. It was just a phrase. I thought maybe we could double-date or something."

The food arrived, sparing further conversation for the moment.

Sabrina sampled her dish. "Mmmmm, this is good." She stole a peek at Tangie. "How's your salad?" She could tell from her friend's expression that Tangie was still stewing over her comment. What was so offensive about her remark? she wondered.

"It's good."

Sabrina continued to watch her friend. Tangie took her time chewing before swallowing. Although she gave the appearance of being one, Tangie was anything but a perfect lady, as far as Sabrina was concerned. "I'm really curious. I can't help it."

Tangie stopped eating. "Are you starting that again?"

"Whenever I mention your love life, you always shut down on me. You never want to discuss the men in your life. I don't do that to you. I'm always talking about my life."

Shrugging, Tangie replied, "My life really is not worth talking about, that's all. Neither are the men, believe me."

Sabrina broke into laughter. "I guess I can understand that. I've had a few men in my life like that."

"*Most* of the ones in my life aren't even worth remembering."

She snatched up that crumb of information Tangie threw at her and pushed for more. "Why is that?"

"They were jerks," Tangie stated. "Now can we change the subject?"

"I've met someone," Sabrina announced. "His name is Elwood Brown. You should see his Jaguar. Girl, it's gorgeous. He also has a Lexus SUV."

Tangie seemed stunned. "When did this happen? I knew you were dating off and on but didn't think you were seeing anyone exclusively. I actually didn't think you had Leon out of your system."

"A week ago. We've talked on the phone three times already." Sabrina took a bite out of her burger.

"So do you like him? All you've mentioned is that he drives a Jaguar and a Lexus. Is there more to him?"

"He's an ex–basketball player. He used to play for New Jersey. Moved back here to take care of his mother. She died six months ago. I'll let you know in about three months whether or not I like Elwood. The newness will wear off by then and his real behavior will come out."

Tangie laughed. "I know what you mean. Wow," she murmured. "That's sad about his mother, but I'm glad to see you're moving on with your life."

"Humph. I won't have it any other way. Elwood is nice and he doesn't seem to mind spending money on me. He treats me like a queen."

"Good for you, Sabrina."

"When was the last time you saw your mom?" This was the only part of her life Tangie willingly shared. Sabrina suspected it was because the whole town knew about Lula Thompson.

Tangie made a face. "You had to bring her up, didn't you? A couple of days ago. She came by my apartment over the weekend."

"Did you let her inside?"

Tangie shook her head no. "I pretended that I wasn't home."

"I thought about doing my mom that way but it wouldn't work. She has a key."

"You and your mother are real close. Lula is always trying to run down somebody else's husband. She's never had time to be a mother."

"She's still seeing Mr. Harris?"

Tangie nodded. "She's thinking he's going to finally leave his wife and marry her. You'd think she would know the drill by now." Hope that Lula would change her ways and become the mother that Tangie needed vanished like soap bubbles in the air.

"Some people will never learn," Sabrina uttered.

22

While they ate, Tangie wondered whether she should repeat what Bonita's cousin had told her. If Leon and Bonita were really getting married, didn't Sabrina have a right to know? She thought so, but then again, why stir up a hornet's nest if it wasn't really necessary? Bonita had announced on more than one occasion that she and Leon would marry, and that had proven to be false. Besides, Tangie doubted that Leon would ever settle down.

She and Sabrina had never agreed when it came to Leon. No doubt she would think this was another ploy to keep them apart, and Tangie wasn't up for drama.

"Now why are you being so quiet?" Sabrina questioned.

"I was just thinking about Dee. I really miss not seeing her in the office or talking to her on the phone."

"So do I," replied Sabrina. "It's not the same in the FFA unit without her."

Tangie agreed. Checking her watch, she announced, "We'd better hurry up. We need to get back to work." She glanced over at Sabrina once more and once again debated whether she should mention Leon and Bonita. This was her friend and she didn't want her to get hurt.

Sabrina met her gaze. "What?"

The woman was already on the defensive. Now was definitely not the right time, Tangie decided. "Nothing. It's nothing."

"Are you okay? You're sure acting strange all of a sudden."

Tangie's leg swung nervously. "I'm fine, Sabrina. Really."

"I know that's what you say, but you sure don't act that way. I can tell something's bothering you."

"Sabrina, have you ever been in love? Really in love?"

"Kind of," Sabrina admitted. "Have you?"

Tangie shook her head no. "I guess I almost came close—I liked this guy a lot, but eventually the relationship just kind of fizzled out."

"How long were you together?"

"About five years."

"That's a long time, Tangie. You sure you weren't in love?"

"I didn't love him. He didn't love me either. We just enjoyed being together. I'm pretty sure he was seeing other women on the side."

"Relationships can be so hard. That's why I'm not looking for love. I just want a man who's financially stable so that he can give me the things I want."

"What will he get in return?"

"Me, of course," Sabrina replied. "I'll look good on his arm and I can throw a mean dinner party. That's the perfect scenario, don't you think?"

"You think you can live without love?"

"Don't you?"

Tangie nodded. "It's overrated. It can make you lose your mind and forget about everything else."

"You're talking about your mother, right?"

"Do you remember the day she came up to the office waving

that tennis bracelet Mr. Harris had given her? I thought I would die from the humiliation. It's bad enough everybody in town knows all about her." Tangie frowned. "She just doesn't seem to care."

"Maybe Mr. Harris loves her."

Tangie shook her head in disagreement. "He'd leave his wife if that were true, and it wouldn't have taken this long. They have been together over ten years."

"You're right," Sabrina agreed. "There's no way I'll stay with a man that long—especially not wearing the title of mistress."

"I just don't know why Lula can't see the truth. I get so tired of people looking at me and whispering. I don't deserve to be treated like this."

"Girl, people aren't blaming you for what your mother does. That's her life—not yours."

"I don't want to be her daughter, Sabrina. I have two sisters and a brother who won't even acknowledge me. The reality is that my father doesn't claim me either. I'm the shame that everybody whispers about, and it doesn't feel good." Tangie felt like she was going to cry. She swallowed hard. "I'm sorry. I didn't mean to go there."

"You have to talk to someone."

"I hate Lula for doing this to me. She was so busy running around with one married man after another, leaving me to my grandmother. I loved MeMa to death, but that was one mean woman. All she did was talk about how I was going to turn out just like Lula."

"But your mother was there. All of you lived in the same house, right?"

"My grandmother raised me," Tangie insisted. "I didn't have a mother. When Lula was there, all she and MeMa did was argue. She wasn't there that much, though. She was always out partying or running after somebody else's husband."

"I'm sure it seems like you had a rough childhood, Tangie—

but in a way you were lucky. It could have been much worse. You know, an abusive situation. Instead, look how you've turned out."

"Yeah, look how I've turned out," Tangie repeated.

23

Within three weeks Cordelia could move her right leg up off the bed, and she could move the fingers on her right hand. Although her speech had improved greatly, she still struggled with words and there was a definite slur. Cordelia also experienced confusion between her right and left.

When the nurse helped her bathe and brush her hair that morning, Cordelia caught a glimpse of herself in a mirror. She looked as if she'd aged ten years.

According to the doctor, her stroke disabled her ability to organize, focus, and plan ahead. Her memory had also been affected.

Cordelia was angry. She didn't understand why God was punishing her this way. What had she done to deserve His wrath? she wondered. *I prayed, attended church, and did all the things I was supposed to do, so why did You do this to me? Lord, what did I do wrong?*

Over and over in her mind, Cordelia tried to figure out where she had gone wrong. There were criminals, nonbelievers, and people ignoring the word of God—yet she was the one being punished. Years ago God had taken away a child, and now He had taken her health.

Betrayal coursed through her veins. Even her mouth was filled with a bitter taste.

God had abandoned her. With that in mind, Cordelia began to view her life differently. God had allowed her marriage to fall apart, one daughter to die, and another to start skipping school, sneaking out of the house, and become pregnant. Now she was to spend her life in a wheelchair unable to care for her own needs. This was a punishment. No, this was hell, she amended.

The thought of dying agitated her, and Cordelia felt her anxiety rise. She didn't want to die. Her initial reaction was to pray, but then she remembered—God had allowed this to happen in the first place. She rejected the idea.

Cordelia could never recall feeling so powerless in her life. She felt backed up against a wall, and there was nowhere to turn. Suddenly the thought of death didn't seem so bad.

There was a soft knock on the door. A young girl stuck her head inside. "I have your lunch," she announced. She brought a tray into the room and placed it on the bedside table. She left as quietly as she'd come.

Cordelia didn't have an appetite so she left it untouched.

A volunteer entered the room pushing a wheelchair. She gave Cordelia a winning smile. "Hello, Mrs. Berkeley. It's time for your physical therapy."

Cordelia's heart began to race. Therapy? Couldn't this woman see that she was sick? *I'm paralyzed,* she wanted to scream. *I can't do anything. How am I supposed to manage therapy?*

"Mrs. Berkeley. It's time for therapy, sugar."

Cordelia shook her head. "Nooo."

The nurse came over to the bed and patted Cordelia on the hand. "Physical therapy is crucial to your recovery," she said in her singsong voice. "The stroke weakened your muscles. Going to therapy can help you gain your physical independence."

She'd been beaten, Cordelia decided. She would never recover enough to become the woman she once was. She had enough of her senses left to comprehend that fact.

After a while the woman gave up and left.

Cordelia was staring up at the ceiling when Gerald strolled into the room. Her eyes strayed to his face, trying to discern the emotions behind his grim expression. She had a strong suspicion he'd been told about her refusal to go to therapy. He most likely thought she deserved this fate. Probably felt vindicated in some way. Gerald had never wanted the divorce and was still angry over it.

He gave her a tiny smile, grabbed a chair, and pulled it over to the side of the hospital bed. Dropping down, he asked, "How're you feeling?"

The very question enraged her. Cordelia rolled her eyes. How did he *think* she was feeling?

Gerald suddenly looked uncomfortable. "Okay . . ." He eyed Cordelia for a moment. "I guess you're feeling better."

She wasn't sure how to take his comment so she turned her head away from him, wishing he would leave. But then she would be alone, and she didn't want that right now. She just didn't want the person with her to be Gerald.

He reached for a Bible lying nearby. Opening it, Gerald began to read aloud.

"Noooo . . ."

"What? You don't want to hear this chapter? Is there another one?"

"Nooo," Cordelia moaned a second time. She wanted to say more but the words just wouldn't come. "D-don't," she finally managed.

Gerald gave her a bewildered look. "What's wrong, Dee? You don't want me to read the Bible to you?"

She nodded as her eyes filled with tears. Cordelia had never felt so frustrated in her life.

He put it away. "Okay. I won't. Don't get upset." Gerald gestured toward the food. "Would you like me to help you?"

Cordelia blinked back tears and shook her head. He had no idea how humiliated she felt right now. The doctors had mentioned that her language difficulties were part of the left-brain stroke symptoms. She felt clumsy, and to add to her misery, food sometimes dribbled out of her mouth. It was an acutely embarrassing ordeal for Cordelia.

The nurse entered the room. "Mrs. Berkeley, you're going to have to do better than this." She pointed to the tray laden with food. "You need to eat, and you're going to have to start going to therapy. You want to get better, don't you?"

The woman acted as if her health and well-being were solely in her control. Cordelia refused to look at Gerald. She felt as if she could almost hear his thoughts. He didn't want to be here any more than she did. But Gerald could leave whenever he was ready. For all his whoring around, he was able to move on with his life. He was an attorney and would be able to defend his clients. She would never be able to be a social worker. Not again. Her career was over.

"Some of your New Hope members are outside," Gerald announced. "I know it makes you feel good to have the support of your church. Pastor Grant is here almost daily to visit and pray with you."

She didn't want to see anyone from New Hope. Cordelia dreaded a visit with Pastor Grant. There were times she would have looked forward to his words of encouragement, but not anymore.

Gerald interrupted her silent ranting. "Dee, you can't just lie around here like this and do nothing," he stated. "You need to eat so that you can get stronger. I don't understand why you're refusing to go to therapy. Honey, it can only help you get better." He stopped. "Are you listening to me? And what about our daughter? She needs you."

Cordelia shook her head. She opened her mouth to speak

but couldn't get the words to come out. "Can't sa . . . say." She paused and tried again. "W-wods ha . . . har."

"Don't get upset, sweetheart. The words are hard right now, but it'll get better. Dr. Wilcox calls your condition aphasia, and he assures me that you'll get better. We just have to take it slowly. Remember, you couldn't say anything before. Give yourself some time—and you've got to trust the rehabilitation team."

Cordelia started to cry. She was afraid. Afraid and alone.

"There is nothing more we can do for your wife," Dr. Wilcox stated. "She's still refusing therapy."

Gerald nodded in understanding. "Is she strong enough to go home?"

"Yes. Your wife is a lot stronger than she gives herself credit for."

"She's given up. I've been trying to talk her into going to physical therapy but she won't go. She won't even take speech therapy." He sighed. "Doctor, I think she's afraid. Dee is so scared of failing that she won't even try. She seems very depressed."

The doctor nodded. "Depression is common after suffering a stroke. It's important to remember that poststroke depression can be the result of a loss of brain chemicals damaged by the brain injury. It can also be a reaction to Mrs. Berkeley's loss of functional abilities. I'm going to put her on some medication to try to counteract the depression."

"My wife has succeeded in everything she's ever set out to do, Doctor. She was very independent—until now. This stroke just robbed the life right out of her. She doesn't even want visitors—especially from her pastor and church members. I hate seeing her this way, and I'm willing to do what I can do to help Dee."

"She may feel uncomfortable because of her speech. Rehabilitation is the way back for Mrs. Berkeley—and for the family as well."

"How does this work, Doctor?" Gerald wanted to know. "Does she start physical therapy for so many weeks, then speech and so on?" .

Dr. Wilcox shook his head. "The different areas of rehabilitation take place within the same time frame. This way the team is able to reinforce an interrelated approach. It's also important that we treat the depression—we want to keep her desire for progress going."

Gerald nodded in understanding.

"Right now, the best thing you can do is try to convince her to go to therapy."

"I will get her there," he vowed.

"Going home may help her feel better as well. Patients have been known to make vast improvements in their recovery once leaving the hospital. But the most important aspect of a stroke's aftermath is rehabilitation."

"I know Dee very well, and she would rather be at home than in the hospital. She doesn't want to have to stay at the rehabilitation center."

When they finished talking, Gerald returned to Cordelia's room. She was watching television when he entered. "I just spoke with the doctor," he announced cheerfully. "You're going to be leaving here real soon. Isn't that good news?"

Cordelia almost seemed to brighten up.

"I thought you'd like that." Gerald sat on the edge of the bed. "Dee, I've taken some time off. My partner is going to handle my current clients for me so that I can stay here in Bridgeport. I've moved into the guest room."

Cordelia raised her eyebrows in surprise.

"You're going to need help for the time being."

His gentle reminder angered Cordelia.

As if he knew what she was thinking, Gerald stated softly. "It's okay to need help sometimes, and I don't mind. I would like to think that you'd do the same for me if our situations were reversed." He smiled. "Maybe?"

Some of her anger faded. Cordelia gave a small smile, as much of one as she could manage.

The knock on her hospital door signaled the dinner hour.

"You're going to have to eat all of your food if you want to come home, though," Gerald stated. "Sweetheart, I'll help you. We're going to make this a team effort to help you recover."

Long after Gerald had gone home, Cordelia sat staring into space. She didn't want him in her house. Not on a permanent basis anyway. He'd done too much to her, and she still had trouble forgiving him. Besides, she didn't need Gerald—she didn't want to need him. Anybody but him. Cordelia was determined to show all of them that she would be fine on her own.

Gerald had taken her outside earlier, and she was still in the wheelchair because she hadn't wanted to get in bed when they returned to the room. Now she had a change of heart.

Instead of paging the nurse, Cordelia decided to prove her independence. She figured all she had to do was push the wheels to roll it closer to her bed. She was wrong. The wheelchair wouldn't budge despite all her efforts. Frustrated and fingers hurting, Cordelia burst into tears. The hospital bed was so close but not close enough.

She was still crying when the nurse checked on her.

24

"Cordelia's going home soon," Bonnie announced. "I spoke with Gerald right before I came here. There's nothing more they can do at the hospital, and she's still refusing therapy."

"In a way that's wonderful news." Sabrina took a sip of her iced tea. "I went to see her yesterday and she didn't really look as if she's getting any better. Maybe going home will be good for her."

"I think it will," Tangie interjected. "I know my grandmother got better once she went home. Of course, therapy really helped."

"How is Dee going to get to her bedroom? It's upstairs."

"She's going to be using the bedroom downstairs, Sabrina. Remember, it has its own bath too," Bonnie replied.

"I'd forgotten about that room. She used it for an office or something like that."

"That was her office," Tangie confirmed.

Bonnie continued: "I'm going over to the house tomorrow after work to help Devon and Gerald get it ready for Dee's homecoming. They had some people there today making improvements in the bathroom, kitchen, and bedroom. I'm going to see if I can help with anything."

"Anything like what?" Sabrina asked.

Bonnie hid her irritation. "Cleaning the house . . . anything I can do."

"Do they need any more help?" Tangie wanted to know. "I don't have any real plans."

"I'll let you know."

"I'd be glad to help out too," Sabrina offered. "But I've already made plans. I'll have to catch y'all at another time. Sorry."

"Dee is going to love seeing you, Tangie." Bonnie played with her fingers, hoping they would notice her newly manicured nails. This was the first time she'd ever done something so frivolous, but it felt good—it felt right. For some unknown reason, she'd felt like pampering herself.

Sabrina was the first to catch on. "Woo woo woo. Bonnie Mae, what's up with you? You've got your nails all done, and it looks like you're even letting your hair grow out. Anything you want to tell us? Inquiring minds want to know. . . ."

"I just felt a need to do something special for myself."

Smiling, Tangie said, "You're always looking out for us—it's time you spoiled yourself."

"I think Bonnie's met a man and she's trying to keep it on the down-low. Come on, girl, you know you can tell us," Sabrina urged.

Bonnie giggled like a schoolgirl. "There's not a man. Maybe one day in the future, but not right now."

"Sabrina's got the right idea. Bonnie, it's time you started going out more. You're still young enough to be a catch," Tangie said.

Bonnie shook with laughter. "You ladies are so good for my ego." She was thrilled that they'd noticed the small changes she'd made. In recent weeks she had decided to work on herself. It may have had something to do with Cordelia's stroke,

Bonnie now realized. It reminded her that each day was precious because it drew you one day closer to death.

"I know you're always sewing something, so what are you working on now?" Sabrina asked.

"I'm making a quilt," Bonnie replied proudly.

Frowning, Sabrina asked, "A quilt? It's too hot for a quilt."

Tangie burst into nervous laughter. "She's making the quilt—not using it."

"I don't like quilts," Sabrina stated flatly.

A gnawing feeling crept into Bonnie's stomach. She reached for her water glass. Sabrina had an amazing talent for putting a damper on everything. She didn't know why she put up with her in the first place.

"When you're finished with the quilt, I'd like to see it," Tangie said. "You know, you should sell them."

"I don't know about that. . . ."

"Really. There are people who'll pay lots of money for a handmade quilt."

"Not me," Sabrina expressed.

"That's already been established," Tangie shot back. "Bonnie, the quilts I've seen are beautiful. You do such a wonderful job."

"You really think so?"

Tangie nodded.

Maybe she should consider it, Bonnie decided. Her church had an upcoming craft show—she would sign up and display a few of her quilts.

Bonnie and Tangie helped Devon clean Cordelia's house from top to bottom.

"Oh, Lord . . ." Devon put away the broom, saying, "I think this house has gotten larger."

Tangie broke into a grin after exchanging a look with Bonnie. "You sound tired, Devon," she teased.

"I am. I don't remember ever cleaning up the house so much. It's got to be spotless."

Bonnie and Tangie burst into laughter. "Devon, you're something else."

Rubbing her back, she said, "Miss Bonnie, I'm tired. It's been a long day."

They settled down in the den. Devon leaned back against the cushions of the sectional sofa.

"Are you all hungry? We could order a couple of pizzas," Bonnie suggested.

"Pizza sounds good," Tangie agreed.

They went through a stack of pizza coupons Devon found in the drawer of a table nearby.

Devon called for her father to join them. "We're ordering pizza. Want some?"

"Sure," Gerald replied. "That sounds good. Pepperoni and pineapple for me." Pulling out his wallet, he said, "This is my treat. I can't thank you ladies enough."

Devon and Gerald brought Cordelia home two days later. Bonnie wanted to give them some time alone before she came to visit. She called daily to check on Cordelia. This time Devon answered. "How's your mother doing?"

"I think she's happy to be home. She hasn't really said anything, though. Mama still has trouble with her words. It's getting better, but I can tell she's embarrassed about it."

"She's probably not ready to talk on the telephone then."

"She's sleeping right now, Miss Bonnie."

"I'll call back later and check on her. Please let her know I called."

"I will, Miss Bonnie. As soon as she wakes up. Mama was up most of the morning. She likes to go out into the sunroom and just sit. I think she likes looking out the windows."

"It's one of her favorite places in the entire house." Playing with a pen on her desk, Bonnie added, "Sweetie, I'm go-ing to hang up now. I'll call back this evening to check on Dee."

"Okay, Miss Bonnie. I'll talk to you later."

Bonnie hung up the phone, ecstatic with the news. She knew Dee would feel better once she came home.

After taking Scotty for a walk, she returned home and set to work on her quilts. Bonnie was in creative mode, and she worked until well after eleven.

That Saturday, Bonnie brought food to Cordelia's house. "I made a peach cobbler for you. I know how much you love them."

Gerald smiled in gratitude. "Thanks, Bonnie. I really appreciate all you've done. Sabrina and Tangie too."

"It wasn't a problem. This was just my way of helping out." Bonnie carried the food to the kitchen. Gerald took it from her and put it away in the freezer.

"How long do you plan to stay, Gerald?"

He turned around, facing her. "As long as I'm needed. I took a leave of absence from work. I want to be here in case Dee needs me."

"You're a good man."

He gave a short bark of laughter. "Don't let Dee hear you say that."

"What's important is that you're here now. For her and Devon."

Lowering his voice, Gerald confessed, "Devon thinks it's her fault. I keep telling her that Dee's stroke had nothing to do with her."

"You just keep telling her that. She needs to stay healthy herself." Bonnie glanced toward the bedroom. "I bet Dee's glad to be home."

"Hard to tell. She just sits and stares at the walls. Dee won't even watch television. I finally had to tell Pastor Grant and her other church members that she doesn't want to see anyone."

"This has to be hard on her, Gerald. A stroke is devastating. Depression is something that a lot of stroke survivors experience."

"I realize that. Bonnie, all I want to do is help her get better. It tears me up inside to see her like this." His voice broke. "It kills me."

"Dee is going to get better. She's too stubborn not to."

"I don't know. It's like she's given up."

"It may take some time, but you know Dee."

"I hope you're right, Bonnie."

"Just be patient with her, Gerald. You can't give up on her— if you do, she might really give up then."

"The timing of it all . . ." He shook his head sadly. "Devon needs her. With a baby coming . . . I don't know, Bonnie. Dee's better at handling stuff like this. Devon was supposed to move in with me. The stroke has changed all that for now."

"She's always said you were the stronger of the two of you."

Gerald gave a short laugh. "Dee said that? That's about the nicest thing she's said in a long time."

Bonnie smiled. "Everything is going to be okay." She headed to Cordelia's bedroom and took a peek inside. "Hello, Dee."

Cordelia turned her face toward the door.

Bonnie stepped all the way into the room. "I'm so glad you're awake. I know you're happy to be home and in your own bed."

"B-Bon . . . nie," Cordelia managed.

"Now, don't you worry about talking. There will always be time for us to catch up." Bonnie pushed a chair beside the bed. She glanced around the room. "I love what you've done to this room, Dee. The wallpaper is perfect." Cordelia had recently redecorated all of the bedrooms in the house. Some flowers would be nice in the room, Bonnie thought. "The tall flower arrangement from your church would be perfect on that table," Bonnie suggested.

"Dee . . . von . . ." Cordelia paused for a second, then said, "Dodder."

Nodding, Bonnie said, "I made the appointment for Devon and went with her to the doctor. She says that everything is fine. Devon just needs to take her vitamins and iron."

Cordelia seemed relieved to hear that Devon and her baby were healthy. This was a good sign.

"The baby is due the twenty-fourth of August. And Dee, you don't have to worry," Bonnie reassured her. "I haven't told anyone about Devon's situation."

A smile slowly formed on her lips. Reaching over, Bonnie took Cordelia by the hand. "I know I keep saying this, but everything is going to work out perfectly."

Cordelia nodded. "Thaa . . . ya," she murmured slowly.

Bonnie gently hugged her. "You're welcome, Dee. You know that I'm here for you."

Not only did Cordelia have trouble pronouncing words, but she also couldn't remember things others told her. She'd already forgotten most of what Bonnie said.

"Gerald worked hard to get this house ready. He did a wonderful job."

Cordelia nodded a second time.

"Have you tried the tub slide chair?" Bonnie asked. "The doctor felt it wouldn't compromise your comfort and safety. You can use it over the toilet and over the tub when you take a shower."

"Bonn . . ."

"You need something, sweetie?"

"Why . . . ha-hap?" Cordelia looked frustrated.

"You want to know what happened?"

"Noo." Cordelia swallowed hard. "W-why . . ."

Bonnie could only respond, "I don't know, Dee. I wish I could answer that question for you. I'm so sorry."

"H-hate been this w-way. Not r-right."

Her heart ached for Cordelia. "You've improved so much in such a short time. It can only get better."

"Never be me 'gain. Not ol' me."

Giving her a bright smile, Bonnie replied, "The new you will be wonderful—just as wonderful as the old you was."

"I doan know. . . ."

"I won't say it's going to be easy, Dee. It's going to challenge you, but as long as you stand proud and encouraged, you'll make it."

Bonnie spent the rest of the afternoon telling Cordelia about her entries in the upcoming craft show at church. When Cordelia fell asleep, Bonnie informed Gerald. She left while he was putting her in bed.

The day arrived for the craft show. Bonnie was nervous. The car was packed and she was ready. She stood in her driveway tempted to change her mind about the show entirely.

"No, I've worked hard for this, and I can't back out now," she whispered to herself. "If I sell just one, then I've made my quota," Bonnie decided.

An hour later she was at the church and busy setting up her booth. Bonnie displayed on top what she considered her best work. She made herself comfortable in the lawn chair she'd brought with her and stuck a straw hat on her head. The sun was beaming already, and it was only eight in the morning.

By eight-thirty she had her first customer. Bonnie stood up and greeted the woman. She didn't look familiar—probably not a member of her church. She held her breath as the woman examined one of her quilts.

"I've never seen anything like it," the woman murmured. "This is a beautiful quilt."

Bonnie beamed at the compliment.

"How much is this one?"

"Sixty dollars," Bonnie stated carefully. She'd had a hard time coming up with the price.

"Only sixty? Hon, I think you're cheating yourself. Look, I'm going to give you one hundred dollars. This quilt is worth it."

"Thank you, but—"

"No buts. This is business."

The customer paid for her purchase and disappeared into the crowd.

Someone walked up behind her and put her hands over Bonnie's eyes.

"Guess who?"

Recognizing Tangie's voice, Bonnie turned around, grinning. She was a little put off to see Sabrina standing there, but she kept it hidden. "This is a surprise. I never expected you all to come."

"I love crafts," Tangie replied. "Besides, I'm in the market for a new quilt."

Sabrina made a face when she thought Bonnie wasn't looking. Ignoring her, Bonnie picked up a quilt in a lavender color and held it out to Tangie. "This one will match your bedroom."

"It sure does," Tangie murmured. "It's gorgeous, Bonnie." She ran her hand gently across the delicate lace-edged panels. "I'm going to have to get this one."

"You don't have to buy anything, Tangie. I'm just glad you both came by."

"I really want this quilt, Bonnie. This has nothing to do with our friendship."

"Can you please hurry up? I'm ready to leave," Sabrina uttered in a brisk tone.

Tangie ignored her. "I want to see if you have something for a little girl. Do you have anything like the one you did for that lady last year?"

Bonnie nodded. "I do. It's not pink, though. This time I did it in peach and ivory."

Sabrina sighed loudly.

Every now and then Bonnie would glance over at her. Sabrina fingered the quilts as if they were contaminated. Bonnie was determined not to let the mood queen get her down today. Not today.

25

Much to Sabrina's frustration, Tangie didn't leave Bonnie's booth until after she'd purchased three quilts.

She'd sighed loudly, tapped her nails on the table, and looked as bored as she could. She was ready to leave this festival of homemade goods. Sabrina didn't have a clue as to why Tangie was carrying on so over scraps of fabric sewn together. She couldn't believe Bonnie had the nerve to charge one hundred dollars for some.

Sabrina glanced around, trying to see if she knew any of the people attending the craft show. She was amazed to see so many people at the church. Most of the stuff sold at the various booths was cheap and tawdry-looking, in her opinion. Bonnie had told them that a percentage of the profits would go toward the summer camp program at the church.

Finally they were on their way.

The first thing she noticed was Tangie's change in mood. "What's up with you?"

"Why were you being so rude today?" Tangie shot back at her as they climbed into her car.

"I wasn't rude." Sabrina thought the line of questioning ridiculous, so she changed the subject. "Are we still going to the mall?"

"We have to. That's where you left your car."

She sighed in irritation. "What I meant to say was, are we still going inside the mall? I need to pick up some things."

"You just want to shop—I doubt you need anything. I'm surprised you have any money."

"I'm not shopping with my money," Sabrina countered.

When they parked in the parking lot of Hudson Belk, Tangie said, "I wish you wouldn't treat Bonnie so bad."

Sabrina glanced over at her friend in confusion. "What are you talking about?"

They got out and strolled toward the store. "You weren't very nice. You made it so obvious you wanted to be anywhere but there."

Shrugging, Sabrina said, "I wasn't feeling like seeing her today."

"It was your idea to go by the church."

"I just wanted to see if I knew anybody who went there. Besides, I didn't feel like stroking her ego, Tangie." Sabrina fingered the silky fabric hanging on the hanger in the lingerie department. "You should see the new suit Elwood brought me. It's gorgeous."

Holding up a chemise to her body, Tangie replied, "I bet it is. I see you're sporting a new Coach purse and a new watch. He get you those too?"

"He sure did." Sabrina picked up a robe and tried it on. "Tell me something, Tangie. Why didn't you like Leon?"

"It's just something about him," Tangie replied.

Sabrina didn't get it. Tangie was extremely negative whenever it came to Leon. As far as she knew, they really didn't know each other. "I really don't understand. Is there something you haven't told me?"

"Just drop it, Sabrina," Tangie snapped. "Tell you what. I'll stay out of your business. Going forward, what goes on between you and Leon is your problem. I have my own stuff to deal with."

Sabrina was stunned by the shift in attitude. "Sorry, Tangie. I didn't mean anything by it. I just asked a simple question."

"Let's just drop this discussion, Sabrina, before I get pissed. You're the one always bringing up Leon. Like I said before, I don't care one whit what you do with or without him."

Sabrina could feel herself getting angry. "Now who's being rude? I'm not trying to argue with you, Tangie. I didn't mean to—"

"Just drop it, Sabrina." Without another word, she stormed off.

She stared after her friend, wanting to call Tangie back. Sabrina muttered a curse. She hated when they argued. But this time she had no idea how things had progressed to this point. It was Tangie's problem, though, she decided.

She was negative about any guy Sabrina had been interested in, and it grated on her last nerve. Maybe she was jealous, Sabrina decided. It was probably true—Tangie was jealous of her. But it wasn't Sabrina's fault that Tangie couldn't hold on to a man.

She spent another hour in the department store before heading out to her car. Her first stop was Jersey Mike's, where she ordered a Philly cheese steak sandwich and a soda to go. On her way out, she bumped into a mass of muscles.

Looking up, she sniped, "I think the door is big enough for the two of us."

Leon leaned down, planting a kiss on her lips. "Hey, pretty lady."

Sabrina pretended that seeing him didn't move her. "Where did you come from?"

"I was in town on some business and I saw your car, so I decided to follow you here."

"I believe they call that stalking." Folding her arms across her chest, she asked, "So what do you want?"

His eyes slid down her body, then snaked back up to her face. "Just thought I'd say hello. I thought maybe you might be missing me."

"Well, I'm not," she lied. "To tell the truth, I haven't given you as much as a second thought."

Pointing to the bag in her hand, Leon questioned, "Is this your dinner?"

"Why?" she countered. "Are you taking me somewhere else?"

"I would but you're mad at me."

Sabrina was never one to turn down a free meal. Her tone softened and turned seductive. "Tell you what. Why don't we have dinner somewhere and talk?"

Just then his cell phone rang. Leon answered it.

Sabrina pretended that she wasn't listening but she was desperately trying to hear his conversation. When he hung up, she said, "I guess that means dinner is off."

Leon shrugged off her question. "I'm sorry, baby."

She hid her disappointment. "No big deal. I'll see you later, Leon."

Her mood shifted for the better after she came home to find that Elwood had called. Sabrina quickly called him back, suggesting that they have dinner together. She threw the sandwich from Jersey Mike's into the refrigerator and rushed upstairs to shower and change. She regretted canceling her hair appointment this morning, but there really wasn't any point in worrying about it now. Sabrina could work miracles with her short hair.

Elwood rattled on and on, but Sabrina was only half listening at this point. All the man ever talked about was his previous basketball days in the NBA. Maybe if she'd told him the truth from the beginning—how she hated sports with a passion—then she wouldn't have to suffer through these aimless conversations.

He didn't seem to notice how bored she was. She sent up a short prayer of thanks when their food arrived. Maybe now he would shut up so that she could enjoy her lobster. She liked Elwood, but that was about it. She would never develop any real feelings for him—they didn't have much in common. Plus the man was ugly.

Leon infiltrated her silent musings. Sabrina missed him a lot. It had been four weeks since that dreadful night of his birthday, and seeing him earlier today brought up feelings she'd tried to ignore.

Elwood was not the man of her dreams, and he did nothing for her in or out of bed. He wasn't the man she really wanted to spend time with, and maybe it was time she told him so. But she was thinking about trading in her BMW for a new model, or perhaps she'd buy the new Mercedes-Benz—the one like Leon's—so she couldn't afford to muddy the waters for now.

She was thankful that Elwood liked to spend money. He enjoyed the better things in life and had introduced her to caviar and fine, expensive wines. Sabrina could personally do without the caviar—she thought the taste was horrible.

The mention of a gold credit card brought Sabrina's attention back to Elwood. "Huh? What did you just say?"

"I just got the new gold card in the mail. You should see the credit limit. It's through the roof."

He had her full attention now. "Well, are you going to tell me?" Sabrina was already thinking of what she wanted to buy.

Elwood blinked twice. "Tell you what?"

"You're sitting here bragging about your new credit card—what's your limit?"

He suddenly looked embarrassed after being called out like that. Elwood recovered long enough to say, "You don't have to worry about the limit. I can pay for our dinner; that's all that matters."

Insulted, Sabrina stiffened her back and folded her arms across her chest. "I didn't bring up the subject of credit cards, Elwood—*you* did."

"I didn't mean to hurt your feelings, sweetheart. I don't think I should give out my credit limits and such. It's like giving out my social security number."

"So you're telling me that you think I'm a skank and can't be trusted," Sabrina accused coldly. She pushed away from the table. "I'm ready to leave."

"For the record, I know you're not a skank, Sabrina. You're a very classy lady. I know that."

Sabrina wasn't going to let him off the hook that easily. "Can we leave?"

Elwood signaled for the check. While they waited, he said, "I'm sorry. I wasn't trying to hurt you."

Sabrina waved off his apology. She was going to make Elwood pay for that insult.

Throughout the drive home, she didn't say a word. Elwood probably assumed he would be spending the night, but Sabrina had news for him—she wanted to be alone.

Elwood was all over her as soon as they entered her condo. Pushing away, Sabrina rubbed her forehead. "Honey, I'm getting a massive headache, so I think maybe you should leave."

"You don't want me to spend the night?"

Sabrina shook her head. "I'm planning to go to church in the morning for prayer, and I wouldn't feel right if you stay."

Elwood burst into laughter. "You don't need to go there, Sabrina. We've had sex before, so the damage has already been done. I don't think it'll matter."

Sabrina hated being laughed at. "Then just go home, Elwood," she snapped. "I'm tired and I want to be alone. I just told you I have a terrible headache."

"What's wrong with you?"

"I'm sorry. I don't feel good, and I don't mean to be rude. I just really want to be alone right now. It doesn't have anything to do with you."

"Why don't you let me stay, sweetheart? I could make you forget—"

"No, you couldn't," she quickly interjected. "When I get terrible headaches they make me moody. You really don't want to experience any of that. I can be a real witch."

"I can see that."

Sabrina held her tongue when a commercial aired featuring the Mercedes-Benz E320 sedan. She couldn't alienate him just yet. She had plans for his money. Hugging him, Sabrina smiled sweetly. "Honey, I'm sorry for being so hateful. Why don't you let me get some rest tonight? I'll call you first thing in the morning, okay?"

"You're sure you're going to be all right?" Elwood sounded genuinely concerned.

She nodded and placed a hand to her temple. "All I need is some rest. My headaches make me evil."

He kissed her gently on the lips. "Give me a call in the morning."

"I will," she promised.

Elwood strode briskly to the front door. When she ran over to the window and eyed him getting into his car, Sabrina threw up her hands, saying, "Thank you, Jesus. I thought the man would never leave."

26

Tangie stared at the letter in her hand. What did Danny Watkins want after all this time, and why did he write a letter? She was surprised that he'd found her at all. She carried it into the house with her and dropped it on the sofa table with the rest of the mail without another thought. She took down her bun as she went upstairs to her room to change clothes.

Tangie slipped into a bright red dress made out of a jersey knit fabric and peered at her reflection in the mirror. Ever since Cordelia's stroke, Tangie had been coming home and staying close to the telephone, but she couldn't take it anymore. She was starving for the touch of a man, and she needed to escape reality for a while.

Looking for a pair of earrings, Tangie ran downstairs to check her entertainment center. She recalled putting them there two days ago. She paused for a moment, carefully surveying the towering oak. Something wasn't right. "Who's been going through my things?" she asked aloud. This wasn't the first time she'd had that feeling.

Nothing really seemed out of place—just moved around.

Tangie knelt down on one knee. She scanned her collection of videos. Right off, she couldn't tell if anything was missing. Standing up, Tangie picked up her earrings and put them on.

The doorbell rang. She went to answer it. Stealing a look through the peephole, she frowned. Opening the door, she said, "Lula . . ."

Her mouth twisted into a frown, her mother asked, "What's wrong with you?"

"I was about to go out. What are you doing here?" Stalking away from the door, Tangie said, "It would be nice if you'd call before you just come over."

"I can't stop by to see my daughter? I was thinking about you and I just wanted to come by and visit for a while. Anything wrong with that?"

Tangie didn't bother to hide her irritation. "I just said I was on my way out."

Instead of turning and leaving, Lula made herself at home on the sofa. Crossing her legs, she asked, "Things going okay for you at the job?"

Releasing a long sigh, Tangie propped herself on the arm of her couch. "Yes."

"How's your love life?"

"Why?"

"Just making conversation, that's all."

"My life is fine," Tangie snapped. "I couldn't be happier."

"I don't see any pictures of your boyfriend. Got one?"

"Why are you so interested in my love life all of a sudden?" Recalling her earlier feeling, Tangie asked, "Have you been going through my stuff?"

Lula looked offended. "No, I haven't gone through your things. I really hate it when you act this way. I'm just trying to get to know you—be a part of your life."

"You are a part of my life, Lula, as much as I hate to admit it. We've never been close and I just think it's too late to try now, so let's just leave things the way they are. Okay?"

Lula shook her head sadly. "I don't want that, honey. I want a better relationship with you." She ran her fingers through her long auburn curls. "I know—why don't I go out with you tonight? It would be fun."

Tangie shook her head. "I don't think so—I mean, I'm going to Fayetteville with some friends," she lied. There was no way she'd consider letting Lula tag along.

"Maybe some other time then. We should spend time together. I'd really like that."

"I'd have to think about it. I'll give you a call and set up something. We'll do dinner and everything." She had no intention of following through. She just wanted Lula to leave. She was putting a damper on Tangie's excitement for the evening.

Her mother nodded. "There's another reason I came here tonight. I wanted to tell you something. Ben and I are through. He's never going to leave his wife." Her voice broke. "It took me long enough to come to grips with the truth, huh?"

Tangie didn't care. The damage was already done.

"I'm not going back to him this time," Lula said firmly. "I haven't even taken his calls for two days."

Seeing the pain on Lula's face melted away some of the anger Tangie was feeling. "You're going to find that it's better this way. A married man can't do anything for you except cause you trouble." She couldn't resist adding, "Besides, you probably need some time alone."

"You must really hate me, Tangie. Otherwise you wouldn't be so mean. Haven't you ever done anything and regretted it later?"

"I'm surprised that anything I say bothers you. People all over town talk about you constantly. That doesn't seem to do anything to you."

"I don't give a flip about what those nosy folks say about me. I only care about you and what you think of me." Lula picked up her purse and stood up. "I guess I'd better get going. . . . You have fun tonight."

Not quite meeting her mother's gaze, Tangie spouted, "That's what I intend to do. Have a real good time."

Stopping at the front door, Lula turned. "Tangie, I know what MeMa thought of me. I know what you think of me. I can't change who I am or what you believe I've become. I'm who I am."

"I know that, Lula. And I can't change the way I feel."

Lula's eyes grew bright. "I've always loved you, Tangie."

"Just not enough," Tangie countered. "Not enough to be a mother. Not enough to put me first." Tangie dropped her eyes to the floor.

"I was young."

She looked her mother in the eye this time. "That's no excuse, Lula."

"I did what I thought was best for you, Tangie. That's why I let MeMa raise you."

"You may have believed you were doing the right thing, but you really have no idea how bad it was for me, growing up. It was horrible."

"What was so bad about it? You had food and you had clothes. You also had MeMa. She taught you how to read and write—she helped you with your homework. I used to watch the two of you together."

"MeMa also told me daily that she didn't know why she was wasting her time. She said I was going to turn out just like you. She used to tell me that on a daily basis. I couldn't wait to get out of her house."

"I can't change the past, baby girl. I can only work on the present." She gave Tangie a tiny smile tinged with sadness. "Have a good time tonight."

It took Tangie a moment to gather herself after Lula left.

As much as she tried, Tangie couldn't get Lula out of her mind. The woman was determined to force her way into her life. *Why?* she wondered silently. *Why is it so important to Lula now? What does she really want?*

Tangie thought back to all those years when she had wanted her mother. There were nights she had cried herself to sleep, exhausted from the deep yearning for Lula's love.

A deep baritone voice cut off her musings.

"Mind if I join you?"

Tangie glanced up from her drink, surveying the gentleman. The man was fine! Just what she needed—a tall, dark, and sexy man in her bed tonight.

Giving him her sexiest smile, she murmured, "Have a seat."

He sat down in the chair opposite her. "My name is Chavis."

She introduced herself. "I'm Tangie. It's nice meeting you."

"I was a little hesitant to approach you because you seemed really deep in thought. I couldn't help noticing you tonight. You're a very beautiful woman. Do you live around here?"

"No, I live in Durham," she lied. "I come here sometimes just to get away. Where are you from?"

"D.C. I'm here taking a couple of classes for my job."

Tangie smiled. "I like the D.C./Maryland area. It's beautiful up there."

"Maybe you should think about coming up for a visit."

She skirted around his suggestion. "So what do you think of North Carolina?"

"It's very southern." He laughed.

"I love the South," she murmured. "I wouldn't think of living anywhere else." The next song prompted her to wiggle in her chair to the music.

Chavis took the hint. "Would you like to dance?"

"Absolutely," replied Tangie. "I love this song."

They got up and strolled to the center of the dance floor. Tangie gyrated her hips as she moved to the music, dancing close enough for him to grab hold of her hips.

"I like your moves, baby."

"I like yours too," she cooed. Tangie closed her eyes, using the rhythm of the music to push the memory of her mother out of her thoughts. She didn't want to think of anything other than this very moment.

Tangie captured Chavis with her eyes as they danced. She knew he would be the one tonight. Tangie would bring this beautiful man to his knees and leave him wanting more. Loving and leaving men like Chavis gave her the power she craved. It made her feel that she was the one in control—she called the shots.

Hours later, Tangie crawled out of a rumpled bed and tiptoed to the bathroom. Normally she liked to shower right after sex, but right now Tangie just wanted to leave. She couldn't stand to be in the room a moment longer with this man.

Tangie slipped around the room picking up her clothes. She dressed as quietly as she could and then found her shoes. She wasn't aware that she was crying until she glimpsed herself in one of the mirrors. Tangie rushed to the door, flinging it open.

The last thing she heard was Chavis calling out her name.

27

Monday morning, Cordelia lay in bed staring up at the ceiling, refusing to start another day.

Gerald burst into her room. "Good morning, Dee."

She groaned in response.

"It's a beautiful day. Let's get you up so that you don't miss a minute of it."

Scowling, Cordelia didn't care how it looked outdoors. She was never going to relish it like she used to—she was sick.

Gerald assisted her out of bed, his cheery attitude grating on her nerves like fingernails on a chalkboard. Every now and then she would mumble a word or two.

With Gerald's help, Cordelia was finally dressed and had managed to brush her teeth. She couldn't deny she felt more comfortable when Devon was helping her. Maybe it was because she and Gerald were divorced.

He wheeled Cordelia into the dining room and placed her at the head of the table. "I made you some oatmeal and toast. I even made fresh-squeezed orange juice."

He was trying very hard to sound normal. The truth of the

matter was that things were anything but normal. They would never be the same.

"Dee?" Gerald prompted.

Cordelia did not respond. She wished she could just block herself from the rest of the world. Almost one month had passed since she had had the stroke, and she was still unable to bathe and dress without assistance. Having Gerald here in the house was another stab of humiliation for her.

He went into the kitchen and returned with a bowl and a plate of toast. Gerald placed it in front of her. "I'll be back with the juice." Turning on his heel, he left, only to return a few minutes later carrying a glass and another bowl. He sat in the chair next to hers.

It took several tries before Cordelia had a good grip on her spoon. She clumsily managed to scoop up enough oatmeal and stick it in her mouth. She glanced over at Gerald. He seemed to concentrating heavily on his plate but she knew it was just an act. Cordelia knew he was watching her every move, because she could feel his eyes on her.

Using all of her strength, Cordelia reached for her glass. It took a few minutes before she was finally able to grab hold. Her hand shook so badly that the liquid sloshed around, spilling on the table. Cordelia tried to set it back down, but ended up knocking it over.

Tears sprang to her eyes. Cordelia was so frustrated that she wanted to scream, *God, why have you forsaken me?* If she had to live out the rest of her life like this, she was going to lose her mind.

Gerald's voice cut into her thoughts. "I'll clean it up, Dee. It's okay." He jumped up from his seat and moved around the table.

Cordelia cut her eyes at him. *No, it's not okay, stupid,* she wanted to say. *I've had a stroke, and what's worse, I have to depend on you. This just isn't fair. I haven't done anything to deserve this kind of punishment.*

He cleaned off the table and brought her another glass of juice.

Cordelia dropped oatmeal in her lap and tried to get it. Gerald reached for her napkin, but she snatched it away with her one good hand.

"Why don't you let me to help you?"

She shook her head. "D-do it my . . . sel."

Anger flashed in Gerald's eyes. "I don't understand you. It's not like you don't need the help. Whether you like it or not, you need me."

"Ge . . . get ow."

"That's out of the question, Dee. Until you can truly take care of yourself, I'm here. I'm not going anywhere."

A hot tear ran down her face.

Gerald's tone softened. "Dee, I'm not trying to hurt your feelings. I know this is very upsetting for you—all I'm trying to do is make this transition easier for you." He wiped away her tears with a napkin. "I don't want to fight with you, Dee."

She could only nod. This wasn't Gerald's fault, and she had no right to take it out on him.

"Let's just try to be friends, okay?"

Again she nodded.

"Dee, I can't begin to know how you're feeling right now or why this happened. What I do know is that it has to be scary and very painful. This is not something I would wish on anybody in the world. I'm so sorry that it happened to you."

Cordelia raised her eyes to meet his. She knew Gerald was being sincere. She read the truth on his face.

"I mean it. If I could take this away from you, I would. But Dee, I know you. I know in my heart that you can beat this stroke. If you want it badly enough, you'll get your speech back and you'll walk again. You can overcome this depression. I believe it."

She shook her head sadly.

"Yes, you can," Gerald insisted. "People recover from strokes all the time, Dee. I've been on the Web site of the National Stroke Association and I've picked up a couple of books on stroke recovery. I even ordered some software to help you with the aphasia."

Cordelia couldn't hide her surprise.

He could still read her, because he asked, "Why do you look so shocked?" Gerald took her right hand in his. "I want to do all I can to help you. This is the only way I know how. There is a stroke recovery support group here. When you're stronger, we should go to a meeting."

"I . . . I scar," she admitted.

"I'm scared too. Dee, I want to ask you something. Do you still believe in God?"

She nodded.

"Why didn't you want me to read passages from the Bible to you? Do you think I'm too much of a sinner or something?" He was teasing.

Cordelia smiled and shook her head no.

"Then what is it?"

"Ma . . . maad."

"Mad? You're mad at God?"

She nodded.

"I don't think God did this to you, sweetheart. I don't know why he allowed it to happen, though—maybe you're supposed to learn something from this experience."

"Nooo." Cordelia shook her head. She refused to believe that anything good could come out of this. It was a tragedy—her tragedy.

When Cordelia woke up from her nap later in the day, she found Devon standing near the window, running her hand over her rounded belly. The T-shirt she wore only served to make her pregnancy more pronounced.

She could recall that right before the stroke, they'd decided that Devon would be moving to Raleigh with her father—instead they were here in her home, both of them against her wishes. The worst of it was that they expected her to be okay with it. Cordelia really didn't have any choice because she needed them both—whether she liked it or not. Gerald had been right about that.

Devon turned suddenly. "Mama, I didn't know you were awake." She crossed the room and sat on the edge of the bed. "How are you feeling?"

"O-okay." Cordelia's expression was guarded. Her daughter wanted something, she could tell. She lay waiting for the other shoe to drop.

"I had a sonogram today," Devon announced. "They gave me some pictures." She paused for a moment. "Wanna see 'em?"

Cordelia nodded slowly. Deep down she wasn't sure she was ready for this.

Devon whipped out the photo. She became animated as she described what they were looking at. Beaming, she asked, "Can you tell the sex?"

Cordelia stared at the photo long and hard. She grinned. "Gu . . . gurl," she announced proudly.

"That's what I wanted," Devon confessed shyly. "A little girl. I even have her name already picked out."

"What?"

Smiling, Devon answered, "I'm going to keep it a secret. Until the baby's born."

Cordelia had never heard of such a thing.

"I know that probably sounds strange, but this is the way I want to do it."

She gave a slight shrug. Cordelia tried to sit up.

"Let me help you, Mama."

Cordelia was impressed with how well her daughter handled her. She worried that Devon could harm herself.

"I'm all right, Mama. You just be careful. I don't want you to fall and hurt yourself."

In virtually no time at all, she had Cordelia settled into the wheelchair and was wheeling her down the hall.

Cordelia now regretted her initial reaction upon seeing Devon in her room. She'd been wrong in her assumption. Her daughter had only wanted to show her the very first photo of her grandchild.

28

Bonnie soaked up the last chapter of the novel she'd been reading. It had been a wonderful story. Closing the book, she got up and stuck it on the shelf, then made her way to the kitchen.

After fixing Scotty a snack, Bonnie made herself a sandwich and ventured back into the den. Her routine didn't vary much from day to day. Things were so different when Edgar was alive. They were always on the go. Bonnie kept herself active but it wasn't the same.

Leaning on the counter, she watched in amusement as Scotty played with a small rubber ball. Bonnie let out a laugh. "Get it, Scotty," she urged. "Get the ball." If she didn't have Scotty, she had no idea what she'd do.

The next morning, Devon called her shortly after she'd arrived at the office. While they were talking about the pregnancy, Sabrina burst in.

"Is that Devon? How's Dee?"

Bonnie prayed Sabrina hadn't overheard much of her conversation. She placed a hand over the mouthpiece. "She's fine." She turned her attention back to Devon.

Instead of leaving, Sabrina made herself quite comfortable in one of the chairs. Bonnie couldn't believe her nerve. She and Devon were having a private conversation—one that Sabrina didn't need to hear—and she wasn't leaving. This confirmed her belief that Sabrina really had no respect for her as a friend or otherwise. She had now crossed the line.

"Devon, hold on for a minute." Bonnie put the phone down. "Did you need something, Sabrina?" She was careful to keep her tone professional.

"No, not really. What's going on with Dee?"

"Dee is okay." More firmly, she said, "Sabrina, Devon and I were having a private conversation. We're just catching up, so would you please excuse us?"

"What? You want me to leave?"

"Please."

Sabrina's eyes narrowed as she got up and sauntered out of the office.

Bonnie picked up the phone. "I'm so sorry, sweetie."

"That must have been Miss Sabrina."

"It was." Bonnie picked up their conversation where they left off. She would deal with Sabrina's ruffled feathers later.

"I wasn't trying to be rude this morning, Sabrina."

She didn't tear her eyes from her monitor. "I didn't know Dee's health was such a big secret," she said snidely. "I was under the impression that we were all friends. Humph! Silly me."

"It isn't a secret, Sabrina. Devon and I were having a private conversation, that's all."

Bonnie could tell Sabrina was still steaming but there was nothing she could do about it—Devon was entitled to her privacy. So was she, for that matter. "I'm sorry if I hurt your feelings," she began.

"Oh, you didn't hurt my feelings," Sabrina shot back. "It wasn't anything like that. I'd let you know otherwise." Her tone held a bit of a threat.

"Well, I'm sorry." Bonnie turned and left. When Sabrina was like this, it was hard to talk to her.

Bonnie avoided her for the rest of the day.

The following Saturday Bonnie stopped by Cordelia's house before going to the shelter. She'd knitted a beautiful throw, which she gave to her as a gift.

"Tank ya," Cordelia murmured softly. She ran her right hand over it, enjoying the cottony feel of the embroidered stars. "I-it's pretty."

They sat for a while in silence.

As Bonnie sat there with Cordelia, one thing was clear to her: Her friend did not belong in that wheelchair. There was still too much life left inside her. "Dee, why won't you even attempt physical therapy?"

Cordelia gave a nonchalant shrug.

"I just don't understand you sometimes," Bonnie confessed. "You have such faith, a wonderful daughter, but you're not trying to help yourself. Gerald's doing the best he can to stand by your side. You have no idea just how fortunate you are."

Cordelia glared at Bonnie. "You doan know anthing."

"I know what I see," she shot back. "I see a bitter woman just sitting around in her wheelchair waiting to die."

Cordelia's eyebrows rose in surprise.

"How can you do this to yourself? I would be grateful just to have my life."

"Wha life?" Cordelia sputtered.

"This is your life—for now. You can't do better until you're willing to try."

"You doan know—"

"No, I don't," Bonnie agreed. "But if I were in your shoes, I'd be going to therapy. Dee, life hit you with a curve, but you can get through this. Who knows—in a few months you could be back to your old self. Maybe even better." Bonnie embraced her. "You've got so much to fight for. Devon's going to graduate in May. She's going to have a baby. I know that you're going to want to hold your grandchild." Bonnie sighed in resignation. "I just wish you wouldn't give up. All you're doing is locking yourself up in this house and staring out windows, watching life pass you by."

Bonnie's words stung her. Cordelia's eyes welled with tears.

"I know what you're feeling. You're scared that you won't be back to your old self, and maybe you won't, Dee. But look at it this way—you have a chance to be a better you. Some people don't get a second chance."

"I jus wan ta know w-why tis hap."

"Dee, even Jesus couldn't explain the mystery of suffering. He tried to relieve it where He could, and as His life ended He took it on Himself. My pastor spoke on this very subject last week. He said the question we need to ask most is not *why* but *how*. How can I draw encouragement and support when I feel so weak and afraid? How can I let His grace be sufficient for my needs?"

Cordelia looked out the window. She had stopped listening.

Bonnie let the subject drop and tried another approach. "It's beautiful out there, isn't it?"

The silence grew between them.

"You used to love the outdoors, Dee. Don't you miss the sunshine? The fresh air?"

"Tired now."

Bonnie released a long sigh. "Okay, sweetie. I'm going to leave, but I want you to at least think about everything I've said. Before I leave, though, I'd like to pray with you and Gerald."

Cordelia gave a nonchalant shrug.

Bonnie went to the door and called for Gerald to join them.

They sat in a semicircle with their heads bowed. She began to pray. "Dear God, open our eyes that we may see You more clearly. Help us not to blame the bad things on You but trust that Your gracious hand will strengthen us in and through all things. Open our eyes more each day to Your steadfast and unfailing love through Jesus Christ our Lord. Amen."

Bonnie left and drove over to the women's shelter.

The shelter had a new resident. She was introduced to Bonnie shortly after her arrival.

Joi was possibly in her mid-twenties, but her face had sustained so many beatings over the years that it made her look older. She would not raise her eyes—just kept them averted to the floor. She reminded Bonnie of a scared rabbit.

"Would you like something to drink? We have coffee, tea, and soda."

"Do you have Sprite?"

Her voice was so soft, Bonnie had to strain to hear her words.

"I believe I can locate one for you. Make yourself comfortable on the couch and I'll be right back."

There was always a chance of Joi being gone when she returned. It happened all the time at the shelter.

Joi was still in the office waiting, however, when Bonnie came back. Bonnie was mindful of not walking up behind her suddenly. She was careful to keep a certain amount of distance from the client. It was important that Joi feel a sense of security in her own personal space.

"Thank you, Bonnie."

"You're welcome. Just let me know if you need anything else."

"I . . . I just need a place to stay for a while. My h-husband . . . he's crazy."

Bonnie listened as Joi poured out her pain. It wasn't that often that a resident trusted the social workers enough to talk. It warmed her heart that this young woman thought of her in that way. They sat in her office talking until the end of Bonnie's shift. She found that she and Joi had quite a bit in common.

At the end of her shift, Bonnie didn't want to leave Joi. She was in such a fragile state at the moment. That night she prayed for all the abused women of the world. Her heart was troubled as she went to bed that night.

In the morning she got up early and dressed for church. Her spirit was still grieving and she didn't know why. After the service, Bonnie stopped by the shelter to see Joi.

One of the other volunteers spotted her and asked, "What are you doing here today?"

"I wanted to check on Joi. How did she sleep last night?"

The room grew quiet.

"What happened? Did she leave?"

"Yes."

Bonnie sighed in resignation. "Oh, God. I wish she'd stayed here. That man is going to kill her sooner or later."

"Sooner. Joi was murdered last night—two hours after she left the shelter."

Bonnie felt sick. She was a basket case by the time she made it home.

"How could you let him kill her, God?" she cried. "Why do you let all these horrible things happen in the world? She was just barely out of her teens." Bonnie's heart ached. "All these evil, vile people in this world . . ." She broke into sobs.

There had been many nights when Bonnie had asked why she'd had to endure the hardship of losing her parents, and of losing the one person who'd truly loved her. She wondered in times like this why her family abandoned her and why Edgar's family hated her so much. Why did people place so much emphasis on the color of a person's skin?

"I don't understand God. I just don't understand and it hurts so much."

She had counseled Dee on suffering just yesterday. On not asking why but how. Despite all the bad things in life, Bonnie knew that this was not God's way of settling scores or teaching a lesson. She knew He wasn't punishing the world for its sinfulness. Bonnie had to ask herself what she could draw from all the suffering of the world and apply it to her own life.

Right now she could think of no answer. Times like this, when she was so emotional, Bonnie really missed Edgar. He had always been her strength, and when she hurt, it was like losing him all over again. Grief flowed through her, bringing with it anger and frustration. She thumped the kitchen counter hard with both fists. Bonnie thumped it again and again. Tears rolled down her face. She cried for a long time.

29

Sabrina had been curious to see how well Cordelia was faring, since Bonnie was sharing information only when she deemed it necessary. She had a strong feeling that they were keeping secrets from her. She was determined to find out what was going on.

She decided to pay Cordelia a visit and invited Tangie along.

They arrived at Cordelia's house an hour later. Gerald welcomed them inside while Cordelia awarded them a polite nod.

Tangie threw her arms around her friend, embracing her. "It's so good to see you, Dee. I've missed you."

Sabrina watched the exchange in silence. She didn't seem all that thrilled to see them, she thought silently. *The woman really should be grateful that anybody came to see her.* Sabrina hugged Cordelia and said, "We were so worried about you."

"I . . . I'm glad ta see ya," Cordelia stammered.

Sabrina promptly settled down and began to update Cordelia on all the office gossip. When there was no one else left to discuss, she started on Bridgeport gossip.

"You know Claire is still walking around as if she owns the place. She thinks—"

Gerald interrupted the visit long enough to inquire whether anyone wanted something to eat or drink. Cordelia seemed relieved when Sabrina and Tangie both declined. She wasn't comfortable eating in front of them, Sabrina reasoned.

Devon arrived home a while later. She peeked into the den and waved. "I have to run to the bathroom but I'll be back in a few minutes to say hello."

Tangie threw up her hand. "Hello, sweetie."

Sabrina eyed Devon and noted that the teen looked as if she'd gained a few pounds. Her mind went to work.

Gerald strode into the room saying, "Excuse me, ladies. It's time for Dee to take her medication." He placed his hand on the handles of her wheelchair. "I'll bring her back in a few minutes."

Sabrina had been sitting across from Tangie, but as soon as Cordelia left the room she got up and moved. Dropping down beside Tangie, she whispered, "Devon looks pregnant." Sabrina was sure of it. Now it all made sense: the secret phone calls, the cryptic sentences, and Bonnie's sudden protectiveness when it came to Devon and Cordelia.

"Girl, you've lost your mind."

"Maybe you'd better put on your glasses, Tangie. I know what I see. That girl is pregnant. And I told you how Bonnie's been acting lately. I guess Dee told her—she didn't think enough of us to let us in on the big secret."

"I sure hope I don't put on a few pounds. You'll be saying the same thing about me."

Sabrina's retort was stilled on her lips when Cordelia joined them. She couldn't stop her next words. "You know, I'm just gonna come out with it. We all want to know. Dee, is Devon pregnant?"

Tangie gasped. "Sabrina!"

Cordelia held up her hand. "I-it's okay. She is."

Devon strode into the den, putting a halt to further conversation. She embraced her mother, and then went around the room hugging Tangie and finally Sabrina.

"We just found out about the baby," Sabrina announced. "Girl, what were you thinking?" She thought of Devon as a little sister and felt she had the right to chastise her.

Tangie sighed loudly. "Sabrina, mind your own business," she muttered. To Devon, she asked, "Is there anything I can do for you? Do you need anything?"

"I'm fine."

Sabrina was not to be outdone. "Devon, you know how I feel about you. I'm here for you, okay?" Sabrina cut her eyes at Tangie. One of these days she was going to tell Tangie exactly what she thought of her. She was tired of her censorship.

"I told you Devon was pregnant," Sabrina announced smugly. "I knew that fat heifer was hiding something."

Tangie unlocked the doors of her car. "Sabrina, don't you know when to keep quiet? It was clear that Dee hadn't wanted to discuss this right away. She probably asked Bonnie not to say anything. Maybe she wanted to tell us herself but then the stroke happened."

"It was probably Bonnie's idea. She wanted to feel important, since she doesn't have a life of her own."

"Not everyone thinks like you, Sabrina."

Exasperated, she replied, "Now what's wrong with you?"

"Dee's upset enough, and so is Devon, I would imagine. You don't need to interfere."

"I wasn't. I'm so tired of y'all thinking the worst of me. Devon is pregnant and she's not going to be able to hide it, so we would've found out eventually."

"I know you didn't mean anything by what you were saying, but I could tell it kind of bothered Devon."

Folding her arms across her chest, Sabrina shrugged. "Well,

she is too young to be having a baby. Devon should be thinking about her future. A child will only ruin it right now."

"I agree she should have been more careful."

"She's so smart, Tangie. She's graduating from high school in May and she's going to college this fall. How could Devon let something like this happen?"

"Only she knows the answer to that question."

"You may get mad at me but I'm gonna say it anyway. This is stupid, big-time. Devon didn't use her head at all. I would've taken her to get on birth control."

"I'm sure we've all lost our heads at one point or another. All we can do is be there for her."

Sabrina agreed. Changing the subject, she said, "Did I tell you that I'm taking my mother to South Carolina for Memorial Day weekend and to celebrate her birthday?" She combed through her short curls with her fingers. "We're going to Pawleys Island."

"That's a great idea," Tangie replied. "At least one of us will be enjoying the holiday weekend."

"We're going to have a great time. Elwood is paying for everything. Girl, we're staying in a luxury five-star hotel."

"Sounds like you have the makings of a unforgettable trip."

"He bought me some new clothes and he's going to give me some spending money. I didn't even have to ask. Now, he's my kind of man. I just wish he weren't so ugly."

"That's not very nice."

"Well, he is ugly. Girl, I woke up one morning and almost puked. He was lying there with his mouth all open and his face all twisted up." Just the memory made her say, "Ugh!"

Tangie threw back her head, laughing. "You need to quit."

"Hey, he's my ugly man." Sabrina had Elwood eating out of her hands. He wasn't much to look at, but the man was generous. "Tangie, I know what you need. You need to get yourself a rich man."

"I'm fine. Whatever I want, I'll buy it myself. I don't need a man for his wallet. Too much of a headache."

Sabrina felt her ire rising. "What are you trying to say?"

"Don't start, Sabrina. You know what I mean."

"I'd rather be with a man who has something going for himself than with a bum."

"I would too," Tangie agreed. "I'm just not looking to be tied to any one man. I'm happy with my life."

"Yeah, right." Sabrina didn't believe that for one second. She didn't understand why people lied to themselves like that. It was pointless.

Tangie burst into laughter. "Well, I thought it sounded pretty good."

Sabrina shook her head. She had a strong suspicion that Tangie was hiding something, but she had no earthly idea what, and it was driving her crazy. She was determined to find out all of her friend's secrets—no matter how long it took.

April gave way to May, the weeks merging into one another. Sabrina and her mother left for Pawleys Island. They departed as soon as Sabrina got off work. Elwood had arranged for them to stay in a villa at Litchfield Plantation, situated in a tranquil wooded area facing the lake. It reminded Sabrina of one of the low-country plantation houses she often admired in magazines.

Sabrina and her mother went from room to room. The villa had three bedrooms, a kitchen, a dining room, a den, a living room, and a washer and dryer.

"This is what I call living, Mama."

"It's nice," Mamie agreed.

"This is the way we should be living. If Daddy had acted like he had some sense, maybe we would be in our summer home right now."

"Your daddy never wanted anything to do with his uppity folks. He wasn't like them at all."

"They're still our family, whether they want to admit it or not."

"Sabrina, be happy with what you have. You have more than most you know."

"Why does it have to stop there, Mama? I'm not going to settle. I know what I want, and nothing is going to stop me from getting it." Sabrina and her mother headed into the master bedroom. "Come help me unpack, and then I'll help you."

Mamie embraced her daughter. "You're such a spoiled brat."

"Mama, I'm glad we did this. This is a beautiful suite." Sabrina hung up one of her shirts.

"Chile, what in the world is this?" Mamie held up a pair of thong panties.

Sabrina burst into laughter. "They're underwear, Mama."

She frowned and said, "They look like they hurt."

Hanging up a dress, Sabrina laughed again. "Mama, you're crazy."

"I guess I'm out of the loop when it comes to this crazy stuff people are wearing."

"They're comfortable, Mama. I love them."

Mamie didn't look convinced. "If you say so." She held them out to Sabrina by the thin strap.

"Why are you holding them like that? They're clean."

Mamie stuttered over her next words. "I . . . I w-wasn't im . . . implying that."

Laughing, Sabrina pulled out a worn-looking cotton nightgown that belonged to her mother. "Now, Mama . . . you know better than this. You need to throw this in the trash."

Mamie placed her hands on her full hips and said, "I don't need any fancy lingerie, Sabrina. I go to bed alone every night."

"That can be fixed, Mama. It's not too late for you to meet someone new." Sabrina broke into a short laugh. "But we are definitely going to have to change your wardrobe first."

"Girl, please . . ."

"Seriously, Mama. I think you should start dating again. We'll get up early tomorrow morning and strut our stuff on the beach. Since tomorrow is Saturday and a holiday weekend, there should be plenty of men around."

"For you, maybe. I'm not interested, Sabrina. I'm too old and too set in my ways."

"Don't you want to live out the rest of your life in comfort and not have to work so hard?"

"I'm happy the way my life is, Sabrina. I own my house and my car. I don't have a lot of bills, and my investments are going well—"

"They're not doing that well," Sabrina cut in. "I told you that you should let someone else look at your portfolio."

"The point is that I'm happy with things just the way they are. A man would only complicate matters." Mamie pulled a blouse out of her suitcase. "Could you hand me a hanger, please?"

Sighing in resignation, Sabrina did as she was asked. Why in the world did she bring her mother with her? she wondered. Mamie Mayhew was going to drive her crazy before the weekend was over.

30

Tangie woke up with a sudden urge to visit Cordelia. She wanted to apologize for Sabrina's mouth. It had been bothering her since their visit. She got up early Saturday morning and dressed quickly. Twenty minutes later she was in her car and on her way to Cordelia's house.

Gerald met her at the door. "Hello, Tangie. Good to see you."

"Hey," she said politely. Tangie didn't care much for Gerald because of what he'd done to Cordelia. "Dee was on my mind and so I thought I would pay her a little visit. I hope I didn't come at a bad time." Tangie fingered her ponytail. "I probably should have called first."

"It's fine. I know she'll be happy to see you, Tangie. I just got her to come out into the sunroom."

"You sure it's not an imposition?" she asked. "I can come back another time."

"She'll love to see you," Gerald reassured her. He led her to the sunroom. "You have a visitor," Gerald announced to Cordelia. "Tangie's here."

"Hello, Dee. How are you?"

Cordelia glanced over her shoulder. "T-Tangie . . ."

Moving closer, Tangie found that Cordelia's face was wet with tears.

Bending down, she asked, "What's wrong, Dee? Why are you crying?" Tangie threw a look over her shoulder. "Why is she crying?"

Gerald looked as dumbfounded as she did.

Cordelia clumsily wiped at her face with her right hand.

"Dee, what's wrong?"

"Cann . . . tal . . . eh." She stopped and tried again. "Cannt t-tal . . . right."

Tangie nodded in understanding. Pulling a tissue from her purse, she handed it to Cordelia. "Here you are, Dee. It's going to be okay, honey. You're sounding better each day. I know you're frustrated, but don't give up."

Gerald cleared his throat loudly. "I'll leave you two alone. Call me if you need anything." He left the room quickly. *Just like a cheating dog,* Tangie thought.

"I-I'm sorr . . ."

"You're allowed." Tangie broke into a smile. "You've been through a lot."

"I wan ta be mee gain."

"I know." Tangie sensed that Cordelia needed to vent. "I understand, Dee. I would feel the exact same way."

"Hate been this wa . . . way."

"Then do something about it, Dee," Tangie replied gently.

"Wha ya mean?"

"Bonnie told me that you won't go to physical therapy and that you refused to even try all that new software Gerald bought for you. Maybe you should change your mind."

Cordelia was quiet.

"It can't hurt, Dee. It could only help."

"What if i-it fa . . . f-fail?"

"Nothing is foolproof, Dee. But as far as I know, even the tiniest bit of therapy can help."

"Wha if I doan . . . doan wawk gain?" Cordelia's eyes filled with tears.

"Oooh, Dee. I don't think that's going to happen. A lot of people recover from strokes every day. I have every reason to believe that you're going to make it too. You have never been a quitter."

"I doan unerstan why this happen. I tried live right and I read tha Bible. Why did God turn on me?" Cordelia swallowed hard.

"God and I don't run in the same circles, but I'm fairly certain that he didn't turn on you. Not you, especially. I think things like this just happen, Dee. It's not a punishment. That much I'm sure of. This is something that just happened."

"I doan wan ta be in this c-chair faever. Cannt b-bear it. I c-cannt."

"Then go to therapy," Tangie urged.

Again, Cordelia was silent.

"Dee, you've never let anything beat you. You can't just give up," Tangie advised. "Give the professionals a chance. Rosewood has a wonderful rehabilitation team. It's rumored to be one of the top rehab centers in the country."

Cordelia nodded.

"If you ever need me, I'm here for you, Dee. Don't you ever forget that."

She nodded again. "How have ya been?"

"Who me?" Tangie laughed. "I've been fine. Just trying to take one day at a time."

"Ya keepen Sabrina out of trouble?"

"Dee, you know how she is. That's why I came by today. I'm sorry about the way she acted over Devon's pregnancy. She had no right and I told her so."

Cordelia smiled at that.

Noting the lines of exhaustion around her friend's eyes, Tangie glanced down at her watch. "Well, I know you're getting tired, so I'm going to go, but promise me that you'll think about what I said." She got up and made her way toward the door.

"How is your motha?" Cordelia inquired after her.

Tangie turned around, facing Cordelia. "She's fine. She wants to get together with me. Like a girls' night out. Can you imagine that?"

"Do it."

Surprised by Cordelia's response, Tangie questioned, "Really? I'm not so sure. Especially with the way I feel about her—we're liable to be out somewhere and end up arguing."

"Tink 'bout it, T-Tangie."

Smiling, she agreed. "I can do that." She gave a tiny wave. "I'll see you later, Dee."

" 'Bye," she practically whispered.

Tangie stood there a moment watching Cordelia. "I'll be back in a couple of days to check on you."

Cordelia nodded.

There was sadness behind Cordelia's eyes. She had given up on life, Tangie realized. She made a mental note to give Bonnie a call later. Cordelia needed their help.

Just as she climbed into her car, Tangie spotted Cordelia's neighbor with her daughter. They were walking along the sidewalk eating ice cream cones. "How special," she whispered, and pulled off.

As she drove, Tangie thought over Cordelia's words. Did Lula deserve to be a part of her life?

Lula straightened her slinky black dress before sitting down. "I'm so excited about tonight. I can't believe we're doing a girls' night out."

Tangie gave a wry smile. "I have to be honest: I'm not real sure about this."

"I appreciate your trying, baby. I really want a second chance with you."

Tangie glanced down at her fingernails, trying to think of something to say. "How are you doing?" she asked finally. "Post-Ben, I mean."

"I have good days and bad. Ben is still calling but not as often as he did in the beginning. I guess he didn't love me as much as he claimed."

"It'll get better, Lula. I promise it will."

"You know we usually go away for Memorial Day, so being with you here tonight is good for me." Lula's face lit up. "Maybe we can spend Memorial Day together?"

"Let's just get through tonight first."

Lula's smile disappeared. "Okay. I understand." She brushed away curling tendrils from her face.

Tangie noted that some of her mother's enthusiasm seemed to vanish. She felt a momentary pang of guilt. Tossing her feelings aside, she continued to get ready.

An hour later they were seated at Marc's Italian restaurant. Tangie knew this was Lula's favorite place to eat.

Leaning forward, Lula said, "Tangie, I made a lot of mistakes with you. I realize that."

"It's all in the past." Tangie took a sip of her wine.

"I don't want you to hate me. I was so young when I had you—only fifteen—and I didn't know how to be a mother. I thought Dave loved me. He even said he was going to leave his wife."

Tangie's stomach churned at the mention of her father's name. "Lula, it really doesn't matter now. I'm a grown woman."

"I'm very proud of you, honey. Just look at you. You were the first one in my family to go to college. Now you're working for the county."

Tangie burst into laughter. "It's really not that big a deal, Lula. I'm a social worker, for goodness' sake."

"It's a big deal to me. I'm the head housekeeper at the Red Roof Inn."

"It's an honest living."

"I know. Ben hated it. He would always tell me that I should go back to school. I got my high school diploma; did you know that?"

Tangie was astonished. "When did this happen? You dropped out of school before you had me, so when did you go back?"

"Right after MeMa died. She made me promise on her deathbed to do it." Shrugging, Lula added, "It's the least I could do for her. I gave her a lot of grief."

Tangie had never seen this side of Lula. "You're sounding a bit regretful."

"I am . . . about certain things." Looking into Tangie's eyes, she said, "I regret not being there for you. I wasn't a good mother and I wasn't a good daughter." Lula took a sip of her wine. "I feel bad about that."

The waiter came and took their orders. They made small talk until the food arrived.

Throughout dinner, Tangie stole peeks at her mother. She didn't know if she could trust what she was seeing. Over the years Lula had spouted similar sentiments, but only when she was between men. Now that she and Ben were not seeing each other . . . maybe it was the same thing all over again.

Tangie raised her eyes and found Lula watching her expectantly. "I'm sorry. Did you say something?"

"I was saying I really mean what I've said. I want us to start over. I'm getting older, as much as I hate to admit it." Lula gave a short bark of laughter. "I'd like for us to become close."

"You're asking a lot." Tangie finished off her pasta.

"One day at a time. That's all I'm asking."

"We'll see," was all Tangie could promise. Lula had disappointed her so many times in the past. She was not going to let her wall down just yet. Her mother would have to work hard to earn her trust.

31

"Devon Michele Berkeley . . ."

Cordelia had a front-row seat to witness Devon receiving her high school diploma. She cried tears of joy and prayed that Gerald had taken lots of pictures.

She was relieved that Devon's pregnancy was hidden beneath the folds of her white robe. Cordelia had lived for this day since the moment her daughter entered the world. She hadn't anticipated being in this condition, but she was grateful to be alive.

Her daughter was beginning her journey as an adult. Cordelia realized that everyone had been right: It was time for her to do some traveling of her own—on the road to recovery. Her pity party had lasted long enough.

The following Wednesday Cordelia had her first physical therapy session. Right after that she started her speech and language therapy. She also scheduled an appointment to meet with an occupational therapist. She was a little overwhelmed by it all, and feeling more than a little discouraged by the time she returned home.

Cordelia was exhausted, so she lay down to take a nap. She slept for an hour.

When she got up, she headed straight to the computer. It was time to see whether Gerald had wasted his money.

Two days later Bonnie stopped by with a couple of casseroles. Cordelia announced, "I go ta therpy. Wan life b-back."

Clapping her hands in joy, Bonnie said, "I'm so glad to hear you say that. When did you start?"

"W-Wednesday." Cordelia made a face. "Lot of wark."

Bonnie smiled. "You can do it. Just don't give up."

"Never," Cordelia vowed. "Wan tis too muck."

One week later, Cordelia was ready to quit. With her physical therapist's help, she got out of her wheelchair and onto the parallel bars. It was a task that took her almost ten minutes.

Cordelia sank back down in her chair. "Nooo. Can't do it."

"Yes, you can, Mrs. Berkeley. Progress comes in small steps." Glancing down at the wheelchair, she continued, "I'm sure it wasn't easy getting this chair to move for the very first time. You couldn't just sit down and push the wheels with your hands, could you?"

Cordelia shook her head no.

"Today it may take ten minutes to get up out of that wheelchair, but the more you do it, the less time it'll take. Stroke can make your muscles weak. They need to be built up and toned. Your treatment includes range-of-motion exercises, strengthening and parallel-bar exercises, balance activities and learning how to use a walker, then progressing to a quad cane."

Cordelia tried it again. It took a while but she didn't give up. She found the belt the therapist placed around her waist irritating, but knew the purpose was to prevent her from falling, so she tried to ignore the rough fabric.

She was soon holding on to the bars for balance.

Toward the end of Cordelia's session, the therapist showed Gerald various exercises that would help strengthen and tone Cordelia's muscles.

Before going home Gerald stopped at Bridgeport Medical Supply to purchase a few items the occupational therapist had suggested. He came out with a couple of sporks—a combination spoon and fork—a swivel spoon, sectioned plates with guards to keep food from going over the edge of a plate, and cups with partial lids.

"That therapist also suggested sliding foam hair curlers over the handles of forks and spoons to make it easier for you to grip them," Gerald stated on the drive home.

Cordelia didn't respond. She stared out the window, wishing she could feel normal once again.

Cordelia pulled herself along, trying to make it to her bed before she collapsed. She was dead tired after such an exhausting day, but she also felt exhilaration and a sense of accomplishment.

There was a short knock, and Devon struck her head inside the room. "Can I get something for you, Mama?"

Cordelia shook her head. "I'm okay. Th . . . ank ya."

Devon strode into the room carrying a small bag. "I bought you something. It's an audio book. You can listen to it. If you like this one I'll get you some more."

She was touched by her daughter's kindness. Cordelia smiled in gratitude. Her anger had long disappeared where Devon was concerned, but she was still filled with disappointment.

"It's by James Patterson. I know how much you love his books. I was looking for the Bible but couldn't find it. I'll keep looking."

Devon gasped suddenly.

Cordelia took her daughter's hand. "Wha wrong?" Her

heart started to pound faster. It was much too soon for her to be in labor. Cordelia wasn't ready to be a grandmother, but she didn't want anything to happen to the baby.

"Mama, it's okay. It was just the baby. The baby kicked."

"Oh."

"Do . . . do you want to feel it?"

Clumsily Cordelia placed her left hand gently on Devon's belly. Her heart jumped to her throat when she felt the demanding kick of her grandchild. Her eyes teared up. "B-baby," she uttered slowly.

Gerald strode into the room. He stood watching them for a moment before saying, "Time to exercise."

"The baby just kicked, Daddy. It was a real kick—not like bubbles popping."

He looked at Cordelia and smiled. "Your grandchild's urging you on. Come on. Let's see that kick of yours."

Rolling her eyes at Gerald, she allowed him to help her get positioned on the bed. She did as she was told without complaint.

32

It was a gorgeous June day. Everyone had survived the madness of returning to work on Monday and was now looking forward to another weekend. Bonnie had decided to treat Cordelia to the movies in celebration of her progress. She was beginning to see glimpses of the person Cordelia used to be.

Sabrina and Tangie met them at the theater as a surprise. They greeted Cordelia with hugs and kisses.

"Dee, you're looking wonderful," Sabrina complimented her.

"You sure do," Tangie threw in.

They followed Bonnie, who was wheeling Cordelia down the aisle to their seats.

When the movie ended two and a half hours later, they decided to have coffee and tea at a nearby Starbucks.

Stirring her coffee, Tangie announced, "My mother and I had a girls' night out over the holiday weekend. I never thought I'd say this, but we actually had a great time."

"That's wonderful," Bonnie stated. "I'm very surprised, given your relationship with her."

"We had a real talk, and I have to admit, I finally understand some things about her. She can still be a pain, though. We're a long way from being friends—much less mother and daughter."

"They all can be pains," Sabrina murmured in agreement. "I know mine can get on my nerves, but I love her like crazy. She is one of my best friends."

"I miss my mother," Bonnie admitted. "She died when I was about thirteen. I felt like she left me when I needed her the most."

Sabrina turned to Cordelia. "Speaking of daughters . . . how is the little mother-to-be?"

"She's fine," Cordelia announced dryly.

"Dee hates Devon being with Tonio but if she had to get pregnant, having a Bradshaw as the father can't hurt," Sabrina announced.

Bonnie gasped loudly. "Sabrina . . ." She couldn't believe that she would say something so insensitive.

"What? Would you rather she be pregnant by a poor boy?"

"I'm sure she would prefer Devon not be pregnant at all," Tangie replied.

"M-money not everthing." Cordelia met Sabrina's smug gaze.

Sabrina merely shrugged and said, "It may not be everything, but it sure helps."

Bonnie didn't want Sabrina upsetting Cordelia. "Why don't we change the subject?"

"Why don't you get a life instead of trying to sponge off ours? You can be so pathetic at times." Rising to her feet, Sabrina stated, "I'm outta here. 'Bye, y'all."

"What a witch," Tangie uttered. "She must be on her cycle."

Cordelia shook her head sadly while Bonnie tried to keep from crying. She had not deserved this—especially from Sabrina. She was the very reason the woman still had her job, but Sabrina wasn't appreciative—instead she was becoming more and more arrogant as time went on.

Bonnie hadn't even wanted to invite her to the movies with them, but Tangie had talked her into it.

"Just ignore Sabrina." Tangie placed a comforting hand on her arm. "You should know better than to take anything she says personally. She's moody."

"She's mean," Cordelia interjected.

Bonnie wiped away a tear with the back of her hand. "I've tried to be a friend to her."

Handing her a napkin, Tangie said, "We know that. Please don't let Sabrina get to you. Just choose not to be offended. She may be dancing in high cotton now, but one day the music will stop. You'll see. Sabrina's going to pay big-time for her actions."

Bonnie was so embarrassed. She was sitting here blubbering like some idiot in public because of Sabrina. She was determined to keep away from her as much as possible. She was tired of getting her feelings hurt.

33

Sabrina muttered curses all the way to her car. She was sick and tired of Bonnie's warm-and-fuzzy attitude. She was sick of Tangie's I'm-so-perfect act as well. Cordelia . . . she was just pitiful. Sabrina was the one who had the most going on—yet they continued to treat her like a child. She was so angry that she wasn't paying attention to where she was going and literally ran into another person.

Strong arms gripped her by the shoulders. "Hey, are you okay?"

Sabrina looked up into the most gorgeous green eyes she'd ever seen. The man stood a sturdy six feet, with shoulders like a bodybuilder and legs like those of a strong gazelle. He was a god compared to most of the men she normally met.

"Are you okay?" he asked again.

Thursday, June twelfth. Sabrina made a mental note of the date. Tonight she'd met the man who would change her life. She couldn't explain how she knew, but she did. "I-I'm fine," she stammered. His bronze features held her gaze.

He released her. "I'm sorry," he said. "I should have been paying attention to where I was going."

"No, it's my fault." Sabrina gave him a warm smile and ran her fingers through her short curls. She should have worn a dress instead of the ratty old jeans she'd chosen.

The beautiful man smiled, causing her body to tingle in anticipation. She had to find out his name. "I'm Sabrina."

"My name is Maxwell. Maxwell Smythe."

She searched her memory. *Where have I heard that name before?*

He stood there gazing at her. As if he'd realized what he was doing, Maxwell said, "I'm sorry for staring at you like this. You're very beautiful—I couldn't help myself."

"Where are you from, Maxwell? You can't be from around here."

"I'm from Richmond, Virginia. I just moved down to Durham. I'm here visiting an old school friend. He and I went to college together." Maxwell's eyes traveled her face once more.

Why couldn't he live in Bridgeport or somewhere closer? she raged in silence. Sabrina had to console herself with the fact that Durham wasn't that far—only two hours away.

They talked over the next half hour and exchanged numbers before getting in their respective cars.

Sabrina was glad that they'd been standing near her BMW. For some reason she wanted to impress him. When he climbed into a Mercedes, she smiled. The evening was looking up, Sabrina decided.

The next afternoon Elwood was waiting for Sabrina in her driveway with a dozen roses when she arrived. Frowning, she demanded, "What are you doing here?"

"I haven't heard from you since you got back from Pawleys Island. Every time I call I get your voice mail."

He tried to kiss her but Sabrina backed out of his reach. "You were out of town for two weeks, and when you called you never left a number," she countered. "Apparently you didn't want me to call you back, or you were somewhere where I couldn't call you." Her interest in Elwood had already been dwindling, but after meeting Maxwell it had completely disappeared. Now she didn't even have to pretend any longer.

"That's not true."

Sabrina took the bouquet of white roses from him. Inhaling deeply, she delighted in their fragrance. Holding them close to her bosom, she asked, "So what are the flowers for? They look like guilt roses."

He laughed but didn't answer her question. Instead Elwood asked one of his own. "Did you and your mother have a good time at Litchfield Plantation?"

"We did."

"I can tell. I just got my credit card bill. Looks like you had a real good time."

"You said we could have anything we wanted." Sabrina handed him the keys, and Elwood unlocked her door and stepped aside for her to enter. He followed her inside, and then closed the door behind them.

To Sabrina, Elwood acted as if he were settling in for the evening. He was going to be disappointed, she thought with amusement. She'd spotted a bigger and better fish—now she had to concentrate her efforts on catching him.

Sabrina went about the business of finding a crystal vase for the flowers. "What are your plans for tonight?" she asked.

"I came over to spend the evening with you. I haven't seen you in a few weeks. I miss you, baby."

In the dining room she glanced up from her task of arranging the roses. "I would appreciate it if you'd call me first—don't just pop over here like this. I'm sure you wouldn't appreciate it if I did it to you." Her mind was racing. How in the world was she going to get rid of Elwood?

He replied from the love seat in the living room, "You're my lady and I'm your man. It wouldn't bother me."

Sabrina walked into her living room carrying the flowers. She placed them on the glass coffee table before making herself comfortable on the sofa. "I care for you, Elwood. But some-times I just want to be alone."

"What are you trying to tell me? You don't want to see me anymore?"

"I didn't say that, did I? I just think that it's not a good idea to spend all of our free time together. I don't know about you but I can't take smothering."

Elwood pushed his glasses up the bridge of his nose. "What?"

"I'm not one of those females who needs to have a man around me twenty-four-seven. Sometimes I just like to be by myself."

Elwood bristled. "I haven't seen you in almost a month. That wasn't enough time?" He pushed his glasses up the bridge of his nose again. Frowning, he uttered, "Girl, I don't under-stand you."

Sighing in resignation, Sabrina said, "I don't want to argue with you. I—"

The telephone reverberated throughout the condo.

Rising to her feet, she said, "I need to get that. It could be my mother. She's not having a good day today." Sabrina broke into a sprint, running through the house like a madwoman. She picked up on the third ring in her bedroom.

"Hello, beautiful. It's Maxwell."

"Hi. I'm so glad you called." Sabrina sat down on the edge of the bed and crossed her legs, putting Elwood immediately out of her mind.

"Were you busy?"

"No, not at all. Actually I was hoping you'd call me today."

Sabrina didn't catch Maxwell's next words because Elwood appeared in the doorway of her room. She sent a stinging look his way. Her nerves were razor-thin, sharpened by Elwood's ob-vious lack of manners. How dare he invade her privacy like this? She gestured for him to leave.

He stood there unblinking, watching her.

Sabrina was seething underneath, but kept an outwardly

composed demeanor. Covering the mouthpiece with her hand, she whispered, "Go. I don't want to talk to you right now."

He stalked down the hall. Before she heard the slamming of the front door, Sabrina was jolted to her feet by the loud shattering of glass. "Maxwell, I need to call you back." Dropping the phone, she rushed into the living room. She stood, stunned at what lay before her. Glass, water, and broken roses were strewn on the floor in the middle of the living room. He'd smashed the vase through the glass table.

Sabrina's body trembled in her fury. "You're going to pay for this, Elwood. Big-time."

Maxwell and Sabrina were having their first date. He'd surprised her by saying he wanted a home-cooked meal. Sabrina didn't feel like cooking so she manipulated her mother into making dinner.

After leaving her mother's house, Sabrina rushed home to prepare the condo. She showered and dressed after adding romantic touches throughout.

Right before Maxwell arrived, Sabrina surveyed her condo once more. Candles were lit everywhere to cast a romantic glow all around. Soft music played through the expensive sound system Leon had purchased for Sabrina in honor of her birthday last year.

Maxwell would be arriving any moment, and she wanted to have everything done. Sabrina caught sight of a magazine lying on her coffee table that featured luxury and elegant resorts, and suddenly remembered where she'd heard the Smythe name. Maxwell's father and grandfather were the owners of the Haddonfield Hotels throughout the country. The family and the hotels had been featured in several magazines and newspaper interviews. Sabrina settled back on the couch and scanned through the magazine. There it was—an article on the hotels and the Smythe family as well. They were an attractive family, she observed. They photographed well.

While she waited for Maxwell to arrive, Sabrina fantasized what it would be like to be married to a Smythe. Maxwell lived in the penthouse of the Haddenfield Hotel in Durham. She hadn't seen it yet but imagined it had to be stunning. She'd never stayed in one of the Haddonfield Hotels. Their cheapest rooms went for no less than five hundred dollars a night.

The Smythe family had more money than Elwood and Leon put together. She'd really hit the jackpot this time. Sabrina couldn't be more pleased.

The phone rang. Sabrina answered it on the second ring, praying it wasn't Maxwell calling to cancel. "Hello?"

"Hey, baby."

Sabrina frowned. "Who is this?"

"Girl, it's Leon. Don't play me like that. You know it's me."

"And?" She responded coldly, but her heart started to pound loudly. He could still get to her. Sabrina cursed him for calling at a time like this.

"Why you acting like that?"

"Why are you calling me? Shouldn't you be in one of your meetings or something?"

"It's like that?"

Staring at her reflection in the bedroom mirror Sabrina responded, "Yeah. It's like that, Leon." She pulled at her red dress, straightening it across her hips.

"I called because I feel like you and I need to talk."

"We don't have anything to discuss, Leon."

"You really believe that, Sabrina?"

"Leon, I can't keep wasting time with you. It's not fair."

"You must be seeing somebody," Leon stated. "He must be paying the bills too."

"It's none of your business," Sabrina pointed out. "What I do is my business, but since you're so interested, I *am* seeing someone—in fact, he's on his way here."

"Who is it?"

"None of your business."

"I hear you messing around with Elwood Brown. That old dog." Leon started to laugh. "He got a mug on him."

"That's old news."

"So you can't fit me in? I really need to talk to you, Sabrina."

"Let me see . . ." she said sarcastically. "How about never?"

"Sabrina, I care a lot for you, but you're running me away with your attitude. The only time you want me around is when you need money. You're a user."

Leon's accusation hurt because she genuinely cared for him. But she definitely wasn't going to tell him that now. "I'm not going to dignify that with a response. If you feel that way, then it's best if we go our separate ways." Sabrina slammed down the phone.

By the time Maxwell arrived, Sabrina had dried her tears and repaired her makeup. She offered him a glass of wine. She'd already had one to calm her nerves.

"No, thank you. I don't drink." Maxwell strode around her living room, admiring her artwork gracing the forest-green walls.

He turned to face her. "Your collection is impressive."

"I love art." Sabrina had invested in art classes and spent hours in museums studying fine art. Her main motivation in life was to educate herself so that she could speak on a number of subjects, including politics. She intended to be an asset to her rich husband. She'd even taken Spanish and French classes but had found them intensely boring.

"Did you hire an interior decorator?" Maxwell was asking.

Sabrina had bought the model with the furnishings included. "Yes, I had a decorator." Tilting her head in a dignified manner, she added, "I simply didn't have time to decorate myself."

"You have a nice place."

"Thank you." She smiled at the compliment.

By the time they sat down to dinner, Sabrina discovered that Maxwell was well traveled and was looking to settle down.

By dessert, Sabrina was planning her wedding.

Her soul was filled with joy.

Sabrina and Maxwell had spent the night making love. He was a magnificent lover. Now she didn't have to worry about taking a lover once they were married.

Sabrina bounced into Tangie's office. Hey, girl, it's Friday. Here's the file you needed."

Tangie eyed her for a minute. "Why are you in such a good mood?"

"Maxwell came over last night. We had a real good time. I have a strong feeling that he's the one."

"The one for what?"

"The man I'm going to marry."

Swiveling around in her chair, Tangie stared at her friend as if she'd lost her mind. "You just met him, Sabrina."

"I know that. It's just a feeling I have."

"I don't know, Sabrina . . ."

"Be happy for me, Tangie. This man is so fine and so gorgeous, plus he's rich."

"Money's not everything," Tangie pointed out softly.

"Neither is love. It gets you nowhere."

"Are you over Leon, Sabrina?"

She didn't respond.

Tangie resumed the task of reading her e-mail. "I didn't think so."

"Leon and I don't have a future together, Tangie. I can't keep waiting forever."

"I understand that. Just take it slow with this Maxwell, okay?"

"I'll be careful." Tangie's words went in one ear and out the other. Nobody was going to rain on her parade.

*   *   *

Sabrina decided to walk the mail addressed to Medicaid over to the right department instead of dropping it into the trash as she normally did. She strolled through the double doors and right up to the receptionist. "This was in our mailbox by mistake." Sabrina turned to survey the Medicaid reception area. She didn't recognize a soul. *Oh, well . . .*

Hearing a strong male voice, Sabrina turned back to the receptionist. There was a man standing there talking to her. She smiled.

He smiled back and said hello.

Sabrina cleared her throat noisily.

Rolling her eyes, the receptionist introduced them. "Sabrina, this is Brandon Jacobson. Brandon, this is Sabrina. She works with the FFA unit. They're across the hall."

An idea quickly formed in Sabrina's head. She said, "Alice, could you do me a favor? I need some day sheets—we're completely out, and our order won't be in until next Friday. Can you lend me a few?"

"I have to get them from the stockroom. Can you come back later?"

"I'll watch the desk," Brandon offered.

Alice got up and ambled off.

To Sabrina, the woman always looked like she was in a daze. *Probably on drugs.* Turning her attention back to Brandon, Sabrina turned on the Southern charm. "Welcome to St. Paul County. I hope you like it here."

"Thanks. I'm enjoying it so far. This is my second day. It's a nice place to work."

Brandon was looking up at her expectantly.

"I hope you don't think I'm flirting with you or anything, but I need to know something. Are you married?"

He laughed. "No. I'm single and looking."

"Would you have lunch with me today? I want to introduce you to someone."

"Who?"

"The woman you're going to marry."

Brandon cracked up at this.

"I'm serious. You're going to love Tangie."

Nodding, he said, "What have I got to lose?"

Sabrina returned to her department and walked straight to Tangie's cubicle. "Have you seen the new guy working in Medicaid?"

"No."

"He's gorgeous. His name is Brandon Jacobson."

"How do you know that?"

"Because I asked him. I wanted to welcome him to St. Paul County."

"I bet you did. . . ."

Sabrina stood her ground. "Girl, not like that. Maxwell is the man for me. Actually I thought he and you would make a good couple."

Tangie eyed her for a moment. *"What?"*

"Tangie, he's got the prettiest eyes and this buttery chocolate skin. He's real sweet. He and Maxwell could be brothers almost."

"I guess I'm going have to meet him."

"Good. I invited him to have lunch with us." Sabrina smirked happily.

Tangie's mouth dropped open in surprise. "Why did you do that? Girl . . ."

"I think you're going to be thanking me for the rest of your life," she promised.

"It's not that kind of lunch, I hope. You know I'm not one for long-term relationships. They're nothing but trouble."

"Just take it slow, Tangie. That's what you told me."

"I don't want to take it anywhere, Sabrina. I'm really not interested in finding a boyfriend. Especially someone working with the county." Shaking her head, she added, "This might not be such a good idea."

"Just meet Brandon for now. If anything comes of it, worry about it then," Sabrina encouraged.

Tangie thought it over. "You're right. I guess it can't hurt to meet the guy. The worst that can happen is that we'll become friends."

Sabrina could have jumped for joy. Everything was working out. If things worked out for Tangie and Brandon, maybe Tangie would start to share more of her life with her. For some reason, she wanted to be a part of Tangie's world. Brandon was the key.

34

"Oh, there he is," Sabrina whispered. "That's Brandon."

"He is fine," Tangie agreed. "Girl, I haven't seen anything look this good in a long time. Hurry up and introduce me." She removed her glasses and wished that she'd worn her hair down and a different suit. Tangie placed a hand to her hair, making sure her bun was still secure.

Sabrina made the introductions.

Brandon shook hands with Tangie, his eyes never leaving her face. The look he gave her filled her with curiosity. What was he thinking? He was the boy-next-door type—his hair cut close, and a very neat dresser. She stole a peek at his nails. They were clean as well. She smiled in approval.

"It's nice to meet you," he said.

Tangie shot her friend a look. "It's nice to meet you too."

They stood there in the middle of the lobby just staring at each other.

Sabrina cleared her throat. "Why don't we head on out to the car? I'll drive."

*   *   *

Tangie really enjoyed talking to Brandon—so much that she hated for lunch to end. Back at the office, she hummed while she worked for the rest of the day. Every now and then Sabrina would peek into her office, grinning like a Cheshire cat.

"Will you stop grinning like that?"

"You like him, don't you?" she asked in a low voice.

"He's nice," Tangie admitted. That was all she could say thus far. She and Brandon had only had lunch together with Sabrina taking in every word. Without voicing the words, they had both known the next time it would just be the two of them.

At the end of the workday, Tangie ran into Brandon again as they walked to their cars.

"I really had a nice time today."

Smiling, she admitted, "I did too. I enjoyed talking to you."

"We'll have to do it again sometime."

"That would be nice."

Brandon walked Tangie to her car. Before going to his, he asked for her phone number.

She wasted no time in giving it to him.

Tangie smiled to herself all the way home. She hadn't felt any real excitement over a man in a long time. She checked her messages as soon as she arrived home, although she didn't really expect there to be a message from Brandon already.

A voice from her past loomed before her.

"Danny," she said in amazement as she listened to his voice. She replayed the message. "Why are you calling me all of a sudden? I'm not going to call you back."

She thought about the letter she'd received weeks ago. Tangie had never opened it. At the moment she didn't even know where it was.

Daniel Watkins III. Danny could drive a woman wild with his sexual prowess. Tangie had not ever come close to finding a partner who could make her feel the way Danny did.

They would do it anywhere: on the beach late at night, in the car with people walking all around them, or on the balcony of a hotel suite. It was the danger of being watched that excited them both.

Then Danny started talking about love and wanting to get married. That was when Tangie ended the relationship. She'd vowed to never marry anyone, because marriage didn't work.

On two separate occasions Danny had tried to get her to change her mind, but Tangie had refused. He warned her on his last visit that he would marry someone else. True to his word, he'd married some plain Jane who attended his father's church.

After a dinner of a homemade chef's salad, Tangie sat down to watch television. Brandon entered her thoughts, bringing a smile to her face. He was such a nice man, soft-spoken and shy. What she liked most of all about him was that he was a true gentleman. His mother had certainly raised him right.

She was so engrossed in the TV movie that she almost didn't hear the phone ring. Tangie picked up on the second ring. "Hullo?"

"How are you?"

Grinning, Tangie answered, "I'm fine. Just a little tired, though. How's everything going with you?"

"You have a hard day at work?" Brandon asked.

"I wouldn't say it was hard. Just very busy. How is your training going?"

"Fine, I guess. It's a lot to learn in a month."

"Pretty soon it'll become so familiar it'll be old hat to you."

He laughed. "You're probably right."

They made small talk. Tangie hid her giggles behind her hand. This was just too cute for words. All of her relationships—if she could call them that—had happened so quickly that small talk was avoided completely. This was a new adventure for her.

"Are you seeing anyone, Tangie?"

"No, I'm free and single. How about you?"

"Same here."

Tangie had a strong feeling that Brandon was about to ask her out.

"Would you like to have dinner sometime?"

"I'd love it." She sent up a silent cheer. "Why don't we get together tomorrow night?"

After making the necessary arrangements, they talked a few minutes more before hanging up.

Tangie called Sabrina next. "Guess who I just got through talking to?"

"That fine Brandon, I bet."

"Girl, he is such a nice man. A real gentleman." Tangie couldn't believe she was acting so giddy after having one simple conversation with Brandon. This was so unlike her.

Sabrina laughed. "You sound like you have a crush on the man."

Tangie's head reeled. She didn't have a crush on Brandon—she'd just met him. "Don't be silly. He's just nice, and I haven't had that in a long time."

"You make Brandon sound like a bore," she teased.

"No, he isn't," Tangie defended. "I love the way he is, Sabrina."

"I think the two of you will make a cute couple."

"We're far from the couple thing, Sabrina. He and I are just talking, and we're going to have dinner. That's all."

"For now," Sabrina interjected. "I predict wedding bells in the future."

"I know you're crazy now."

"I'm serious, Tangie. I knew it the moment I met Brandon. You know it too."

Sabrina's words sent a shiver down Tangie's spine.

35

Saturday afternoon Cordelia wheeled herself into the living room when she heard voices. Gerald and Devon were talking and laughing as they brought in huge shopping bags.

"W-what is a-all that?"

"We went shopping for baby clothes," Devon stated. She pulled out a tiny gown. "Look how cute and little it is."

Cordelia muttered in obvious disappointment. She waved her daughter away, not wanting to see another item.

The smile vanished from Devon's face and she eyed her mother for a moment before snatching up the bags and storming from the room.

"What is wrong with you, Dee? Why are you treating Devon this way?" Gerald questioned.

"You like this? Buying b-baby stuff?"

"I'm not crazy about this situation, Dee. Not at all, but there is nothing I can do to change it. Our daughter is going to have a baby."

"I know that." Was she expected to carry her burden quietly? she wanted to ask.

"Devon has been so supportive of you throughout this ordeal. She's bathed you, brushed your teeth, and combed your hair. Why can't you return the kindness by supporting her through this pregnancy?"

"B-baby not coming til A-Au . . . gust. Doan know what can hap . . . happen. All I'm saying."

"I understand your point, Dee. But Devon wants to do this now. Tonio's father gave her the money—it's hers to do with as she wishes." Lowering his voice, Gerald added, "You know something? Even God forgives. No matter what we've done, He can forgive us. You should consider following in His footsteps. Remember we weren't married when you got pregnant."

Cordelia knocked lightly on Devon's door. "D-Devon, I wan to talk . . . to you."

"Come in." Devon held the door wide open so that Cordelia could easily navigate through.

"I sorr foe h-hurt feelings."

"You really hate this baby, don't you?"

Guilt consuming her, Cordelia shook her head no. "Doan h-hate b-babe."

"Then it's me you hate."

Cordelia thought her heart would crumble at those words. "I don't hate you, Devon."

"Why did you get so upset about the clothes? I'm going to keep my baby, and it's going to need stuff."

"I know." It was hard for Cordelia to convey her thoughts to Devon verbally. She wanted to shout, *Devon, you're just barely seventeen and you're going to have a baby. This is not ideal, and I don't think you're aware of how real your child will be. Right now you're excited about baby clothes, but before long you will hate the sight of them. You don't like doing laundry now—with a baby you have to do it more often.*

"Mama, I'm not crazy about being pregnant," Devon confessed. "But I am. I also know that this baby is very real." It was almost as if she'd heard her mother's thoughts.

"I wan mush moe foe you."

"I know, Mama. I wasn't planning on being a mother—not for a long time. I'm sorry I disappointed you. I just wish . . ."

"Wha?" Cordelia prompted.

"I wish you could still love me even though you're disappointed."

"I do lub you, Debon."

"Can you love the baby too? We're a package deal, Mama. You have to love both of us."

Cordelia nodded. *This baby is my grandchild. Of course I'm going to love her,* she railed silently.

Devon started to cry. "I'm sorry, Mama. I can't say it enough."

Cordelia reached out with her left hand. "Don't c-cry. It will be okay. I sor . . . ry."

"I just want you to love me, Mama."

"I do. You are my h-heart. Always."

Devon took her mother's hand in hers. "Please don't hold this against me. I know I messed up, but I intend to make the best out of this situation. I'm not perfect."

"I w-want you to have a g-good lift . . . life."

"I will. I just have to know something, though. Mama, are we going to be okay?"

Cordelia nodded. "Yes. We'll be fine." It was only at that moment that she knew it for sure.

36

Bonnie was going to get a life.

Dressed in her bra and panties, she stared at her reflection in the mirror. Bonnie was full-figured, she acknowledged. Slightly overweight. Although in her current shape, she wore a size eighteen, Bonnie decided that she was going to lose some weight. She wanted to be able to wear a sixteen comfortably. She mainly wanted to lose some of the inches around her middle.

Ever since Sabrina had mentioned her needing to get a life, Bonnie had been on a mission to do just that. She was getting her hair done on a regular basis and wearing just a touch of makeup.

She was going to brighten up her wardrobe as well. Bonnie planned to hit the department stores later this afternoon. She'd even withdrawn a thousand dollars from her savings to shop for new clothes. She'd been in mourning long enough.

Bonnie tried to remember the last time she'd done anything for herself. She was so used to taking care of everyone else. Stepping into her walk-in closet, she found a pair of royal blue knit pants and a white T-shirt.

After getting dressed, she strolled to the kitchen to pour fresh water into the bowl for Scotty before leaving for the mall.

"Mommy will see you later. She's going shopping to spruce up her wardrobe."

Bonnie returned home three hours later laden down with shopping bags from several department stores. Scotty jumped up and down in excitement, as if he thought the purchases were for him.

"Mommy brought something for you too. You know she did." Bonnie dropped her purchases on the sofa. She then made some room for herself and removed her shoes. Shopping was exhausting. She couldn't understand how Sabrina and Tangie could do it all day long.

Bonnie leaned back against the plump cushions of the sofa and closed her eyes. She just wanted to rest for a few minutes.

An hour and a half passed before she woke up. Bonnie glanced at the clock on the mantel. "Oh, my. I didn't mean to fall asleep." Her eyes searched the room and found Scotty lying near the front door. "Why didn't you wake me?" she scolded softly.

She rose to her feet slowly. "I'm going to freshen up and then I'll take you out for a walk." Bonnie walked past the photo of Edgar and she blew him a kiss. "You'd be proud of me. I'm taking baby steps—and I'm scared."

37

Maxwell was driving down on Sunday.

After church, Sabrina decided to clean out her closet while she waited for him to show up. She sorted through her shoes, placing the worn pairs in a plastic bag. She'd already gone through her clothes. When she was through, she put the bags near the front door. She was going to give them to Bonnie for the women's shelter.

Things were going well with Maxwell. Even she and Tangie had grown closer. Sabrina liked the way things were now. Before Tangie was very closemouthed about her relationships, but she now confided everything to her.

She went into the kitchen and tore open the plastic containers containing dinner. Sabrina had stopped at a nearby restaurant and ordered takeout. She would have had her mother cook, but Mamie wasn't feeling well. Sabrina thought it was an inconvenient time for her to get sick.

She changed her clothes for the second time since she'd been home from church. Sabrina wanted to impress Maxwell with her sense of style and elegance.

After finally deciding on what she was going to wear, Sabrina settled down in her living room. She thumbed through a bridal magazine. "Here comes the bride . . ." she sang.

Sabrina and Maxwell sat side by side on the sofa staring into each other's eyes. She offered him a second cup of coffee.

"I'm fine. Thank you."

"Tell me about yourself, Maxwell. I want to know everything about you."

"Let's see. You already know that my family owns Haddonfield Hotels. You know that I work in the family business at times. Other times I do what I really want to do."

"What's that?"

"I provide analysis and guidance to businesses and individuals to help them with their investment decisions. I'm a financial analyst."

Sabrina was visibly impressed. "Really?" *I'm going to marry a financial analyst.* She could just imagine everybody's faces when they found out.

"I don't really want to talk about me. Tell me about you." Maxwell glanced around the condo. "There's definitely more to you than meets the eye. Besides working as a social worker, what else do you do?"

She laughed. "I take care of my sick mother. She's not terminal—just sickly." Sabrina had been telling that lie for years. Each time she sent up a prayer that nothing serious happened to her mother.

"This is going to sound tacky, but how can you afford to live like this? Social workers don't make that much money."

"How do you know?"

Maxwell laughed. "I know a couple, and they sure aren't raking in this kind of dough."

"I have a trust fund," Sabrina lied. She wanted Maxwell to believe that their backgrounds were similar. *Money begets money,* her mother used to tell her all the time. "My father's family owns a couple of banks—Heritage First National Bank in Raleigh." That much was true; however her father had been a drunk, and the family disowned him long before he married her mother.

Sabrina and her mother went to visit them once. It was right after her father's death and turned out to be a big disappointment. The high-and-mighty Mayhews sent them away with a check for fifty thousand dollars. Her mother had put the money in a savings account and touched it only when absolutely necessary.

One day the Mayhews would regret sending her away.

"It's an honor to meet you. My family has been doing business with your family for many years."

Sabrina smiled and took a quick sip of her wine. She made mental notes of her lies as well. She still couldn't believe her good fortune. Her dreams were going to come true—she'd landed herself the heir to a hotel fortune.

Over dinner they talked more about the hotel business and the Smythe family in general. Sabrina wanted to know as much as possible about them. From the way Maxwell talked, they were very close-knit. She liked that.

When Sabrina found that Maxwell wouldn't be staying, she was a little disappointed. He promised to come down on the weekend.

Sabrina giggled through the cleaning of her kitchen after Maxwell left. She was so happy, she even mopped the floor instead of leaving the task for the housekeeper, who was coming by on Wednesday.

As she readied for bed, Sabrina turned on the music and danced in her bedroom. She was giddy. She was happy. She was going to be rich.

38

Tangie was having a great time with Brandon. They'd seen each other every night so far. She was surprised to find herself having such a wonderful time without touching. Brandon hadn't even kissed her yet.

They'd spent most of their time just talking about themselves—their likes, dislikes, social work, and dreams for the future. Tangie couldn't remember having these kinds of conversations with a man in a long time. *If ever,* she amended. She discovered during their talks that she and Brandon had a lot in common.

Tonight they decided to take in a movie after dinner. Tangie wasn't much into comedies but found that she was really enjoying herself. She wasn't looking forward to the evening ending.

Brandon drove her home and escorted her to the front door. He politely turned down her invitation to come inside.

Putting aside her disappointment, Tangie said, "I had a wonderful time, Brandon. I really enjoy your company."

"I feel the same way. I enjoy being around you."

"I hope we can do this again."

He gave a big smile. "Count on it. Now you go on inside. The mosquitoes are going to eat you alive if you don't."

"Good night, Brandon. Drive safe." Standing on tiptoe, Tangie planted a kiss on his cheek.

"Tangie, would you mind attending church with me next Sunday?"

She was a little thrown by Brandon's invitation. "Church? You want me to go to church with you?"

Brandon nodded.

"Sure. I would love to go."

It was obvious he was pleased. "I'll see you tomorrow. At the office."

" 'Bye." Tangie walked into her home without looking back. But, when she got to her door, she couldn't resist turning to watch him stroll to his car. Brandon's confident stride drew her to him like a magnet.

After getting settled into her bed, Tangie called Sabrina. She had so much to tell her.

It wasn't long after Brandon had gone home that Tangie felt the all-too-familiar throbbing. She needed sex. She'd planned to seduce Brandon until he invited her to church.

He thought she was a nice girl. Tangie smiled. Brandon liked her and he seemed to enjoy spending time with her. She liked him too, but his perfect-gentleman routine was wearing on her nerves. She was ready to take their relationship up a notch.

Tangie finished off her soda. The movie *Love and Basketball* was coming on, so Tangie picked up the remote to change the channel. The last thing she wanted to watch was a love story.

She and Brandon were officially dating, and this was definitely new to her. Tangie needed sex—only her boyfriend was being coy. She didn't want to cheat on him. She really didn't.

When a shower did nothing to cool her libido, Tangie searched through her closet for something to wear.

"Just this one time," she repeated over and over to herself.

Shortly after eleven Tangie was on her way to Cypress City, a small town west of Bridgeport. Club Classic was another one of her haunts.

Lula was parked in Tangie's driveway when she arrived home Monday after work. She got out of her car. "I was just about to leave. I thought you might be working late."

"I stopped by the mall. What did you want?"

"I just thought I could visit for a while. You don't mind me coming by, do you?"

"No," Tangie uttered. "Besides, it wouldn't matter to you whether I did or not." She laughed.

Lula followed her into the town house. They walked straight through to the family room.

"I went by MeMa's grave this morning," Lula announced. "I wanted to put some fresh flowers out there."

"Since when did you start going to MeMa's grave?"

"I go once a month."

Tangie's eyes rose in surprise. "I didn't know that."

"There's a lot you don't know about me," Lula pointed out.

"You're right." Gesturing toward the kitchen, Tangie asked, "Would you like something to drink?"

"I'm fine." Patting the empty space beside her, Lula said, "Come. Sit down and let's talk."

Tangie did as she was told. "So what do you want to talk about?"

"So you and this Brandon are going strong, huh?"

Tangie grinned. "Things are going great. I think he really likes me."

"Why wouldn't he? You're a wonderful catch."

Tangie felt strange discussing a man with her mother. Changing the subject, she inquired, "Lula, what's going on with you? Have you heard from Ben lately?"

She shook her head. "He's stopped calling. It's really over between us. Hard to believe I stayed with that man for almost fifteen years. He really played me for a fool."

"Don't think that way."

"How am I supposed to think?"

"Mr. Harris was never yours, Lula. He's been married all this time." Tangie hesitated, then said, "Brandon asked me to go to church with him."

Lula didn't seem surprised. "You going?"

Nodding, Tangie asked, "Any reason why I shouldn't?"

Shaking her head no, Lula stated, "Maybe that's where we went wrong. We didn't go to church like other people."

Tangie dismissed her statement with a small wave of her hand. "I don't think that has anything to do with it."

"I don't know, baby. Maybe it really does. Church seems to do something to folks. My parents didn't take much stock in it, but they all had bad luck too."

"And you think not going to church is the reason behind their troubles?"

Shrugging, Lula uttered, "I don't know. I just think church can't hurt, so you should go. Do whatever it takes to make your life a better one."

Tangie eyed her mother. "You really mean that, don't you?"

"Yeah. Why wouldn't I?"

Shrugging, Tangie answered, "I don't know, Lula. I guess I really didn't think you cared one way or the other. Not about my life, anyway. We should change the subject," Tangie said quickly. "What have you been doing for yourself?"

"Just working and trying to keep my head above water."

Tangie decided to test Lula. "Do you need anything? Money?"

"I've been saving, so I'll be fine." Smiling, Lula added, "I've learned a little something over the years. I even have stock in Coca-Cola, Microsoft, and Yahoo."

Tangie was impressed. Maybe Lula was telling the truth. Maybe she sincerely wanted a second chance.

39

This particular Tuesday was no different from the others. It began with Cordelia going to physical therapy as she did all the other days. On Tuesdays and Thursdays she also had speech and occupational therapy.

She was proud of herself, as she'd made significant strides with her speech. Every now and then her words would slur, but it no longer bothered Cordelia as much. It had become a part of her life.

A few members of her youth group from church had stopped by to see her earlier. As much as she missed them, Cordelia dreaded having them see her this way. She didn't miss the looks of pity the teens bestowed her way. She also didn't miss the whispers whenever they spotted Devon.

When they left, Cordelia couldn't have been happier. She wished Gerald would discourage visits from Pastor Grant and other well-meaning New Hope members, but every time she tried to broach the subject, he would argue that she needed to be among friends. He refused to let her hide behind her stroke.

Cordelia didn't know how to make him understand that

they were only reminders of all that she'd lost. When she had the stroke, she'd lost her connection to God.

"Mom, can I come in?" Devon asked from the doorway.

She lay across her bed, every muscle aching. "Sure. Is something wrong?"

"No. I just thought you might like me to help you wash your hair."

Cordelia nodded. "I'd like that. You know it's been a while."

Combing through her mother's hair with her fingers, Devon said, "Daddy says your therapy is going great. You really sound good, so that software is helping, huh?"

"It is. Today I sound more like me. But I still have t-trouble with some words."

"You sound real good to me."

"Today I used a walker. I'm clumsy with it."

"Mama, that's great!" Devon bent down as much as her swollen torso would allow. She gave Cordelia a hug. "I'm so proud of you."

When Devon straightened up, Cordelia placed a hand on her daughter's belly. "What did the doctor say?"

"She says I'm doing fine. The baby's healthy."

"That's good. How is Tonio acting?"

"He's okay." Devon sighed and glanced down at her hands. "I don't know what I ever saw in him."

Turning around so that she could face her daughter, Cordelia asked, "What happened?"

"I just found out that he got this other girl pregnant. Our babies will be a month apart."

She gasped in surprise. "Are you serious?" Cordelia had always known that Tonio was no good, but to impregnate two girls at the same time . . . She shook her head. "His mother has probably lost her mind by now."

"I heard she threw him out. He's living with his grandmother now." Devon's mouth turned downward. "I feel like such a fool."

"I'm sorry, baby."

"You tried to tell me. I wish I'd listened to you, but I guess it's way too late for that now."

Cordelia's heart went out to her daughter. "I want you to know that I really wish I'd been wrong about him." She noted the water in Devon's eyes. "I'm sorry, baby. I r-really am."

"He's such a jerk. Tonio used to get so mad whenever I talked to another guy. All the time he was cheating on me."

"Maybe things will work out for you two in the end."

Devon shook her head. "I just want him to be a father to his child. Nothing else. I'm going to go to college and raise my baby."

"Are you okay?" Cordelia wanted to know. "I know what it feels like to have your heart broken."

"It's the worst pain I've ever known, Mama. Actually, that's not true. It hurt worse when I thought you didn't love me anymore." She met her mother's gaze. "That was the worst feeling. Then I thought I was the reason you had the stroke—"

Cordelia cut her off by saying, "The stroke had n-nothing to do with y-you."

"It might have," Devon countered. "I was putting you through so much."

She shook her head. "This is my journey." Cordelia put her hand back on her daughter's stomach. "I was pregnant with you before your father and I married. I was so scared."

"I kind of figured that's what happened. The dates didn't quite add up."

"We wanted the best for you. We still do. We also want the best for your child."

"I try not to think about it sometimes . . . but then I get this hard kick." A lone tear rolled down Devon's cheek. "I wish things could be normal again. You know?"

Wiping her daughter's tear away with her one good hand, Cordelia smiled and whispered, "I know."

40

Part of Bonnie's getting her life back was learning how to be happy being alone. She had to force herself out of her comfort zone and do things like dine out or take in a movie or play without Cordelia or Tangie. She kept a polite distance from Sabrina these days.

She sat inside her car for a few minutes longer, nervous about going into the restaurant. Bonnie didn't relish the idea of eating alone, but she was determined to follow through this time.

She took a long, deep breath and stepped out of her car. Bonnie switched on the alarm and entered the restaurant.

"Well, Bonnie, look at you. Don't you look nice."

She recognized a woman from St. Paul County Human Services. "Thank you. It's good to see you."

"You too. I didn't feel like cooking so I decided to come here."

"Same here," Bonnie confessed.

They talked for a few minutes more before Bonnie was seated. She noticed that there were several other people in the restaurant eating alone. Smiling to herself, she picked up the menu. This wasn't going to be as bad as she thought.

After dinner Bonnie returned home, feeling a true sense of accomplishment. She was proud of herself and vowed to spend more evenings like this.

She changed into a pair of pajamas and went into her study. She and Cordelia were hosting a surprise baby shower for Devon in a few weeks, and the invitations needed to go into the mail.

"Surprise," the guests shouted in unison when Devon walked into the room with her father.

Putting her hands to her face, the guest of honor burst into laughter. "Oh, my!" Turning to her father, she cried, "Why didn't you tell me? Look at me."

Gerald grinned. "It's a surprise party, honey. I couldn't tell you."

"You look great," Cordelia complimented her. "Now sit over here. Your throne awaits."

Bonnie fingered the twenty-two-inch-high centerpiece to make sure everything was securely in place. She had put it together yesterday in the shape of a cake. It consisted of one eight-ounce baby bottle, fifty-five medium disposable diapers, two receiving blankets, a hooded towel, a gown, a one-piece underwear, one pair of socks, and a pair of booties, along with twenty other small baby items.

She caught sight of Sabrina standing off to the side, her eyes surveying the room. The woman didn't want to miss a thing.

Bonnie hadn't wanted to invite her, but Cordelia talked her into it. She was still resentful of the way Sabrina had treated her. Their eyes met briefly. Bonnie turned away and found Tangie. She went over to talk to her.

"What's going on between you and Sabrina?" Tangie asked.

"Nothing. I'm just tired of the way she treats me. I stay out of her way, that's all."

"Just tell her off, Bonnie. Don't let her trip on you like that."

"How are things going with you and Brandon? There are some awfully jealous women down at St. Paul County Human Services. You snatched him up quick."

Tangie broke into laughter. "We're going good. I'm going to see him after I leave here. We're going to play miniature golf."

"How fun."

Bonnie moved to the center of the room and announced, "It's time for games. Does everyone have a pen?"

As the day wore on, even Sabrina had loosened up enough to join in the fun. She had managed to remain pleasant to Bonnie as well. After the cake had been cut and served, it was time for Devon to open up the gifts.

Bonnie stayed on her feet, going from person to person, making sure everyone was comfortable and having a good time. She did grab a meatball, a carrot stick and a couple of drumettes to eat while playing hostess. She made sure Cordelia ate and took her medicines on time, however.

The baby shower ended on a high note, and Bonnie couldn't have been happier. Tangie offered to stay behind and help her clean up but she refused. "You have a date. Don't worry about this mess. I'll take care of it."

When everyone was gone, Bonnie did something she had never done in her life—she let everything go until the next day.

41

Haddonfield Hotel Durham served as testimony to the enduring qualities of the antebellum South. Flowering trees, neatly trimmed shrubbery, and colorful gardens fronted the building.

Once inside, Sabrina entered a majestic lobby with soaring ceilings, tasteful Southern furnishings, and a splendid fireplace. The hotel offered an array of athletic activities matched by only a few American hotels. Sabrina didn't play golf but there were three championship golf courses.

"There are fifteen outdoor and five indoor tennis courts, jogging paths, and bowling."

"I like playing tennis," Sabrina had stated. "I'm glad I brought my racket."

She had spent the last couple of days swimming, playing tennis, being pampered, and being waited on hand and foot in the penthouse of the Haddonfield Hotel. She felt like she'd died and gone to heaven. Sabrina had driven to Durham on Friday to spend the weekend with Maxwell.

Snuggled up against him, she said, "I'm going to hate leaving here."

"Then why don't you stay here another day?"

"I can't. I need to get back to check on Mama. She didn't sound too well on the phone last night."

"What exactly is wrong with her?"

"She's sickly," was all Sabrina would say. "It just doesn't take much to weaken her. I guess you could say she's very fragile."

Maxwell nodded in understanding. Turning her face toward him, he covered Sabrina's mouth with his.

Before he allowed her out of bed, he made love to her once more.

Sabrina sang all the way back to Bridgeport. She stopped by her mother's house to eat before going home.

Shortly after five, Sabrina arrived home. The first thing she did was check her messages. She grimaced when she heard the first two.

Leon was up to his old tricks again. As soon as she had moved on, he was sniffing after her again. "I'm tired of this mess," she muttered. "I'm not falling for your crap anymore. It's finally over, and for good."

The doorbell sounded.

Sabrina practically stomped over to the door, ready to blast her unwanted visitor. She was really surprised to see Leon standing there. "Why yo—" She stopped short.

"Girl, you always looking so mean," he teased. "You should show off that pretty smile of yours more often. Especially when your man comes around."

"When *my* man comes around I will smile. Right now it's just you, Leon."

His smug look disappeared. "What you mean by that? You seeing another man?"

"What if I am?"

"I thought I was your man."

"I used to think so too. I guess we were both wrong."

"You know something? You're a evil little somebody," Leon

muttered nastily. "That's why I don't come around that often anymore. All you do is complain when I do. I'm only good enough for you when you spending my money."

Sabrina didn't care what Leon thought. "That's all you were good for. You sure didn't know how to be faithful to me. Do you actually think I believed you about all those meetings? You were probably messing around with the jolly green giant—that witch Bonita."

"Bonita has nothing to do with this. This is about you and me."

"Leon, it's over. Why don't you go to a meeting or something? I just got home and I'm very tired."

"You're going to need me one day, pretty lady."

"I don't think so," she shot back.

"I don't know why you act like this. I really care about you but you're always trying to drive me away."

"Then take the hint," Sabrina uttered nastily. "I don't need you, Leon. I have someone new in my life."

"So that's it? You have a new sugar daddy. He must really be rolling in it."

"He is. So what?"

Leon shrugged. "What's his name? I can tell you if he's legit or not."

"He's legit—I already know that for a fact."

"Then why won't you tell me who it is? Is it some big secret?"

"No, it's not a secret. I just don't feel like discussing my love life with you." Sabrina pointed to the door. "I would appreciate it if you'd leave. As I stated earlier, I'm tired."

"You're never going to be able to keep anybody. You're too coldhearted. But then again, you'd actually have to have a heart." Leon headed to the door. "Good luck, Sabrina."

"Good-bye. And do me a favor, Leon. Lose my number."

42

Brandon took Tangie home with him to Charleston, South Carolina, for the Fourth of July to meet his family. She immediately fell in love with his mother and sister, Sherry.

"Can I help you with something?" she asked.

"No, sugar. You just sit down over there in that lawn chair and enjoy yourself."

Tangie awarded Mrs. Jacobson a warm smile.

Brandon wrapped his arms around her. "I hope you're having a good time," he whispered.

"I am," she whispered back. He had such a way of making her feel so special. Tangie found herself falling for Brandon. Initially it scared her, but she no longer fought it. She felt guilty, however.

She and Brandon still hadn't made love. He had been practicing celibacy for the last two years. Tangie hadn't found a way to control her urges, so she was still sneaking out of town for her trysts. More and more she was finding them unfulfilling, but she couldn't stop. It was like they were her life's blood.

Brandon's mother sat down beside her. "I hope you're having a good time, dear."

"I am. You have a beautiful home, Mrs. Jacobson. Thank you for including me."

"My son speaks highly of you." Lowering her voice to a whisper, she added, "He adores you."

"I think a lot of him as well. Brandon is a wonderful man."

"He's a lot like his father." Having said that, she pulled out a stack of photo albums. She handed one to Tangie. "These were taken when Brandon and Sherry were babies."

Tangie scanned the pictures. She burst into laughter over the one with Brandon posing on a fur rug in the buff. He had the biggest toothless grin on his face. She felt his presence before she saw him in the room. Tangie met his gaze and grinned. "Hey, you."

Brandon crossed the room and joined them on the sofa. "What are you doing?"

"Looking at your baby photos. You were so cute."

He put a hand to his face. "Mom, why are you doing this to me?" He groaned. "I thought you liked me."

Embracing him, Tangie burst into laughter. "They're nice pictures. Stop giving your mother a hard time."

Together they sat there for the next two hours going through photo albums and telling stories from Brandon's youth.

"What were you like as a child?" he asked Tangie.

She sobered up. "There isn't much to tell. I didn't socialize much. I was a bookworm. Just stayed home and read books all the time. My grandmother was very strict."

Brandon's mother went to the kitchen to check on dinner.

"She really likes you," Brandon announced. "I can tell."

"I like her too. Your sister is a sweetie."

"Sherry's a good kid. I just wish she would slow down some."

Inclining her head, Tangie asked, "What do you mean?"

"My sister thinks that she has to be intimate with every boy she likes—it's wrong and I keep telling her that."

Tangie shifted in her seat. Her palms suddenly felt damp. She chewed her bottom lip.

"She should be saving herself for her husband." Brandon glanced over at her. "Honey, you okay?"

"Huh? Oh." Tangie gave a choked laugh. "I'm fine. I couldn't be better."

Brandon's words continued to stab at her.

What would he think of her if he knew what she'd been doing behind his back? Tangie knew the painful answer. *How can I treat you like this?* She resolved that things would be different from now on. She was not going to cheat on him again. If the roles were reversed, she would be furious.

As if to mock her, Tangie felt the stirrings of desire igniting. She curled her body into a ball. *"No,"* she whispered harshly. "I can beat this. I don't have to keep doing this to Brandon." She sat up in bed and rearranged her pillows.

Sleep was not going to come easily to her tonight.

43

The night of August fourteenth, Cordelia woke up with a start. She'd heard moaning in the hallway outside her bedroom door. "Devon," she called out. "Honey, are you okay?"

Her fear grew when she heard Gerald's voice, filled with concern.

Moving as quickly as she could manage, Cordelia tried to get into her wheelchair. She gritted her teeth in frustration because she just couldn't seem to move as swiftly as she'd like. There was something wrong with Devon. She wasn't due for another ten days, but babies had a way of coming whenever they wanted, and Devon had been having contractions for the last day or so.

There was a strong knock on the door before Gerald stuck his head inside. "Dee, are you awake?"

"What's wrong? Is Devon in labor?"

"Yes. The contractions are about six minutes apart."

"Find me something to slip on, please. I'm coming to the hospital with you."

Gerald strode into the room and headed straight to the closet. He pulled out a dress and assisted her with getting dressed.

Devon walked into the room saying, "I have everything. I'm ready." She placed her hand to her stomach when another contraction hit. She groaned in pain.

Cordelia wanted to reach out and take her daughter's pain, but that was unrealistic. The urge to pray hit her. She prayed for her daughter's health. She was still angry with God but not enough to keep him from watching over the birth of her grandchild.

Gerald wheeled her out to the car and helped her inside. He then made sure Devon was comfortable. Her contractions hadn't progressed any faster. They rode to the hospital in silence, each caught up in their own thoughts and fears.

Cordelia only had to look upon Gerald's face to see the worry in his eyes. This was his little girl and she would soon be having her own daughter.

Devon was sleeping peacefully after being in labor for eight and a half hours. Her daughter was nearby in a bassinet sleeping. Tonio sat in a chair beside the crib staring at the baby. His parents were outside the room. Gerald wheeled Cordelia out into the hallway.

Margaret Bradshaw spoke up. "How have you been feeling?"

"I'm doing okay. Each day I'm able to do a little more." Cordelia was extremely proud of the progress she'd made with her speech. The slur was hardly noticeable these days, and she had little trouble with the words.

"The baby is beautiful." Margaret seemed to be searching for things to say. "She looks like Tonio did when he was a baby."

Cordelia thought she looked just like Devon. "She is beautiful." She glanced up at Gerald. "I need to get something to eat."

He nodded. "I'm going to take Dee down to the cafeteria. Would you all like something?"

"No, thank you. We're fine," Margaret murmured. "I think we'll just wait here for Devon to wake up."

Cordelia waited until they were on the elevator before saying, "I'm surprised they're hanging around. I didn't think they would have much to do with Devon and the baby."

"She's their grandchild too."

"I wanted to strangle Tonio. I know this sounds bad, but I really wish you hadn't called him. I didn't want him anywhere near Devon—especially after the way he's hurt her."

"I didn't want him here either, but he is the father." Gerald frowned as he added, "I wanted to strangle him myself."

Devon was awake when they returned. She had the baby in her arms and was playing with her fingers. She looked up when they entered the room. "Mama . . ."

"Congratulations, sweetheart." Cordelia smiled. "She's beautiful."

Gerald agreed. "You did good."

"Tonio, would you tell your parents that Devon's awake, please." She hated sharing this moment with them, but Cordelia realized just how selfish that sounded.

Margaret and her husband joined them in the room.

Devon's eyes traveled the room. "I have a name already picked out. I know everybody thought I was crazy for keeping it a secret, but now I'll tell you—her name is Christina Cordelia Bradshaw."

Tears filled Cordelia's eyes.

"Cordelia is pretty obvious," Devon was saying. "You all don't know this, but I had a little sister. She died when I was five years old. Her name was Christina."

"Honey . . ." Gerald couldn't finish his sentence. He put a hand to his mouth.

"We . . . we're so honored, Devon." Cordelia couldn't quite put her feelings into words. Losing her baby daughter had been so hard for her and Gerald. Now, looking back, that was when her marriage had started to crumble. She'd been so immersed in her grief that she'd shut herself off from her husband. Even after she sought solace in the church, she continued to push him away. Maybe Gerald was right: Cordelia had sent him into the arms of other women. It was strange, but she'd never considered it before.

44

Near the end of the second week in August, the trees were beginning to change color. Bonnie thought she could smell rain in the air. She prayed that it wouldn't come because it was time to go out to the cemetery.

She got up early Saturday morning and drove out to Forest Memorial Gardens, the final resting place for many of Bridgeport's citizens. Bonnie parked and climbed out. As she walked the trail leading to Edgar's grave, she fingered her wedding band. The gold of Bonnie's ring seemed to grow warm. She stared down at it. "I know you loved me more than anyone," she whispered.

When Bonnie reached the grave, she ran her fingers across the engraved lettering. She fell to her knees. "Oh, Edgar. I miss you so much."

Bonnie yanked out a weed, careful to uproot the full length. "I don't know if I will ever fully accept your leaving me. I know that you didn't do it on your own—I just wish you could have stayed with me a little longer. Sometimes I'm scared of what the future holds." She gave a little laugh. "I'm getting much better. Guess what? I'm actually going out and having dinner alone."

She pulled another weed. "I have a good time too. It was a little uncomfortable at first, but then I realized that there wasn't anything wrong with it."

After she'd pulled out all the weeds, Bonnie retrieved a book from her tote. Edgar had been a very religious man and loved reading the Bible. Today she read from the book of John. The verse that stuck out was John 4:39: *Many Samaritans from that city believed in him because of the woman's testimony. He told me everything I have ever done.*

Bonnie spent time reflecting on those words. She began to pray.

"My heavenly Father, I come before You humbled by Your majesty and magnificence. You are truly Lord of all. You know me, the work of Your creation, so well. It is a comfort and relief to know that I need not hide from You, that I can bare my soul before You and lay my shortcomings at Your feet, for I know that there is no end to the depth of Your love for me.

"Continue to mold me, teach me, and shape me to be the image of Your son, ever more Christ-like. Fill me with such love that it will allow me to continue to reach out to others in true acceptance. I ask all these things in the name of Your son, our Lord, Jesus Christ. Amen."

Bonnie felt like a new person. She ran her fingers lovingly across the name of her long departed husband. "Edgar, honey, I'll be back next week. Every time I come out here, I leave feeling uplifted and refreshed. Even in death, talking to you always helps. I cherish the time we were together and I carry those memories in my heart."

Bonnie rose to her feet and made her way back to her car.

45

Spending a lazy Sunday afternoon in the condo, Sabrina picked up one travel brochure after another. She was on the hunt for the perfect romantic vacation. The Labor Day weekend was coming up, and Sabrina wanted to get away. "Why don't we go to Hawaii?"

Maxwell scrunched up his face. "Been there. Done that. Come on, admit it: Hawaii is boring."

Sabrina had never been to Hawaii but she didn't tell him that. "I love it there. Especially Maui. My mother and I haven't been since I was in my teens." She stared at the pamphlet longingly. It had been a dream of hers to own a condo on Maui.

Reaching for one of the carrot sticks on the vegetable tray, he asked, "Is that where you really want to go?" Maxwell swung his legs off the sofa and sat up. He took a bite off the carrot. "We can go there if you want."

"Honey, we don't have to go there. We could go somewhere in the Virgin Islands. Maybe St. Thomas or St. Croix?"

Shrugging, Maxwell said, "I love Martinique, French West Indies. We should go there."

"That sounds nice." Sitting cross-legged on the floor, Sabrina searched through her stack of brochures. She was sure she'd had one on the West Indies. She felt herself getting irritated. "I know I had some information on Martinique." She muttered a curse.

Maxwell burst into laughter. "It's not that serious, baby. Don't get so intense."

Sabrina forced herself to relax. "Well, I guess we're going to Martinique then."

He reached for another carrot stick. "You know what, babe? I had another idea. I was thinking about going to Los Angeles. We could hang out with some musician buddies of mine."

"That's not exactly what I would call a romantic vacation, Maxwell." Rubbing his thigh, she added, "I was hoping it would just be the two of us."

"We can make it a couples weekend, baby. It'll be more fun that way. Los Angeles is a lot of fun."

Sabrina was offended. "Excuse me? You think you need other people around to have fun with me?"

"No, that's not what I'm saying. Baby, that's not it at all." Maxwell rose to his feet. "Sabrina, we can do whatever you want to do. Just let me know."

"I want your input as well. This trip is not just for me—it's for both of us."

"Really, whatever you decide is fine with me. Just pick the place."

Sabrina stood up and removed her dress. "I really want to go back to Hawaii. I want to be wined and dined in Maui. I want to go shopping in Maui. . . ."

Maxwell didn't take his eyes off her. "Baby, I'll take you anywhere you want to go."

*   *   *

Three hours later, Maxwell and Sabrina showered and dressed.

"I'm going to have to get out of here. I need to get back to Durham. My parents are flying in tonight. I wish you could meet them."

"I do too. If I didn't have to work tomorrow . . . Although I could call in sick."

"No, don't do that," he said quickly. "You'll get to meet them another time. Count on it." Lowering his head, Maxwell planted a kiss on her lips.

"I'm going to miss you. I wish it were Friday already. And don't forget, we're having dinner with my mother on Saturday," Sabrina said as she walked him to the door.

When she opened the door she found Elwood standing there. Sabrina sent him a sharp look.

He looked Maxwell up and down. Holding out his hand, Elwood introduced himself. "I'm a friend of Sabrina's."

Smiling, Maxwell replied, "I am a friend of Sabrina's also. It's nice to meet you."

"What are you doing here?" Sabrina asked.

"I would think it's obvious," Elwood shot back. "I came to see you."

"I—"

Maxwell interrupted her. "Honey, I've got to get on the road. I'll see you this weekend."

"Have a safe drive," Sabrina called out. Folding her arms across her chest, she glared at Elwood. "If you don't leave, I'm going to call the police."

"For what? Because I came to talk to you?"

"It's over. Why can't you get that through your head?"

"I don't like being used, Sabrina. I really cared for you, but all you wanted was my checkbook."

Rolling her eyes, she said, "Think what you want. The truth of the matter is that I didn't want you. We're not a good fit. Now leave my house and don't come back. Ever."

"I ought to sue you for every penny I spent on you."

"Whatever!" Sabrina turned and slammed the door shut. She stood with her back against the door, trying to calm her nerves.

The Haddonfield property was located in the northern portion of west Maui. Kapalua Bay had been voted in previous years by *Condé Nast* as the best beach, so Sabrina thought it the perfect choice for their vacation.

Maxwell chased Sabrina into the water. She squealed when he splashed water on her, getting her hair wet. Angry, she tossed curses at him.

"I'll have a stylist come up and do it for you when we return to the penthouse."

"Really? Just like that?"

He nodded. Moving closer to her, Maxwell reached for her. "There's something I want to tell you."

"What?"

"I love you, Sabrina. From the moment we bumped into each other." Maxwell kissed her.

They were the words she'd been waiting to hear. "I love you too," she uttered. Sabrina wished she really felt that way, but she didn't. Her heart still belonged to Leon, even though the dog didn't deserve it. But Maxwell was gorgeous and very rich—she could live with that, she decided.

They spent the next four days shopping and playing tennis or just lying around on the beach during the day and taking moonlit walks at night. Sabrina managed to convince herself that she was having the time of her life. Once she and Maxwell were married she would spend the rest of her life traveling to exotic islands for weekend getaways and touring Europe. Not bad for a girl from Bridgeport, North Carolina.

46

Tangie and Brandon eased into the last pew at church. They were late because of her. She'd gone to Fayetteville last night and didn't get in until six that morning and ended up over-sleeping. Although she'd been attending church services with Brandon for a few months, Tangie hadn't gotten much out of it. But today's sermon got her attention.

"This morning our topic is 'God Wants to Get to Know You.' That's good news. The better news is that God does not care where you are, how you look, what you've done, or what you wear . . . God just wants to spend time with you, and He wants you to spend time with Him."

Tangie felt the hair on the back of her neck stand up. Heat rushed to her face and she felt uncomfortable. She tried to block out what the pastor was saying, but his words pene-trated.

"Do you think that God is so stern that He's only looking to see where we fail? Do you think that God is so unforgiving that He would never see past your sins? Do you think God is so busy that He has very little time for us? Then think again, because you are wrong."

Tangie stole a peek at Brandon. He seemed captivated by the message and was nodding vigorously.

"It really does not matter how badly man has messed up . . . God still wants us the way He created us. He loves us and offers a wonderful plan for our life."

Suddenly she felt eyes on her. Tangie looked up. The minister was gazing directly at her. He repeated his words. "No matter how badly a person has messed up, He wants us to come back to Him. God wants you back."

Yeah, right, Tangie thought silently. *He definitely doesn't want me. I'm a soiled dove. Like my mother.* She felt her eyes water and she blinked rapidly. *I have no place being here in this church.*

Leaning over, she whispered to Brandon, "I need to go to the bathroom. I'll be right back."

Tangie stayed in the rest room until she feared Brandon would come looking for her. She forced herself to go back inside. She was strong, she told herself. She could face whatever the pastor had to say.

"Some of you may want to know how to give your life to Jesus Christ. How can you come into this fellowship with the Lord?"

The minister seemed to be looking at her once more. Tangie played with the folds of her skirt.

"We already know that God loves us, but there are things that can block us from that love. When we sin, we become separated from God. . . ."

That counts me out, Tangie thought.

"Some people scoff at the concept of sin because they consider it a prohibition against fun. The Bible tells us that sin is anything but fun, nor is it beneficial. You see, sin has devastating consequences of which we need to be aware. The Book of Romans points out the truth." He paused to allow what he'd said to sink in. "Sin enslaves people and demands that they obey its lusts. Because of sin, a great gulf separates God and man, but this is how we can bridge that gulf. Romans 5:8 says: 'But God showed His great love for us by sending Christ to die for us while we were still sinners.' Praise God." The pastor picked up the microphone and stepped down from the altar. "John 14:6 tells us, 'I am the way, the truth and the life. No one can come to the Father except through me.' "

Those words sent a chill through Tangie.

"Honey, are you feeling okay? You were so quiet on the way home."

Tangie glanced over at Brandon. "I'm fine. Just tired. I didn't sleep well last night." She cast her eyes downward because she couldn't face him right now. Last night was spent in the arms of another man. *I've got to stop this madness,* she raged silently.

When they arrived at her town house, Tangie made up an excuse. "Sweetie, I'm not feeling all that well. I don't think I'd be much company. Would you mind if I just spent the rest of the day alone?"

He looked concerned. "Are you sure?"

She nodded. "I just want to crawl into my bed and sleep. I'll call you later, okay?"

"Sure. You get some rest."

"I will." Tangie watched him drive off and waved. He was such a good man—too good for her. Her heart heavy, she turned and unlocked her door.

Inside, she settled down on the sofa in her den. Tangie placed a pillow beneath her head and closed her eyes. She could still hear the words of the sermon reverberating inside her head. She frowned. "Stop it," she whispered.

Tangie fell into a troubled sleep fifteen minutes later.

47

The Berkeley home was in a state of disarray with the new baby in the house. Six-week-old Christina Cordelia Bradshaw slept during the day and was awake most of the night. Devon wasn't going to start college until the winter semester, but she'd started a new job and was trying to function on little or no sleep.

Cordelia wanted to help out more but she couldn't. She felt the baby was still too small for her to hold comfortably. Hearing footsteps, she cast a look across her shoulder. "Is Christina asleep?" she asked Gerald.

He nodded. "I just told Devon to lie down and try to take a nap too. She's so tired." Gerald fell back on the sofa. He stretched out his legs and yawned.

"I know. She's trying so hard to take care of everything. Tonio has been over here just once to see his daughter." Cordelia had seen Devon crying over him on more than one occasion. She could choke the life out of Tonio for hurting her daughter like that. That was how she made it through her physical therapy sessions—visualizing Tonio.

"His son was born a few days ago. That young man is going to have his hands full."

"What about college? Is he still going?"

"I spoke to his father last week. Tonio's not trying to do much of anything these days. Outside of making babies." Gerald glanced over his shoulder to see if Devon was up. Keeping his voice to a whisper, he said, "Another girl has come forward saying she's pregnant."

"Humph! I'm not surprised."

Cordelia reached for her walker. She'd been out of the wheelchair for about a week and was still feeling a little insecure. She looked to Gerald for assistance. "I'm ready for my daily exercise. Ready, drill seargent?"

Gerald burst into laughter.

Cordelia couldn't get over how handsome he looked.

48

Bonnie admired the new dress she'd just finished sewing. She'd started it last week and now it was finished. She couldn't wait to try it on.

She put the dress on and stood in front of a full-length mirror. Bonnie ran her hand down the side. "Not bad . . ." She loved the turquoise color against her skin and decided to wear it to church on Sunday.

She was talented, Bonnie acknowledged. She wasn't a bad person either. But for years she'd had this feeling of being alone and unloved. It didn't matter whether she was on a crowded street, or with her friends—she always managed to feel as if she were all on her own.

It had been only lately that Bonnie was able to see herself in a more positive light. Her own insecurities had forced her into becoming a wallflower, and those same insecurities had motivated her into trying to buy others' friendships. She found the latter bothersome and exhausting, and she'd grown tired. Bonnie wanted to be liked for who she was—not for what she could do or provide.

*   *   *

Sabrina knocked on the door to Bonnie's office. "Hey, can I talk to you for a second?"

Bonnie became guarded. She and Sabrina were still on shaky ground as far as she was concerned. "Sure. Come in."

"I feel like we haven't talked for a long time. How have you been?"

"What did you need?"

Sabrina was a little taken aback. "Uh . . . I . . . Have you spoken to Claire lately? She wants me to create another data sheet. What's wrong with the one we're already using?"

Bonnie didn't respond.

"Did you hear me?"

"I heard you." Leaning back in her chair, Bonnie said, "I guess you should do what Claire asked you to do."

"Excuse me?" Sabrina sat up straight. "Bonnie, what's up with you? Why do you have such an attitude lately? I haven't done anything to you."

Anger flashed in Bonnie's eyes. She got up and closed the door to her office. Turning, she said, "I've put up with your attitude for the last time, Sabrina. I've never tried to be anything but a friend to you—all you've done is take advantage of that. If you come in late, I cover for you; I have helped you keep your job here, but all you've done is be mean and rude in return. I'm tired of it. From now on you're on your own."

Sabrina's eyes grew large but she didn't say a word. After a moment she got up and brushed past Bonnie. She opened the door and left the office.

Bonnie released the breath she was holding.

49

Sabrina felt like she'd been hit with a brick. She didn't have a clue as to what had just happened back there. She sat at her desk trying to shake off the effects of Bonnie's words. Curling her hand into a fist, Sabrina vowed that everybody would soon bow down to her. Nobody had the right to treat her like dirt. *Just wait until Maxwell and I are married. You'll all pay.*

Her phone rang.

"Sabrina speaking."

"I want my money back. Every penny."

She felt a shred of fear. "Stop calling my job, Elwood. Stop calling me, period. If you don't stop, I'm going to call the police."

"Once you give me back every penny, you won't ever hear me mention your name."

Sabrina slammed down the phone. Elwood was getting on her nerves. He was calling her at home and at work, threatening her. A couple of times she suspected he'd been hanging around her condo. She was tempted to confide in Maxwell but couldn't risk the truth coming out.

After work she would go by her condo and pick up a few things, then stay with her mother. It was probably a wise move, since Elwood was acting so crazy. Sabrina picked up the phone and placed a call to Maxwell.

He wasn't home, so she just left a message. "Honey, my mother is really sick, so I'm going to spend a few nights at her house. You can reach me on my cellular. 'Bye for now."

Sabrina left work an hour earlier than normal and rushed to her condo. She ran through the house like a madwoman, grabbing cosmetics, clothing, and lingerie. She tossed them into a suitcase.

She worked quickly because she didn't trust Elwood. He had a habit of showing up whenever the mood struck him. She wanted to avoid another run-in with him.

Sabrina was packed and ready to go. She ran out to the car, threw her Louis Vuitton bag in the backseat, and climbed in. Making sure all the doors were locked, she sped off.

Her nerves had calmed down by the time Sabrina parked in her mother's driveway. At least Elwood didn't know where she lived.

She let herself into the house and went straight to the kitchen. "Hey, Mama."

Mamie looked down at the luggage in her hand in confusion. "Where are you going?"

"I'm staying over here for a couple of nights. You don't mind, do you?" Sabrina dropped into one of the chairs at the breakfast table. "I'm having my condo sprayed for bugs. That smell lasts for a couple of days and I can't stand it."

"Hungry?"

She shook her head. "No, thanks, Mama."

Mamie stood over her with her hands on her hips. "What's wrong with you? You never turn down a meal."

"I'm just not hungry. Maybe I'll eat something later." Sabrina rose to her feet. "I'm going to go lie down for a little while." Elwood had succeeded in scaring her, she acquiesced.

She decided to call the phone company and have her phone number changed. If he came back to her house she would take out a restraining order.

Sabrina felt much better when she woke up two hours later. She got up and went in search of her mother. She found her in the den.

"What are you doing?"

Mamie glanced up. "Just watching some television. You've been in there sleeping for a long time. Anything you want to tell me?"

She laughed. "I'm not pregnant, Mama."

"Then what's wrong with you? I know something is wrong. I know you, chile."

"An old boyfriend has been hounding me."

"Not that Leon?"

"Someone else. Elwood Brown. He wants me back, and I keep telling him that it's over."

"Call the police."

"If he bothers me again, I will."

"There're some crazy men out there, sweetie. I think we should call the police now." Mamie reached for the phone.

"No, Mama. Just let it go. I don't want to overreact, okay?" Sabrina picked up the television remote. "Mind if I change the channel?"

"No, go ahead."

Lifestyles of the Rich and Famous was just coming on. Sabrina enjoying seeing how the wealthy lived. She studied and memorized the actions of the affluent and fantasized that one day she would live as they did. Even Maxwell was under the impression that she'd been raised in a lifestyle similar to his. He had no idea that she and her mother were Mayhew outcasts.

50

The first weekend in October, Brandon and Tangie drove to Virginia Beach. The weather had turned chilly but they didn't mind. They both preferred the cool weather to the hot. She was stunned when he announced that they would have separate bedrooms. It was clear to her that he was determined to stay celibate.

Tangie admired his fortitude. As much as she wanted to be faithful to him, she couldn't. That hunger was still there within her—only it wasn't as if she enjoyed satisfying her lust. She needed it. Then afterward she felt sick. Tangie was scared because she didn't know what was happening to her, and there was no one she could talk to about her problem.

Brandon kissed her on the forehead. "What's going on in that head of yours?"

She looked up at him. Pasting a smile on her face, Tangie said, "I was thinking about this weekend. I'm very excited."

He embraced her. "I'm going to make this an unforgettable weekend for you. I promise."

"Wow. I can hardly wait."

Brandon paid for both rooms. They followed the bellman to the elevators. Less than five minutes later, they were standing at the doors of their respective rooms.

Leaning against her door, Tangie said, "I'm going to unpack and freshen up. I'll meet you in your room in thirty minutes."

"Works for me. We'll get something to eat. Do you want to venture out for dinner or just eat downstairs?"

Tangie considered his question for a moment. "Let's just eat here at the hotel."

"See you in thirty."

Gracing him with a winning smile, Tangie turned and entered her room. She stepped aside to let the bellman exit.

From across the hall, Brandon said, "I've got the tip." He held out a ten-dollar bill to the man.

When Tangie closed her door, they were still outside Brandon's room talking. Her boyfriend met no strangers. He would talk to anyone. She couldn't stop grinning as she put away her clothing, and she knew the reason why. She was in love.

"Wow," she murmured as the realization hit her full force. Tangie dropped down on the edge of the king-size bed. She loved Brandon. But then why couldn't she stop sneaking around with other guys if she loved him? The question bothered her.

"I know I love him. I love Brandon," she whispered. "Those other guys don't mean a thing. It's just sex. . . ."

Tangie rose to her feet and began pacing the room. *That's it. Brandon and I aren't sleeping together and I need sex. Some people need more sex than others. As soon as he and I make love I won't need those other guys anymore.*

She stopped walking. "This is crazy. I love Brandon, and if I'm going be with him I have to be faithful. Starting from this point on." Tangie didn't want to disappoint him. "I can do this."

Looking at the bed brought on a familiar tingle. She closed her eyes and repeated, "I can do this. I don't need sex."

Tangie strolled into the bathroom and undressed. She stepped into the shower.

Brandon came looking for her not too long afterward. She'd just gotten dressed when he knocked on her door.

"I was getting worried about you."

"I'm all right, baby. I felt dirty, so I took a quick shower." Tangie put a trembling hand to her hair. "I think I wet my hair." She moved around Brandon to peer into a mirror.

Her curls were now hanging limp due to the steam and the spray of the water. "I'm going to have to pin my hair up," Tangie announced with a frown.

Brandon eased up behind her. Wrapping his arms around her, he said, "It doesn't matter how you wear your hair. I love it."

She leaned into his body. "You are such a sweetheart. I don't know what I'd do without you."

"If I have anything to say about it, you won't ever have to find out."

Staring at his reflection, Tangie's eyes met his gaze.

"I love you," he whispered in her ear.

"I love you too," she whispered back.

Tangie read the lust in his eyes. Before she could suggest that they stay there and order room service, Brandon stepped away from her, saying, "I think we should go on downstairs. I'm starving."

Grabbing her purse, Tangie swallowed her disappointment and followed him out the door.

The next morning Brandon and Tangie got up early to start their day. The weekends didn't last long, and they wanted to savor every moment. After a full-course breakfast, they spent the morning on the beach, the afternoon shopping, and then went to dinner.

"Let's take a walk along the beach," Brandon suggested. "The moon is full and it's beautiful out. Don't forget your jacket, though. It's cold out there."

"Moonlit walk on the beach . . . How romantic . . ."

"It's perfect for what I have in mind."

Tangie was intrigued. Grinning, she inquired, "Oh, really? And what is that?"

"It's a surprise."

Her body began to throb in excitement. Brandon was ready to give up celibacy. He wanted her; she could tell. Tangie wanted him too.

Brandon embraced her, pulling her close to him.

They walked for what seemed like a mile from the ocean-front hotel where they were staying. It was cold being near the water but Tangie didn't care. She could have walked home to North Carolina in her euphoric state.

Brandon stopped walking. Looking down at her, he said, "There's something I want to say. I know you'll probably think I'm crazy but I'm going to say it anyway."

"What is it, Brandon?"

"I love you so much, Tangie—"

"I know, baby. I love you too," she cut in. "You're the best thing that's ever happened to me."

"That's exactly the way I feel, baby. I can't see me without you." Brandon ran a finger gently down her cheek. "I don't want to ever lose you, Tangie."

She couldn't discern the strange look in his eyes. "Brandon, what exactly are you saying?"

"I . . . Tangie, would you do me the honor of being my wife?"

She was stunned speechless. Brandon had proposed. They hadn't even had sex and he wanted to marry her.

"Baby . . ." Brandon prompted. "Will you marry me?"

Tangie found her voice. "Y-yes. Yes, I'll marry you." She threw her arms around him, holding on to Brandon for dear life. He'd told her once that she was his destiny. She knew he was her salvation.

51

"I haven't seen you this excited in a long time," Gerald observed.

"I'm getting together with the girls. We're having lunch. This is the first time they're going to see me without the walker." Cordelia had progressed to using a quad cane in the last week. She was getting stronger day by day.

"That's good. You're on the road back to being yourself."

"I feel good."

"Dee, when are you going back to church? You hardly talk to any of the members anymore. They're always calling here and leaving messages but you won't return their calls."

"I don't know if I'm going back," Cordelia stated firmly. How many times had she talked to others about God's love? How could she go back to church when she was so angry with God? Trusting Him had caused her nothing but pain. Cordelia had once called His name in joy, but now it was like a bad taste in her mouth. God had long since forsaken her.

"Your pastor wants to come by one day soon for a visit."

Cordelia tossed a look over her shoulder. "He's not my pastor anymore. I haven't been in church in a long time."

"I think you should reconsider."

She turned around to face Gerald with the aid of her quad cane. "When did you become so gung ho for going to church?"

He met her gaze straight-on. "We're not talking about me, Dee. We're talking about you. You were the one running down there every time the door opened." Gerald's words were laced with bitterness.

"Well, you don't have to worry about that anymore, do you?"

He ignored her last statement. "This isn't right, Dee. I know you feel that God let you down somehow."

"He did."

"Sweetheart, that's your anger talking. God is still here for you."

Cordelia looked over at him. "So now you're an ambassador for the Lord? I guess things have changed."

Gerald laughed at that. "I see you didn't know me at all. I have always had a relationship with God. I worship Him in my own way."

"I thought I knew everything about you. I can't remember you ever mentioning God—I don't even remember ever seeing you pray."

"I didn't exactly do it in front of you, Dee. It was private for me. Maybe I was a little embarrassed."

"Or maybe you were ashamed?"

"No, it was never that. I just felt uncomfortable when it came to worshiping God in public. But you're right—a lot has changed in recent years. I will worship God however and whenever. He's brought me through some things. . . ." Gerald's voice died. "What? Why are you looking at me like that?"

"I've never heard you talk this way. I'm just a little stunned."

"Life takes us through twists and turns, Dee. It changes us— sometimes for the better and sometimes for the worse."

Cordelia couldn't have agreed more.

The doorbell sounded. "That's probably Bonnie," she announced. "I'll get the door."

Bonnie greeted her with a hug. "Look at you!"

"I'm ready."

"I can see that." Bonnie waved at Gerald. "Let's go."

"I'll be back in a couple of hours," Cordelia told him.

"Have fun. I'm going to run out myself for a while. I may not be here when you get back."

"Okay."

Inside the car, Bonnie said, "You are doing so well, Dee. I'm so proud of you."

"I feel good about the progress. It's been a long road and it's not over yet. I still have a ways to go."

"God is good, isn't he?"

Cordelia didn't respond. She could feel Bonnie's eyes on her. "How is everyone back at the FFA unit?"

"The same. Nothing ever pleases them."

Cordelia laughed at this.

The ride to the restaurant was short. Tangie and Sabrina arrived shortly after they did.

They giggled through the appetizers and salads. Cordelia noted that Tangie seemed in a particularly strange mood. It was as if she knew something everybody else didn't.

Their entrees arrived and everyone dug in.

Cordelia finally had to inquire, "What's going on with you, Tangie? I notice you've been grinning all through lunch."

"Yeah, she sure has," Sabrina uttered. "She even has this strange kind of glow going on."

Tangie burst into laughter. "Actually, there is something I've been dying to tell you all."

"Well, what is it?" Frowning, Sabrina asked, "You're not pregnant, are you?"

Tangie's smile disappeared. "No, it's not that."

"Then tell us," Cordelia urged. "I already have an idea of what it is, but I'm not going to say anything."

"Brandon proposed to me while we were in Virginia Beach."

Bonnie clapped her hands in glee. "Really? That's wonderful."

Sabrina's mouth dropped open in surprise. "You're engaged?"

Nodding, Tangie replied, "Yes. Brandon and I are getting married."

Congratulations rang out around the table.

"I'm so excited. I can't believe that I'm actually getting married."

"Have you set a date?" Bonnie asked.

"Not yet." Tangie took a sip of her iced tea.

Cordelia noticed that Sabrina was unusually quiet. "This is wonderful news, isn't it, Sabrina?"

"I already said congratulations," she snapped. "Tangie, when did you and Brandon go to Virginia Beach?"

"We were there this past weekend. Why?"

"You never mentioned that you were going. Why would you go to Virginia Beach of all places? It's cold—"

"I don't see where any of that matters," Tangie shot back. "It was a last minute decision and we went." She reached into her purse and pulled out a tiny box. "He gave me a ring. I took it off this morning because I wanted to surprise you all." She placed the emerald cut diamond engagement ring on her finger.

"Oooh," Bonnie moaned. "It's beautiful, Tangie. Brandon sure has good taste."

Cordelia agreed. "It is beautiful. That's what? About a carat and a half?"

"Yes," Tangie confirmed.

"Well, I'd check to see if it's real, if I were you," Sabrina advised. "There are some real nice fakes out there on the market."

"What's wrong with you?" Tangie questioned.

"Nothing." Sabrina rose briskly to her feet. "I'm going back to the office early. I've got some work I need to do."

Cordelia stared after her, wondering what in the world was going on with Sabrina.

52

_____

"Well, my goodness," Bonnie announced. "What just happened here?" She looked over at Cordelia. "I'm beginning to think she's crazy."

"I think Sabrina's just a little jealous of Tangie's good news, that's all."

"She'll just have to get over it." Tangie reached for her water glass. "If she were getting married, I would be happy for her."

Cordelia took a sip of her water. "I'm sure she's happy for you, Tangie. You know how much Sabrina wants to be married. She's had her wedding planned for years."

"Dee's right." Bonnie finished off her salmon. Sabrina was acting childish, as usual. She didn't know how to share the spotlight with others. If she didn't grow up, she was headed for some rude awakenings.

Tangie agreed with them both. "I have to admit I didn't think about how she would feel."

"You don't have to consider her feelings. This is all about you."

The waiter brought their check.

"It's been so good having lunch with you ladies. I really miss our time together," Cordelia said.

Smiling, Tangie replied, "I miss you so much, Dee. You know something? I think we should try to get you out of the house on a weekly basis."

"I agree. We're going to try to do this at least once a week." Bonnie opened her purse. "Put those wallets away. I'm buying lunch today."

"I'll buy next time," Tangie promised.

Outside, Bonnie announced, "I'm going to drop Dee off at home, then head back to work. I should be there in half an hour."

"I'll let Kayla know."

"Thanks, Tangie."

True to her word, Bonnie was strolling into the FFA unit thirty minutes later. She spied Sabrina at the copier. Their eyes met. She was wearing a sour expression, so Bonnie didn't bother to say anything to her.

Tangie walked up to her and whispered, "Stay away from Sabrina. She's in witch mode."

Bonnie was happy for Tangie. She had enjoyed being married to Edgar and wished the same happiness for her friend. Brandon was a nice man and he genuinely seemed to love Tangie.

On the way to her office, a coworker halted Bonnie.

"I was just looking for you. My cousin showed me the quilt you made for her. I love it."

"Thank you."

"Could you please make one for me? I would love to have something similar to hers. Maybe in a beige color or ivory. Ivory would be nice."

Nodding, Bonnie said, "I would be more than happy to make one for you. Give me a day or two to come up with a sample of something I have in mind."

53

Sabrina was happy for Tangie on one hand, but on the other, she was jealous. She deserved to have a husband and family, too. She fought back tears as she drove back to the office.

"It's not fair," she whispered in the car. *It's just not fair. Why does the ho of the group get the husband?* Sabrina wondered. She didn't deserve to get married.

She had always assumed she would be the one getting married first. Tangie wouldn't be faithful—she probably didn't have a clue how. A tear slid down her face. If only Maxwell would get a clue and propose.

She'd been patient long enough, Sabrina decided. It was time she gave her future some serious thought. She was getting older, so she needed to have children soon. She wondered briefly if she'd be able to conceive quickly and whether there was any damage to her body from the abortions.

Sabrina made a mental note to schedule an appointment with her doctor. She wanted to know in advance whether she would be able to become a mother. She'd heard of women unable to have children because of multiple abortions. "God, please don't hold them against me—I just wasn't ready to be a parent."

54

Tangie was a little hurt by Sabrina's distance since the news of her engagement. She'd attempted on two separate occasions to make conversation with her, but Sabrina just brushed her off.

A week passed and she was still getting the cold shoulder. Tangie decided to confront her after work. She waited beside Sabrina's car in the parking lot.

Sabrina walked out of the building. She paused for a split second when she spotted Tangie. Coming toward her, she asked, "Something wrong with your car?"

"No. I was waiting to talk to you. I'm bothered by your attitude, Sabrina. You're supposed to be my friend. If you'd announced your engagement, I would be happy for you. I wouldn't be tripping like this."

"I am happy for you, Tangie. But I don't have to do flips all over the place, do I?"

Surveying her up and down, Tangie questioned, "What's up with you? Why are you acting like this? It's hard to even talk to you."

"Excuse me?"

Shaking her head in dismay, Tangie responded, "You know what? Forget it, Sabrina. I'm sorry it's not you. I'm sorry, okay?"

"I said I was happy for you, Tangie. The problem is that you are always saying we're friends but you don't trust me. You don't treat me like a friend."

"What are you talking about, Sabrina?"

"You couldn't even tell me you and Brandon were going to Virginia Beach. You couldn't tell me first that you were engaged. I'm always sharing my life with you—you want to keep secrets."

"I'm not keeping secrets, Sabrina. I just don't discuss my private life with people—even friends. It's not a reflection on you. It's just the way I am."

"I'm happy for you, Tangie."

"So you think we're not friends because I don't tell you my business?"

"It just seemed to me that the relationship is one-sided."

"I never asked you to tell me anything, Sabrina. You don't have to share your intimate details with me."

"That's what friends do, Tangie."

"Friends don't envy one another either."

"Are you saying we can't be friends anymore?"

Tangie shook her head no. "That's not it at all. You are my friend, Sabrina. I trust you as much as I can trust any one person. It's not something that comes easily for me. I'm sorry if you feel I've shut you out. I really didn't mean to do so."

"I'm sorry too. I know I fly off the handle at times but I didn't mean to diminish one second of your joy. I guess I expect my friends to be like me." She broke into a smile. "Here comes your fiancé."

Tangie turned in time to see Brandon walking toward them. She grinned when he blew her a kiss.

"Hello, ladies." He embraced Tangie and planted a kiss on her cheek.

"Congratulations on your engagement. I didn't say you could take my friend from me."

He laughed. "You brought us together."

"I'll be looking for a bouquet of roses tomorrow as thanks."

"You got it," he promised. "And dinner." Brandon looked down at Tangie. "Why don't we take Sabrina to dinner?"

Tangie was quick to agree. Maybe this would smooth Sabrina's ruffled feathers for a while.

Singing to herself, Tangie cleaned her house from top to bottom. She was getting married, and it was still hard for her to comprehend. Marriage had been the farthest thing from her mind.

Since her engagement, Tangie hadn't felt the strong tug of sexual urges as she had in the past. Brandon had indeed given her a new life. From the moment she spoke her vows, Tangie determined to make her marriage work and to remain faithful always.

She finished up in the formal dining room and moved into the living room. Tangie always saved this room for last because it was the least used and it took virtually no time to clean. She picked up a stack of junk mail and was headed to the trash with it. A letter floated down to the floor. Tangie bent to pick it up.

The letter from Danny. She'd forgotten all about it. Tangie held it over the trash can, preparing to throw it away. There wasn't much point in looking back into the past, she decided. Something stopped her.

Looking down at the neat scrawl on the envelope, she went through a mental debate. *Maybe I should at least read it. What harm can it do? It wasn't like he hurt me or anything. The relationship just fizzled out. Last I heard, he was getting married. Maybe it didn't work out or something. He probably just needs a shoulder to cry on.*

Tangie opened the letter. She read the contents twice before fainting.

*   *   *

The blood pounding in her temples, Tangie slowly opened her eyes. She tried to sit up. Dazed, she struggled to remember what had happened, then spotted the letter on the floor.

Recalling what happened moments before darkness assailed her, Tangie reached for the letter. "This is a joke. A horrible joke."

She pushed herself to her feet and went into the den. After taking several deep breaths, she picked up the phone and dialed.

When someone answered on the other end, she said, "Hello, I need to speak to Danny, please."

"Who is this?"

"Tangie Thompson. I'm an old friend of his. He . . . he sent me a letter a few weeks ago." She paused. "I . . . I just got it."

"Danny has spoken of you a few times, Miss Thompson. I'm his mother, Maybelle Watkins."

Tangie wasn't sure what to say. "How is he doing?"

"He's . . . Miss Thompson, Danny died yesterday. I'm sorry."

Fear gripped her. "H-he's dead," she stammered. "Danny is d-dead." Tears streamed down her face as she let the receiver drop to the floor. Tangie sobbed uncontrollably with the realization that the news was true. "Oh, my God . . ."

In the distance, she heard a whisper. "Miss Thompson, are you there?"

Tangie picked up the phone. "I'm . . . I'm sorry for . . . your l-loss. I'm sorry." She hung up.

Danny was gone forever. He had had AIDS and now he was dead. In his letter, he stated that he'd contracted HIV unknowingly several months before meeting her, and that he might have infected her with it. Terror chilled her to the bone. What could she tell Brandon?

The clock ticked off her escalating fear.

When she felt strong enough to stand, Tangie ripped off her

clothes and rushed into the shower. She scrubbed vigorously. "I can't believe this," she screamed. "How can this happen to me?"

The telephone rang while she was getting dressed, causing her to jump at the sound. Tangie stared at it a moment before picking up the phone receiver. "H-hello."

"Hey, girlfriend, what's up?"

"Sabrina, hey. Look, I can't talk right now."

"What's wrong?"

"Nothing. I just can't talk right now. I'll give you a call later, okay?" Tangie just couldn't do it. She wasn't in any condition to deal with anyone right now—especially Sabrina. Yet if she stayed in this house alone, she would lose her mind.

"This is a surprise," Lula murmured when Tangie showed up at her door.

"I . . . I was driving around and I ended up here." Tangie pushed her hair out of her face. She couldn't remember driving to her mother's house.

"It's okay. Come on in. You look a sight." Lula ushered her daughter into the apartment. "Tangie, what's wrong?"

"I needed to get out of my place—I couldn't breathe," she managed to get out. "I just needed to leave."

Lula sat down beside her on a floral sofa. "Honey, what happened? I can tell you're upset."

Tangie shook her head. "I can't . . ." She stood up. "This was a mistake. I'm sorry. I shouldn't have come here." She ran out, leaving behind a perplexed Lula.

55

Pastor Grant entered the sunroom, where Cordelia was staring out the window watching the squirrels play.

"Hello, Sister Berkeley. How are you feeling? You sure are looking well these days."

She glared at her ex-husband. He'd gone against her wishes, and she was furious. "I'm fine, Pastor," she answered tightly. Cordelia gestured toward the love seat. "Please sit down."

"Why, thank you, sister."

"Would either of you like something to drink?" Gerald offered.

Pastor Grant declined. So did Cordelia. She was so angry with her ex at the moment.

Gerald left them alone.

Smiling, Pastor Grant said, "We'd sure love to see you in the congregation. Everybody misses you."

Cordelia couldn't meet his gaze. She suddenly felt guilty, as though she'd been caught in some wrongdoing. "I don't think I can go back, Pastor."

"Why, Sister Berkeley?"

Her chin quivered. "Because of the way I feel about God. I'm very angry with him." Shame crept into her eyes after her confession. It didn't change what she felt, however.

"That's when you should come to church."

"I wouldn't feel right, Pastor."

"I hope you don't mind my asking this, but why are you so angry with God?"

"Because I did right by God. I got up each morning with a prayer on my lips and a song of praise in my heart. I glorified Him from sunup to sundown. Then I find out my baby girl is pregnant and I had a stroke." Her eyes misted over. "My life as I knew it is no more. I have every right to be angry."

"Sister Berkeley, Jesus teaches us that we shouldn't give in to sickness, but instead we should fight to regain our health. Not all suffering is bad, though. Sickness, for instance, can sometimes bring about blessings."

She met his gaze, not believing what she'd just heard. "Blessings? What kind of blessing is this? Tell me, Pastor."

"It can remind us just how dependent we are on others, but mostly on God. It also reminds us just how precious life is to us."

Cordelia shook her head slowly. "I'm sorry, Pastor Grant. I don't see it that way."

"In times of trial, we have to lean not on our own understanding. We have to call on God's help to accept God's way and believe with our whole hearts that no matter what lies ahead, all will be well."

"I have no faith in God. Not anymore."

"You're still faithful, Sister. If you weren't, you wouldn't be struggling now. Sometimes it's easier to be mad at God than to change ourselves."

"I used to believe that God would take care of all of my needs. I thought he would protect me from all harm. I used to think that when real bad things happened to people, it was because of where their relationship stood with God—or lack of one. But I see now that it has nothing to do with that at all. No matter how hard I pray, it won't stop fate."

"Faith is not fate; nor is it passive, Sister Berkeley. We have to take on a more active role."

"What did I do wrong, Pastor? Why did all this happen to me?"

"I don't know why the stroke happened. As far as Devon goes, it has nothing to do with you per se. It is a consequence of your daughter's actions. You did the best you could to raise her. Sometimes you just have to let go and let God."

"I just wanted what was best for her. I feel responsible. She's my daughter."

Pastor Berkeley nodded in understanding. "It's not your fault. Devon has a mind of her own—all of us do. This pain you feel now is what our heavenly Father feels whenever we stray. Remember, though, His love for us never wanes."

"I still love my daughter. That's why it hurts so much. This is not the life I wanted for Devon."

"This is something that is beyond any of our control, sister. In times like this we have to give our children over to God."

"I know that," she murmured softly.

"Don't give up on the Lord."

Cordelia did not respond.

"As I've gone through illnesses and other setbacks, it's helped me to know that while we can't see the whole plan, God does. Relying on God helps me through all my trials."

"How do I let go of my anger, Pastor? I've held on to it for so long."

"Prayer, Sister Berkeley. Prayer and God's word."

56

Bonnie couldn't help but notice how quiet Tangie was through-out dinner.

"Are you okay?" she whispered. "You seem so sad."

"I'm okay."

"Come on, Tangie. There's something wrong—we can all tell," Sabrina announced. "We're your friends, and you know you can talk to us."

Bonnie reached over and patted Tangie's hand. "If you want to talk, we're here to listen."

Tangie's eyes bounced from one person to the next.

She looked to Bonnie as if she were struggling with some-thing. Her eyes were filled with turmoil and pain.

Her eyes glassed over. "I need to talk to someone."

"Honey, what's wrong?" Bonnie asked. She had never seen Tangie look so upset.

"A friend of mine died recently. He died of complications due to AIDS."

Bonnie wiped the corner of her mouth. "I'm sorry to hear that. Were you two very close?"

Tangie took a sip of water. "Danny was an old boyfriend. Actually, that's not true. We were lovers—only it was just about sex."

"You and he . . ." Sabrina's voice died. She cast her eyes downward.

Everyone was quiet, each one staring at their plates.

"He sent me a letter months ago but I misplaced it. Actually, I had no intention of reading it." She gave an embarrassed laugh. "I thought maybe it was a letter declaring his love or something like that. Danny even called me a couple of times, but I didn't return any of the calls. I finally called after I read the letter, and he was already dead." A tear slipped down her cheek.

Bonnie reached over and patted her hand. "Tangie, you should get tested."

She nodded. "I know. I'm scared, though. I've had a couple of tests done in the past and they were all negative. But now . . ."

"That's a good sign, I think. You've tested negative all those times."

"I'll go with you, Tangie," Sabrina stated. "I should probably get tested myself. It's been a while. We'll be a team."

"You'd do that for me?"

Sabrina smiled. "You're my girl, Tangie."

"I'm so thankful I have you ladies. I was so scared." Tangie finished her water but hadn't regained her appetite. She signaled for the waitress and asked, "Could you please get me a to-go box? I'm going to take it with me."

Bonnie tried to sound cheerful. "We're all going to think positively, Tangie. And remember that you're not alone."

"She's right," Cordelia threw in. "You all didn't abandon me. I wouldn't be sitting here today if it hadn't been for each of you."

"Have you told Brandon anything?" Sabrina asked what everyone had been thinking.

"No. This is not something I can tell him."

Bonnie and Cordelia exchanged looks.

"You're going to have to tell him, Tangie. You owe him that much," Bonnie said gently.

"Brandon and I have never made love," she announced. "We're waiting for our wedding night."

"You're going to have to be tested every six months for the next couple of years," Cordelia stated. "Tangie, you're going to have to say something to him."

She was quiet for so long, Sabrina called her name. Tangie looked over at her.

"You okay?"

Tangie nodded.

"When the time is right, sit him down and tell him," Bonnie advised. "Brandon loves you and he'll understand. I know he will. He's a good man." She rose up out of the chair. "We should be getting back to the office."

"Oh, Edgar, this world is becoming such a horrible place to live," Bonnie said in a moan. She'd come straight home from St. Paul County and climbed into her bed. Her heart was heavy from Tangie's news.

"I used to think that you got the worst of it, but Edgar, I was wrong. You are so blessed that you didn't have to suffer. You left this world on a pillow of peace and embraced by love, honor, and respect. You were a blessing to so many people. Your kind spirit ministered to all kinds—the heartbroken, the needy. . . ." Her voice died. Tears filled her eyes, but they were tears of joy. "Your work was done and so it was time for you to go. You lived your life according to God's plan, so you died knowing you would get everlasting life. How happy I am for you."

Bonnie began to feel a small pleasure in the knowledge that Edgar would be in heaven for all eternity. It renewed her motivation to get her own house in order. "Lord, I want to see Your face and live in the kingdom with You. I want to see my dear Edgar again. Give me the strength to live as You ordained. Just show me Your plan for my life . . ." she prayed in earnest.

When Bonnie finally fell asleep, it was with her Bible in her hand.

57

Maxwell opened up his arms for Sabrina to sink down on his lap. "I've been doing a lot of thinking, honey. I'm ready to settle down," she said as she picked up his hand and began playing with his fingers.

"Settle down? You?"

"Yeah, me. What do you mean by that?"

"Nothing."

Sabrina rose to her feet, her arms falling to her sides. "You think I don't ever plan on getting married? I want it all—marriage, children, the works."

Maxwell was strangely quiet, resting his hands on his knees.

"Well . . . don't you have something to say?"

"That's not something I ever really expected to hear out of your mouth."

"Why not?" Sabrina tilted her head in a curious study of Maxwell. Was it possible that she'd read him wrong? She couldn't afford to be wrong. She started to panic inside.

"Because you seem so happy with your life."

"I am happy with my life, but I want to get married too. I

thought that you wanted the same thing. Was I wrong, Maxwell?"

He reached out and pulled her down on the chair. "Sabrina, you know I'm crazy about you."

"Then what's the problem?"

"I have to do some thinking."

Sabrina didn't bother to hide her disappointment. Folding her arms across her chest, she mumbled, "I see."

"Don't go getting upset with me. This is a big step. I don't know if I'm ready for something like this."

"When will you know?" Sabrina questioned. "Because I'm ready to move on. As much as I hate admitting this, I'm not getting any younger."

Maxwell was quiet. He seemed deep in thought.

"Well?" Sabrina prompted.

"What?"

"When will you know?" she repeated.

"I don't know, Sabrina." He stood up. "Let's finish this discussion later. Right now I just want to go to bed."

She eyed him. "I don't want to be a girlfriend forever. I want to be a wife. If not yours, then I'll be somebody else's."

"Just like that?"

Sabrina nodded. "In a heartbeat." She stifled her yawn. "I'm going to bed. You can sleep in the guest room."

"Guest room?"

"I didn't stutter. I assume you remember where the clean linens are. Good night, Maxwell." She left him standing there with his mouth hanging open.

An hour later she was still having trouble sleeping, so Sabrina got up and went into her office. Maxwell found her in there thirty minutes later. "I missed you. What are you doing up so late?"

"I couldn't get comfortable, so I decided to come in here and do some work."

"What kind of work?"

"I was going over my bank statements," she lied. They actually belonged to her mother, but both of their names were listed on the account.

Maxwell looked over her shoulder. "This is impressive. You should think about investing. You'd get a better return on your money."

Sabrina looked up at him. "I own quite a few shares in Microsoft, Disney, and a few other companies. But I would like to find a way to double this."

"There are ways to double, even triple your money. Tell you what. I'll research some things and get back to you."

"You'd do that for me?"

"I love you, Sabrina. I want the best for my lady."

She gave him a skeptical look. "You're not just saying this to get back into my bed, are you?"

Maxwell pointed at himself. "Who, me? Would I do something like that?"

Laughing, Sabrina took him by the arm. "Come on. Let's go to bed." Maxwell was back in her good graces. He was going to help her make some money. Her mother would be thrilled.

Two days later, Maxwell called and said, "What are you doing?"

"Nothing. Why?"

"I was thinking about coming to see you. Actually, I'm in the car and on my way there right now."

"How far away are you?" Sabrina's eyes bounced around the den. Everything looked okay. She ran her fingers through her short hair.

"I'm about half an hour away."

"What's wrong? You miss me?"

He laughed. "I love you, and yeah, I miss you."

"I'll see you when you get here." Sabrina didn't care what the reason was behind Maxwell's visit. She was thrilled that he'd decided to come back before the weekend. She'd been a little fearful that he might not return after her announcement. She meant what she'd said, however. Sabrina would not hang around if Maxwell wasn't interested in marrying her.

Maxwell arrived with a dozen white roses. "I thought about what you said, baby. And you're right. Let's get married."

Sabrina couldn't believe her ears. "What did you just say?"

"You heard me. Let's get married. Right away."

"Yes." Sabrina threw her hands around his neck and wrapped her legs around his waist. *"Yes!"* she screamed.

When Maxwell pulled out a tiny ring box, Sabrina thought she would faint. She held her breath while he opened it. The ring was a princess-cut diamond, and she estimated it to be at least three carats. She wanted to do flips across the room but held her composure.

"Put it on my finger," Sabrina urged. "Hurry. Put it on my finger. I want to see how it looks."

Maxwell did as he was told. "Baby, I wish you could see your face."

"I'm happy. I've never been so happy in my entire life. All my dreams are coming true." Sabrina pulled his head to hers. "Thank you, Maxwell."

The next day Sabrina was supposed to meet Tangie at the clinic at noon. They both had taken sick leave, but now that Maxwell was in town, Sabrina wanted to spend the day with him. They also had a wedding to plan.

Maxwell wanted to get married on the day before Christmas, which was fine with Sabrina. She didn't want a long engagement either. They were now one week away from Thanksgiving, so that didn't give them much time.

Around ten, she called Tangie. "I know I promised to go with you to the clinic, but I can't. You're not go—"

Tangie angrily cut her off. "Sabrina, how can you do this to me?"

"I got engaged last night. Maxwell is in town and we've got a lot of planning to do. We're getting married Christmas Eve." Sabrina wanted to have her wedding before Tangie's so that anything her friend did would pale in comparison.

"Congratulations," Tangie said dryly.

"Tangie, don't be mad. This is important to me—"

"What I'm going through is just as important," she snapped. "This *is* my life we're talking about."

"Look, I'm sorry. Why don't you reschedule it for tomorrow? I'll—"

Tangie slammed the phone down in her ear. Sabrina had known Tangie would be upset, but she hadn't expected her to sound so hurt. But right now she was in too good a mood to worry about it.

She and Mamie spent the day going over wedding plans and visiting suitable locations for the reception. Sabrina already had an idea of what she wanted, so the planning portion of it came easily.

That evening, when Maxwell came out of the shower, she was in the middle of her bed with bridal magazines sprawled all over.

"What are you doing?"

"Trying to pick out bridesmaids dresses. What are you doing?"

Maxwell climbed into the bed. He pulled Sabrina to him. "Missing my bride-to-be." He took the magazine out of her hand. "No more wedding talk. Right now I want some loving."

Sabrina giggled and tried to sit back up. "I should make you wait until our wedding night."

"Then we'd have to go to the justice of the peace. I can't wait a month to make love to you."

Straightening her pajama top, Sabrina gave him a sidelong

glance. "You know, I could use your help with this wedding. There's a lot to do in a short time."

Maxwell released a sigh and then sat up in bed. "Do you need any money?"

"No, I'm going to pay for the wedding—you take care of the honeymoon."

"That's fine. Speaking of money . . . it's been really bothering me the way you have that money sitting in your account not earning anything. It's not a good use of your assets."

"What should I do with it?"

"I have a few friends in the music industry, and they're looking for a select few silent partners. These are short-term investments. You can double, even triple your investment."

Sabrina's eyes grew large. "Really?"

"That's what I do, babe. I'm a financial analyst. Think you'd be interested?"

"Sure, I'm interested, but I am going to have to give it some serious thought, Maxwell." She didn't add that she would have to talk to her mother.

"Honey, I wouldn't do anything to hurt you. Right now you're going to miss out on a big deal that's going down soon. I put in some of my own money."

"Is it too late to get in?"

"In a couple of days it will be. You have to have at least twenty-five thousand cash."

"I have that."

"Think about this carefully and get back to me. Because if you're interested we're going to have to move quickly."

The last thing Sabrina wanted to do was let Maxwell down. The man was going to marry her, after all. She had to come up with a way to convince her mother to let him invest the money.

58

All Tangie could think about was having to face a doctor today and hear the verdict. She prayed it wasn't a life sentence.

The knock on Tangie's door startled her. Composing herself, she went to answer it.

"Hey, Sheryl. Come on in." The last thing she wanted was company, but Tangie didn't want to be rude.

When they were seated in the den, she inquired, "What have you been up to?"

"Girl, I met this guy and I think he's the one. We've been seeing each other almost every day."

Smiling, Tangie murmured, "Good for you." She tried to stop her hands from trembling.

Sheryl didn't seem to notice. She just kept on talking. "I can't believe you're engaged. You sure you're ready to settle down?"

"I don't know. I think so. Brandon is a dream come true." And she didn't deserve him. Tangie didn't want to think about what she'd have to say to him. How could she even begin to explain what had happened? She hardly understood it herself.

"Girl, I got something to tell you. You're not going to believe me. Bonita and Leon got married. They eloped."

"Leon married Bonita?"

"Yeah, girl. They went to Vegas and got married. Gonna have a big reception in a couple of weeks."

Sheryl lapsed into a conversation about her latest boyfriend, but Tangie wasn't listening. Her mind was on Sabrina. She wondered how she was going to take all this.

"Tangie, are you listening to me?"

"Of course," she lied. Tangie couldn't concentrate on anything other than her current situation. She was glad when Sheryl finally decided to leave. She loved her to death, but the girl was long-winded. Today Tangie just wasn't in the mood.

Tangie had tried to cancel her evening with Brandon but he insisted on coming over. They sat in her family room not really saying much at all. She was too caught up in her misery to be good company.

"You've been very quiet, sweetheart. What's wrong?"

"Nothing's wrong." Tangie hated lying to Brandon. She searched for an answer to her dilemma. Was there a way to keep this from affecting him in the long run?

Brandon surveyed her face. "You're sure? You look so sad, honey."

"Everything is perfect," she lied. There was just no way she could break the news to him. Brandon didn't deserve this type of misery.

"I couldn't keep my mind off you. All day long I kept thinking about you and this evening. I couldn't wait for the day to end."

Tangie wrapped her arms around him. "You're such a sweetheart. That's why I love you so much."

He kissed her. "I love you too, baby."

Brandon was happy; she could tell just by looking at him.

Tangie could also tell that his feelings for her were real by the way his eyes caressed her body and his gentle touch. He was everything she wanted in a man.

Brandon was such a wonderful man, and he deserved a good woman. Better than her, she sadly acknowledged.

Right now she needed a miracle to get her through this mess. Her heart beseeched her to fall on her knees and pray. All she'd heard from Bonnie and Cordelia and, most recently, Brandon, was how loving God was—well, she didn't see it that way. He was cruel. He had allowed her to find Mr. Right, only to snatch him away from her. He had also possibly handed her a death sentence. She was definitely being punished for all of her sins.

Tangie had been granted a reprieve. The results of her HIV test were negative. She was in tears by the time she reached the car.

"Thank you, God. I don't know why you did this, but I'm so grateful. You won't regret it. I promise."

59

Cordelia sat on Devon's bed playing with Christina. "What are you doing with that foot? Huh?"

"That was Miss Sabrina on the phone," Devon announced when she came into the room. "She wants me to be a bridesmaid in her wedding."

"What did you tell her?" Cordelia wanted to pick up her granddaughter, but her left arm was still a little on the weak side. She stroked the baby's chubby cheek and was awarded a smile.

"I told her I'd do it." Devon sank down on the bed. "Hey, cutie! What are you doing? Playing with Grandma?"

Eyeing her daughter, Cordelia smiled. She was turning out to be a good little mother. "She's such a sweet baby."

"She sure is." Devon broke into laughter. "What? Why are you laughing at your mommy? Do I look funny?" She tickled the bottom of Christina's foot. "Gotcha."

Cordelia joined in the laughter.

Devon picked Christina up and started to rock her. "Mama, have you met this guy Sabrina's marrying?"

"No. Bonnie and Tangie have. They say he's a nice guy. Good looking, which is a big switch for Sabrina."

"Is he rich?"

"His family owns the Haddonfield Hotels."

"Wow! He's loaded. There's hundreds of those hotels all over the world." Devon kissed her baby's forehead. "I hope they'll be happy together."

"They might have a chance if Sabrina learns to keep her mouth closed. Sometimes she talks entirely too much."

"She can work a nerve," Devon agreed. "This Maxwell Smythe really is going to have his hands full with Miss Sabrina."

"He sure is," Cordelia agreed.

Gerald and Devon made Thanksgiving dinner. Cordelia was touched by the gesture. Even though she was still feeling resent-ful, Cordelia realized that she had much to be thankful for.

Bonnie dropped off a red velvet cake, and Cordelia asked her to stay.

"No, this is a family day. I don't want to interrupt."

"You wouldn't be. Besides, you're like family anyway." She grabbed Bonnie gently by the arm and led her over to the couch. "Now have a seat. Devon's changing your goddaughter but they'll be out here shortly. You should see Christina. . . ." Cordelia's voice died when she saw the expression on Bonnie's face. "Are you okay?"

Snapping out of her reverie, Bonnie said, "I was just think-ing about Edgar. I miss him terribly during the holidays. I miss him all the time . . . but during the holidays it's much worse."

"He was a good man. I miss him too."

"Dee, you're really blessed. You have so many people who care about you. And you have such a wonderful daughter and granddaughter." Stealing a look over her shoulder, Bonnie added, "Gerald really cares for you."

Cordelia waved off her comment. "I am lucky." She found

she couldn't consider herself blessed. It wasn't that she didn't think so—she just couldn't say the words right now.

"You're blessed," Bonnie said again. "You know, for years I've felt so lonely, Dee. I felt like nobody in the world cared for me—"

Cordelia cut her off. "That's not true, Bonnie."

"I know. I learned that I was so busy caring about other people, I didn't care for myself. I had to learn to love myself, and it's not been easy. There were days when it was downright hard."

"You've always been there for everyone, but I guess we were too involved in our own problems to think of you. I'm so sorry, Bonnie." Cordelia embraced her. "You have been a wonderful friend. I want you to know that."

"One of the things that has come out of my journey is that I have a talent and I've found a way to use it. You know the quilts I've made? Well, I've made some that have a family's history on them. Some with pictures and family trees. I'm going to do that—help families preserve their history on quilts."

"That's a wonderful idea, Bonnie. I like it. In fact, I wouldn't mind having one of those. My old family Bible is so worn, it's not going to hold up much longer. I would love to pass a quilt on to Christina."

60

Bonnie parked her car and climbed out. Walking around the car to the other side, she opened the door and took out a quilt encased in plastic. She carried it gently toward the front door and rang the doorbell.

A young woman appeared. Smiling, she said, "Come in, Miss Bonnie."

"I was in the area, so I thought I'd just deliver this quilt to your grandmother. I brought your pictures back too."

"She's gonna love it. This looks just like the other one. The difference is that this one will have photos of our family. Have a seat and I'll go get Nana."

Bonnie did as she was told.

Molly Odell made her way slowly into the living room. "Bonnie, it's good to see you, dear."

"How are you feeling today, Mrs. Odell?" she inquired.

"Today is a good day."

Bonnie broke into a small laugh. "I understand."

"You're such a dear." The woman ran her hand over the pattern. "This is beautiful." Her eyes filled with tears. "It looks just like the one I lost in the fire. That one had been in my mother's family for years."

Bonnie held back her own tears. It gave her such joy to see the happiness on the face of Mrs. Odell. She was the oldest member of their church and a real sweetheart.

"Thank you so much. You have no idea how much this means to an old woman like me."

"The pleasure is all mine, Mrs. Odell. I know how much your mother's quilt meant to you."

"This one will become a part of the Odell legacy, thanks to your kindness."

The old woman's words and tears of joy were worth more than any amount of money Bonnie could ever receive.

61

"The seamstress finished the alterations on your gown. You can pick it up tomorrow," Mamie announced when Sabrina walked into the house.

"Thanks. Did you pay her?"

"Of course. You asked me to, didn't you?"

Sabrina sat down on the sofa beside her mother. "Maxwell and I have been talking. He knows of a way you can double your money."

"Things are fine the way they are, honey."

"But you could have more—you could get yourself a new house or a car."

"I don't want a new house or a new car." Mamie smiled. "Honey, I know you think you're helping, but don't worry about it. I don't mind doing the things I do for you. I'm okay financially. You don't have to try to replace the money I've given you."

Sabrina hadn't even considered that idea, but she went along with it. "Mama, you do so much for me. . . ."

"Just put it out of your mind. I'm all right. That money got me through my lean years—I don't see fit to mess with it now, Sabrina."

"Whatever you say, Mama," Sabrina replied.

Maxwell called as soon as she got home. "Hey, baby. Where have you been?"

"I was over at my mother's house."

"Have you given any thought to what we talked about? I know how important it is for a woman to have her own security. We can double your money, and you don't have to worry—I won't touch it. You have my word."

"It's our money, Maxwell. What's mine is yours." However, the money she was referring to belonged to her mother. But as soon as she and Maxwell married, she would receive a monthly allowance three times her salary. He would never know the truth.

"I can come down to Bridgeport tomorrow and pick up a check—"

"Excuse me?"

"The check. You remember what we talked about? I'm going to invest it."

"How soon can we double it?"

"Thirty, forty-five days at the max. This is not something long-term. We get in and we get out. Just like that."

"Are you sure about this?"

"Honey, I would never lead you wrong. Look, if you're worried, don't do it."

"No. I trust you, Maxwell."

"Sabrina, if something goes wrong, I'll just give you the money back. Better yet, I'll have an agreement drawn up."

"You don't have to do that."

"No, I want to. I want you to know that you can trust me."

They made plans for Maxwell to come up to her job and pick up the check.

Sabrina hung up with mixed emotions.

*   *   *

Sabrina ignored the doubts in the back of her mind. She'd been up most of last night trying to decide if what she was about to do was the right thing. She was standing in her office holding a check for over thirty thousand dollars. This was her mother's entire life savings. But then again, Maxwell said he was bringing a letter from his attorney. She didn't know why, but it gave her no comfort.

She didn't want to hurt her mother. Mamie Mayhew had been good to her—probably more so than she actually deserved. How did she pay her back? By lying to her and manipulating her. Sabrina had even instigated the breakup of her mother's marriage.

"You're in deep thought."

She turned in her chair. "Hey, Brandon."

"Having prewedding jitters?" he teased.

Smiling, Sabrina shook her head. "That's probably the one thing I'm really sure about. What are you doing up here; dare I ask?"

He laughed. "Where is my fiancée? She's not in her office."

"I haven't seen her much today. She's around here somewhere, though." Tangie hadn't had much to do with her since the day Sabrina had bailed out on her. Sabrina had tried to apologize twice, but the gesture was met with silence.

She heard Maxwell's voice and rushed to her feet. "My honey's here."

Brandon laughed. "Let me get out of the way before you run me down."

"Funny," Sabrina shot back. She brushed past him and greeted Maxwell with a kiss on the cheek.

"Hello, sweetie."

"Hi, yourself," he said. "You look beautiful."

"Thank you." Taking him by the hand, Sabrina led him to her office. "I have something for you."

Once inside the cubicle, she handed him a key. "This is for

you. Since we're going to be married in a couple of weeks, I though you might need a key." Smiling, Sabrina said, "You know, this is a pretty special moment. You are the first man I've ever given a key to my home."

Maxwell just stood there staring at the key in his hand. She couldn't read his expression, but Sabrina assumed he'd be happy.

"Well?"

He raised his eyes to hers. "What?"

"I thought you'd be happy."

"I am. I guess I was expecting something else."

Confused, Sabrina asked, "What? What were you expecting?"

Maxwell lowered his voice. "I guess you changed your mind about the investment."

"No," she mumbled. "No, I haven't. I just wanted to give you the key."

Maxwell wrapped his arms around her. "Thank you, baby. I'm honored. Really, I am. I wasn't surprised about the key because we're going to be married."

Sabrina pulled the check out of her pocket. "Here you go."

Maxwell kissed her as he took the check from her. "I have something for you, too." He pulled out a legal-looking document. "Here's the agreement."

"I told you that you didn't have to do this."

"This is business, honey. I'll take care of pleasure this evening when you get home."

"You're staying?"

"Just for tonight. I need to get back to Durham tomorrow."

Sabrina spotted Claire coming in their direction. "I'll see you when I get home. My supervisor is heading my way. Probably with another one of her projects for me." She couldn't wait until she and Maxwell were married. She was only going to work up until the week before her wedding.

Sabrina had originally given her notice the week after Thanksgiving, but Claire and Bonnie had both asked her to reconsider, which she did. Now she regretted her decision. *Oh, well*... She only had another week. She could manage that. At least tonight she would leave work and go home to Maxwell.

The last time Sabrina saw Maxwell was when he came to her office to pick up the check. That had been one week ago. She'd called the hotel and was told that he'd checked out with no forwarding address.

She sat cross-legged in the middle of her bed, her eyes swollen from crying. She hadn't been to work for the last three days and had no intention of going in tomorrow. Sabrina couldn't even summon up the strength to get out of bed and shower.

She heard her front door opening and closing. Hope welled inside her, and Sabrina jumped out of bed. She ran out of the room, nearly knocking her mother down. "Mama, what are you doing here?"

"Girl, you nearly scared the life out of me." Mamie put a hand to her chest. "For goodness' sake."

"I thought you were Maxwell."

"I came here to check on you. Why haven't you gone to work? I've been calling and there's been no answer. What's going on with you?" She surveyed Sabrina carefully. "When was the last time you showered?"

"Maxwell's disappeared. I think he's been kidnapped."

"Girl, please. He's probably out of town. You can be so dramatic at times."

"I've tried to call his cell phone but it's been disconnected. They said he's checked out of the hotel too."

"Honey, that don't sound like a kidnapping. It sounds like he's moved on."

"We're supposed to get married next weekend. He wouldn't do this to me, Mama. I know him."

Mamie didn't look like she was so sure.

"He loves me. Something happened to him. I just know it."

"Have you talked to his parents? Maybe they can tell you what's going on."

"They're out of the country most of the time."

"Somebody at the hotel has to know how to reach them, Sabrina. You go on in that bathroom and take a long bath. You'll feel like a new woman afterward. In the meantime, I'll make some calls."

Sabrina was relieved to have her mother with her at a time like this. She did as she was told. Her mother was right—she felt much better after her bath.

Mamie had a strange look on her face.

"What's wrong, Mama? Something happened to Maxwell, didn't it?"

"I . . . Honey, his parents didn't even know he was getting married. His mother said they hadn't spoken to him in years."

"That's not true. They were just in Durham five months ago visiting him. Why are they lying?"

"His mother said they had the hotel in Durham close his account. They hadn't known he was there until someone called from the finance department. From what I could gather, he's the black sheep of the family. She asked if you were pregnant when I told her about you."

Sabrina felt sick inside. This could not be happening to her. After all of her careful planning . . .

"Baby, I hate to say this, but I think this man pulled a fast one on you. I told his mother that he'd better stay gone, 'cause if I ever got my hands on him, I was gonna hang 'im high."

Sabrina shook her head sadly. "Mama, he wouldn't do this. He wouldn't do this to me." The realization loomed before her. She'd been left nearly at the altar. *What am I going to say to everyone?* she wondered wildly.

"I'm so sorry, my sweet baby. Well, maybe it's best that it ended early."

Sabrina suddenly remembered the check. Nausea consumed her and she stumbled to the toilet. She wanted to die.

62

Tangie was worried about Sabrina, so after work she decided to pay her a visit. As she drove, she tried to remember whether there had been any indication of her being sick in recent days. The truth was that Tangie had been very distant with Sabrina since she'd backed out of going to the clinic with her. Now she felt a small measure of guilt.

Her mother opened the door and greeted her.

Laying her purse on the sofa, she hugged Mamie. "I've been so worried about Sabrina. How's she doing? It's not like her to miss so many days of work."

"She's taking it hard. She's been in bed all day long. I had to make her get up and take a shower."

Confused, Tangie asked, "Does she have the flu?"

Mamie shook her head. "Oh, goodness, no. Sabrina's not sick. She's heartbroken. Maxwell's gone."

"Gone?"

"That rat has gone somewhere—he had no intention of marrying my Sabrina. His parents' didn't even know he was engaged."

"Oooh, no. I know she's devastated. Where is she now?"

"She's back in bed. I finally got her to stop crying." Mamie shook her head in dismay. "I don't know why this happened. Sabrina doesn't deserve this."

"May I see her?"

"Go on. It'll do her good to have a close friend nearby."

Tangie made her way to Sabrina's bedroom and knocked softly on the bedroom door. "Sabrina, it's me, Tangie," she announced softly.

"Come in," came a muffled voice.

Sabrina sounded so sad it was heartbreaking. In all the time that she'd known her, Tangie had never seen her so down. She couldn't even remember ever seeing her without makeup. Her eyes were swollen from crying and her hair was simply tousled on her head. For once, Sabrina didn't seem to care.

"Hey, girl," Tangie said.

"What are you doing here?"

"Something told me you might need a friend. Your mother just told me what happened."

Sabrina's eyes filled with tears and overflowed. "What did I do to deserve this?"

"Nobody deserves to be treated in this manner. You can't blame yourself, Sabrina."

"Leon was the only one who cared about me. I'm sure of that."

Tangie didn't respond.

"He wasn't ready to settle down. I know that much. Maybe if I'd been more patient with him, things would have been different. I never told him how I felt about him."

"You didn't?" She was surprised.

Sabrina shook her head. "I loved him so much, Tangie. It was just something about him—he could make me laugh, but then he could make me so mad. . . ." Sabrina started to cry.

Tangie passed her the box of tissues off her nightstand.

Wiping her face and blowing her nose, Sabrina climbed out of bed. "I'll be right back." She rushed to the bathroom.

Tangie heard water running and then the door opened. Sabrina had washed her face and combed her hair.

"I've been thinking about giving Leon a call."

"Why?"

"Just to talk. I could see where his head is at. I don't mean it the way you think. I just want to know if I'm right."

"About what? His feelings for you? You already said that you know he cares for you."

"I could be wrong. I thought Maxwell cared about me as well. I was wrong. Tangie, I'm just not real sure of anything anymore. I've messed up big-time."

"What are you talking about?"

"Mama spent so much money on this wedding. It was going to be classy and very elegant." Staring off into space, Sabrina repeated, "So much money."

"I'm sorry."

"Tangie, I did something horrible. I gave Maxwell money. A lot of money."

"Like how much?"

"Thirty thousand dollars."

"Stop lying."

"Girl, this is one time I wish it were a lie. Maxwell is a financial analyst—" Sabrina stopped short at the look Tangie gave her. "Well, that's what he said he was. Anyway, he was going to double the money for me."

"Where in the world did you get thirty thousand?"

"It was my mother's savings. My father's family gave it to her after he died. They gave her fifty thousand—she only touched it when she really needed it."

"What possessed you to give him that money?"

"He said he could double it—I believed him, Tangie. He even gave me a legal document saying that he would replace the money should the venture fail."

"Sabrina, the letter could be worthless."

"Maybe not." She brightened up. "I'll call that attorney in the morning. I don't care about marrying Maxwell or the Smythe millions anymore—in fact, I don't ever want to lay eyes on him again. I just want my mother's money back."

Tangie could hardly believe what she was hearing. Sabrina had never not worried about money. Perhaps it took something like this to change her for the better. It was definitely something she could understand. She had been struggling with whether she should tell Brandon the truth. But seeing Sabrina in all this pain, she decided to leave well enough alone.

63

Cordelia stood at the back of the church staring up at the pulpit. Pastor Grant was talking to one of the deacons. Her eyes bounced around, looking at the various artistic renditions of Jesus Christ.

The only reason she'd come was for Christina's christening. Cordelia could not disappoint her daughter by not attending. She took a deep breath and then exhaled slowly. She walked slowly, supporting herself with the quad cane. She nodded in greeting to a few familiar faces.

Cordelia was tired by the time she made it to her seat, three rows from the front pew. Gerald joined her there a few minutes later.

Right before the service started, Cordelia saw the Bradshaw family come in. They were seated right behind her. She turned around to greet them. Cordelia couldn't resist sending a glare in Tonio's direction.

Cordelia was pleased that Devon had moved on. Between working and taking care of Christina, the poor girl barely had time for herself.

The choir stood up to sing, capturing Cordelia's attention. She met the gaze of Pastor Grant. She awarded him a tiny smile, then looked away like a disobedient child. Being back here in the church made her nervous. Cordelia felt as if she could feel the very eyes of God on her, watching and waiting. . . .

What do You want of me? her heart questioned. *I trusted You and believed in You with all my heart. You let me down.* Her disappointment in God lent itself to tears. Cordelia pulled a tissue from her purse and wiped them away.

Gerald glanced over at her but didn't say a word. He just embraced her.

Cordelia leaned into him, needing his strength right now. She was so confused at the moment. Gerald had been going home three days a week to check on his clients and caseload. She knew that he would be moving back to Raleigh permanently soon. It had been only in recent weeks that she was able to sleep through the night without fear of another stroke. She had regained most of her functional abilities and was getting stronger every day. The one thing she constantly avoided was resuming her relationship with God.

Why?

The question leaped from her heart.

She was still angry with God for allowing the stroke to happen. Cordelia realized that it was through His grace that she was able to recover—even being alive was a blessing bestowed by God. *I know all this, yet I'm still very angry.* Her eyes filled with tears. *You hurt me, God. You scared me with the stroke. I've never been so scared in my entire life.* When her Christina had died, her grief drew Cordelia closer to God. She needed her faith just to help her make it through each day. God had saved her. The stroke had not only crippled her—it crippled her faith as well.

The ceremony began.

Cordelia was pleased with Devon's choice for Christina's godmother. Bonnie would do a fabulous job. She'd noticed all the subtle changes in her friend's personality that had taken place over the last few months. Bonnie was finally coming into her own.

She smiled when Christina squealed from the pulpit. The baby objected strongly to having water sprinkled in her face.

Cordelia was hardly aware of Gerald taking her hand in his. She didn't look over at him, instead settling back to enjoy the rest of the service.

64

Bonnie kissed the forehead of her sleeping godchild. "You are so precious, sweetheart." This was the closest she would ever come to having a child, and she didn't plan on wasting one moment of it. She laid the baby inside her traveling playpen, which had been set up in one corner of the den. Scotty was locked in her bedroom, so she wasn't worried about him bothering Christina or any of the other guests.

She ventured off into the kitchen to take out another vegetable tray. Tangie followed her.

"Do you need help with anything, Bonnie?"

"Thank you, but no. Just sit down and enjoy yourself. Brandon couldn't make it?"

"He was at the church earlier. The single men at his church are getting together today. He's one of the coordinators, so he couldn't get out of it."

"I understand. How is Sabrina feeling? I thought for sure she would come to the christening."

"She's really embarrassed, but it's also been pretty hard on her, Bonnie. But you know Sabrina. She's not going to be down for long."

"It was terrible how Maxwell treated her."

"You don't know the half of it," Tangie said cryptically. "Sabrina's gunning for him now. She's giving his parents a fit."

"Why?"

"Because she believes they know exactly where Maxwell is and just won't tell her."

"Maybe it's for the best," Bonnie pointed out. "If I were him, I'd be very scared. I wouldn't want Sabrina as an enemy."

Tangie burst into laughter. "I hadn't thought of it that way, but you're absolutely right. Maxwell should be scared."

Bonnie moved about her house, nodding and waving to guests. It had been a long time since she'd had so many people in her house. She loved it. Her home had life once more, like it used to when Edgar was still alive.

"Oh, Bonnie, you have a lovely home. Thank you for inviting us," one of her guests said.

"Thank you for coming," Bonnie replied. "And please come back. Don't be a stranger."

Every now and then she stole a glance at the photo of Edgar on the fireplace. Bonnie smiled because she knew he was with her in spirit, sharing in her happiness. They were four days into the new year, and she felt that this one was filled with lots of promise. "Thank you, God," she whispered in prayer. "Thank you for showing me how to live again."

65

Sabrina stared down at the legal document in her hands. "I don't believe this. Elwood's suing me." Tossing the papers on the couch, she curled her hands into fists. First Claire had given her a written warning for being late, and now she was being sued for ten thousand dollars. "Jesus, why is this happening to me?" she cried. "What have I done to deserve all this?"

"Goodness! What's wrong with you?"

Sabrina wiped away a tear. "I'm just having a very bad day, Tangie."

"I heard Claire was giving you a hard time. You need to get out of this office. Why don't we take a walk?"

"For what? It's not going to do me any good. Nothing will change. I'll still be embarrassed and humiliated. To make matters worse, Elwood Brown—that rat—is suing me for ten thousand dollars."

Tangie's mouth dropped open in surprise.

"Yeah. Can you believe that?"

"Why is he doing that? Did he loan you money?"

Sabrina shook her head. "He's mad because I dumped him

for Maxwell. Now he wants me to pay him back all the money he spent on me."

"He's angry right now. Maybe he'll calm down and forget about this lawsuit."

"I don't know, Tangie. He was really mad."

"He probably feels used."

"Well, he shouldn't," she snapped. "I never made any promises to him—I never even told him I cared about him. In fact, he didn't have to do any of those things he did for me. I really should have just stayed with Leon. Then none of this mess would be happening."

"Sabrina . . ."

She grew impatient. "Well, what is it?"

"There's something you should know about Leon."

"What?"

"I probably should have told you sooner, but it just—"

"Just tell me, Tangie," Sabrina cut in. "Lord knows I can't take the suspense any longer."

Clearing her throat, Tangie said, "This is probably going to make your day worse, but I think you have to know." She took a deep breath before continuing. "Leon and Bonita got married."

Sabrina paled. Clearing her throat, she asked, "Excuse me?"

"Leon's married," Tangie repeated.

"How long have you known about this?" Her tone had turned terse.

"Sabrina, I heard about it a couple of months ago. You were so happy with Maxwell—I didn't feel the need to tell you. I'm sorry."

"You know how I feel about him—why wouldn't I want to know?"

"I thought you'd moved on, Sabrina. I had no idea that you still had feelings for Leon. I assumed you were in love with Maxwell."

Sabrina was furious. "I still had a right to know. I thought you were my friend." Putting a hand to her face, she asked, "Why is everyone betraying me?"

"I'm sorry. I wasn't trying to betray you. Really, I wasn't."

She wasn't listening anymore. Sabrina wasn't sure how much more she could take. "I can't deal with this right now. Could you leave me alone, Tangie?"

After calming down at the end of the long day, Sabrina could understand why Tangie didn't say anything sooner. She was only trying to protect her. Now she was ashamed of her actions earlier. Before she knew it, Sabrina found herself standing in the doorway of Tangie's home with a peace offering—pizza.

"Hello, Sabrina. I just tried to call you." Tangie stepped aside so that she could enter.

Putting the pizza on the coffee table, Sabrina said, "I want to apologize for the way I acted earlier. It was just too much at once."

"I understand. I'm really sorry about the way I handled the situation. We're friends and I should have told you."

"Tangie, you were only looking out for me, and I really appreciate it. I'm so lucky to have a friend like you. As you know, I don't have many, so I cherish you dearly."

They embraced.

"I feel the same way about you," Tangie responded. "I still feel bad, though. I should have said something about Leon and Bonita getting married."

"Well, let's forget it," Sabrina suggested. "May Leon and Bonita be miserable for the rest of their lives."

"Wait! Let me get some sodas and we'll toast properly. In the meantime, find a movie and put it in the VCR."

While Tangie was in the kitchen, Sabrina fingered the collection of videos stored in the bottom of Tangie's oak bookshelf. She spotted one stuck way in the back, and her curiosity kicked in. There was no label, which further piqued her interest. Most likely it was something Tangie had recorded off the television. "Hope it doesn't have any commercials." She stuck it in the VCR.

"Find something?" Tangie asked. She carried a glass of soda in each hand. "I hope you picked out something good to watch."

"Me too," Sabrina muttered.

Tangie dropped down on the floor beside her. "Okay, start the movie."

When a naked Leon appeared on the screen, Sabrina's eyes opened wide with shock, but when she noticed that the naked woman on the bed was Tangie, she dropped popcorn all over the floor. "Oh, my God . . ."

Sabrina turned to look at her friend. "Y-you and Leon. How long has this been going on?"

"Sabrina, listen to me. This happened a long, long time ago. There has never been anything else between me and Leon. I swear to you."

Pointing at the TV, Sabrina screamed, "You call this nothing? Apparently he wasn't enough man for you—is that why you had to try his friend too?" Tears streamed down her face. "Everything makes so much sense now. You never wanted us together. You wanted Leon for yourself."

"Leon and I were only together that one time, and it happened long before he met you and Bonita. I was in college and he was still in the military. It was only about sex, Sabrina— nothing but sex."

"Why did you keep the tape?"

"I really don't know. I never look at it, Sabrina. I wanted to forget it."

"This is what you won't talk about, isn't it? All the little freaky things you like to do in bed."

"What are you talking about?"

"I know about all your little sex toys upstairs by your bed. Now I see you're into videos—"

"What?" Tangie interjected. "How do you know what's in my bedroom drawers? Have you been going through my things, Sabrina?" She put a hand to her mouth. "Oh, my God, you have. . . . I've noticed that things looked moved around."

Sabrina didn't respond. She was too angry to speak.

"You're standing here in my house talking about friendship and you've been invading my privacy—breaking what little trust I had in you." Tangie picked up the pizza and threw it on Sabrina. "Get out of my house, you witch!"

"I'll be glad to. I don't want to be around a ho any longer than I have to," she uttered nastily. "I should have known though, since you run around with that slut Sheryl." Picking up a glass of soda, she tossed it at Tangie's feet. "That's to go with your pizza."

Sabrina stormed out of Tangie's town house as fast as her feet could take her. Once she made it to her car, she drove to an empty parking lot and screamed in fury.

Sabrina wasn't ready to go home, so she continued to drive around town. She stopped long enough to pick up a bottle of cognac, then drove awhile longer. Her next stop was Brandon's apartment. She knocked on his door as loud as she could.

He was clearly surprised to see her at his door. "Hey, come in."

She followed him into the apartment. Sabrina glimpsed the photograph of Tangie on the end table. Picking it up, she asked, "Have you spoken to Tangie?"

"Not today. I was planning to call her later. Why?"

"Brandon, I have to apologize to you. I introduced you guys, but now I think I've made a terrible mistake. You can't marry her."

"What are you talking about? Sabrina, I know things didn't work out for you—"

"That's not it at all, Brandon. I'm trying to tell you that

Tangie has not been honest with any of us. She's . . . she's not what we think she is."

"What are you trying to say?"

"She's a ho, Brandon. The woman you want to marry is a ho. She may also have HIV—some guy recently told her he might have infected her with the disease. He's dead now."

"Sabrina, you're drunk. Why don't you have a seat and I'll call Tangie over to come drive you home. It's just the alcohol talking."

"I don't want Tangie anywhere near me," Sabrina shouted. "She and my ex-boyfriend were lovers." She started to cry. "I thought she was my friend."

Brandon sat down beside her, wrapping an arm around her shoulder to console her. "Start from the beginning. What's going on?"

66

Tangie was on the lookout for Sabrina the next morning, but she never showed up. Bonnie told her later that she'd called in sick. She tried reaching her at home, but apparently Sabrina was screening her calls. There was still some confusion on her part—how did things get so out of control? She and Sabrina really needed to talk, although Tangie wasn't sure she could forgive her for invading her privacy.

"You're not going to call me a whore and hide from me," she muttered. Tangie decided she would stop by Sabrina's condo after work.

Brandon suddenly loomed in the entrance of her office. "Tangie, I need to talk with you."

She greeted him warmly. "I was just about to call you."

Normally he always had a smile for her, but today he looked so grim.

Tangie's smile vanished. "Honey, what's wrong? You look upset."

"Can you take an early lunch? I'd like to talk to you."

"Sure. Just let me get my purse." Tangie rose to her feet and grabbed her handbag. The air between them was taut. She took several deep breaths to calm her palpitating heart.

Brandon drove over to a nearby park. They got out and walked over to a picnic table. Once they sat down, he asked, "Do you have something to tell me?"

Tangie had a feeling something was terribly wrong. Her hands suddenly felt weak and clammy. "What are you talking about, Brandon?"

"I think you know," he replied.

Tangie didn't know what to say. She suddenly felt sick inside. Sabrina had taken their fight to another level. She'd gone to Brandon.

"For starters, Tangie, tell me about Danny—and about Leon. How could you do that to Sabrina? She was your friend."

Tangie recovered from her shock. "Honey, I can explain everything."

"I can understand your not telling me about Leon. But Danny . . . You were going through something that could change your entire life—you didn't want to share that with me?"

"I didn't know how to tell you, Brandon. I know I was wrong, but I was so scared. Not only of having HIV, but of losing you."

"Tangie, I love you. I believed you loved me too—"

"I do," she cut him off. "Brandon, I love you with my entire being."

"If we're going to get married, we need honesty between us, Tangie; I mean it. There can only be honesty between the two of us from now on."

Her hand shook in reaching out for his. Brandon was right, and he was owed the truth. Tangie was in a world of conflicting emotions.

"What is it, honey? We can talk about anything."

"Brandon, there's something else I need to tell you."

"What is it?"

Tangie averted her eyes to shield her anxieties. "This is not easy, but I owe you this much." She met his gaze and took a deep breath before continuing. "Brandon, I love you so much. You are the first man I've ever said this to—the first time I've ever felt this way. But you have to understand that I was in a bad place before I met you. Trusting a man was out of the question."

Brandon never took his eyes off her face.

"Leon wasn't the only time I've done something like that. There were no videos or anything like that—however, there are times when I get these urges . . . sexual urges. Anyway, I'd go and find a man to have sex with. That's all I wanted—sex. I didn't care who they were, and once it was over . . . I just wanted them to disappear. Then I started to feel different afterward. I started to feel guilty."

"Did you have these urges while we were together?" Brandon asked quietly.

His eyes seemed weighed down with disappointment, and Tangie felt her own fill with tears. If she said another word, she was going to lose Brandon.

"Tangie, are you going to answer the question? Did you have these urges while we were together?"

"Yes," she whispered. Tangie knew exactly what was coming next.

"Did you act on them?"

God, I've kept my word. Do I have to lose Brandon too? Please don't do this to me. I'll do whatever I have to do. Tangie had never prayed much in her life, and she didn't really know how, but she was willing to learn. *Help me out of this, God. Please.*

"Tangie, did you sleep with other men while we were involved?"

Breaking into a sob, she nodded. Tangie couldn't say the words.

Brandon didn't reach out to comfort her. He just sat there beside her, staring out into space.

Tangie could almost feel his heart withdrawing from hers. This was too much for Brandon. An apology wasn't enough, she knew.

"We should get back to the office."

Wiping her face, Tangie glanced over at him. "Work? You think I can just go back to work like this?"

"I'll drop you off at your car then. I have to get back."

"Brandon, we need to talk about all this. . . . We can't leave things unsaid."

"We should have talked a long time ago. It's too late now. I'm not sure I even know who you are."

"I see." She wasn't surprised. She'd known from the beginning this was where they would end.

Tangie was in luck.

She pulled up just in time to see Sabrina getting out of her car. Tangie resisted the temptation to run her over. She parked her SUV and stormed over to her former friend.

Sabrina was clearly surprised to see her. "Tangie—"

"How dare you run to Brandon. Don't bother denying it, because I know you were the one. I just spoke to him."

"I felt he had a right to know the type of woman he was marrying. But don't worry—I'm sure he's going to forgive you. It wasn't like you cheated on him or something."

"You had no right telling Brandon anything. I should have been the one."

"I agree with you on that, but the fact remains that you didn't, Tangie."

"You don't care about me or Brandon. You're just mad that I had sex with Leon. What made you so angry?" she snapped. "The fact that he said on the tape he could spend the rest of his life with me?"

Sabrina glared at her. "This is not the time or place. I did it—I told Brandon and I can't take it back."

"Stay out of my life, Sabrina! If you don't you're going to be sorry. You mess with me and I will destroy you."

Tangie was seething by the time she arrived at her mother's house. She got out of the car, slamming the door behind her.

"Boy, you sure are in a foul mood," Lula observed. "Bad day at the office?"

"The worst day of my life. Actually, it's one of a few."

"I'm so sorry to hear that. What's going on with you? Do you want to talk about it?"

Tangie turned to leave. "You know, this is not a good day, Lula. I think I should just be alone."

Lula stood in her path. "You were upset the last time you came here. I'm not going to let you walk out again. That bothered me for a long time." She took Tangie by the hand and led her to the sofa. "Talk to me, honey. Now, I know something's been bothering you for a while. Tangie, I may not have been a good mother, but I am a good listener."

"Sabrina and I had a fight last night. And then this morning Brandon and I had a fight, too. Sabrina is the cause of my fighting with Brandon."

"I see."

"No, you don't. You don't have a clue as to what I'm talking about."

"Then why don't you tell me?"

Tangie started with the letter from Danny and brought Lula up to speed. "I felt I owed him the truth."

"Sabrina had no right to do this to you."

"Maybe I was wrong in keeping secrets about Leon from Sabrina. But I've had it with her."

"Forget about Sabrina. Is it something you and Brandon can get past?"

"I don't know, Lula. That's what really scares me. I could lose him over this situation."

Embracing her, Lula murmured, "Honey, I'm so sorry."

"I just hate Sabrina so much. All of this is her fault."

"You're just very angry right now."

"I'm never going to forgive her," Tangie vowed. "Never."

"Honey, Sabrina didn't know about the men," Lula reminded her.

Tangie wiped away a tear with her hand. "How could I be so stupid?"

"I don't think you were acting out of stupidity. I think it was something more."

Giving Lula a sidelong glance, she asked, "Like what?"

"I think it's a problem we both have. We're addicted to sex. Only I crave married men."

Tangie frowned. "Sex addiction?" She broke into a laugh. "I don't think so. At least not me."

"Do you enjoy those encounters?"

"I used to—I found them intensely exciting—but no, not the last few times. I mean, I love sex. . . ."

"Can you go more than a day without it?"

Tangie didn't respond. It had been hard. She'd been faithful to Brandon since their engagement. But then three days after finding out she was HIV negative, Tangie had picked up a guy in a mall in Fayetteville. After that, she'd vowed no more.

"Hon, did you hear me?" Lula questioned.

"I don't think I can. There are times when I'm stronger. . . . I think I might have a problem." Tangie burst into tears.

Lula pulled her close. "We're going to deal with this, honey. The two of us together. I won't let you down this time."

67

Cordelia burst into laughter. She and Gerald sat in the den watching a rented movie. She reached over and stuck her hand in the bowl of popcorn.

"How is Sabrina doing?" Gerald asked suddenly. "Did they ever find that guy?"

"Not that I know of. As for Sabrina, she's resilient. She's humiliated, but in a way it's hard to feel sorry for her. She's so self-centered."

"That she is."

"I feel bad for her mother, though. He took her life savings. It's so strange, Gerald. His family owned the Haddonfield Hotels—he didn't need the money, so why did he do it?"

"I heard he and his parents have been estranged for years. They basically pay him to stay away. He's always been a problem child."

Tossing Gerald a look, she asked, "Do you think this guy has done this before?"

He nodded. "I'm sure of it. He probably thought Sabrina

had some money. He probably goes from place to place swindling unsuspecting women. It'll catch up with him eventually."

"Poetic justice, I guess. Sabrina has always wanted a man with cash—turns out she found a man who wanted a woman with money. Such a shame." Cordelia reached for the popcorn but Gerald moved it out of her reach.

"Have you taken your medicine?"

"Yes, I have. Now give me the popcorn," Cordelia said smugly. She was going to miss Gerald when he left next week. She had grown used to having him in the house again.

One year ago, she'd suffered the stroke.

Cordelia stared at the dust-covered Bible on her bookshelf. She hesitated a moment before picking it up and taking it over to the sofa.

Her Bible fell open to the Book of Proverbs. Cordelia's eyes scanned the page, stopping at Chapter Three. Verses five and six jumped right out at her.

Trust in the Lord with all your heart and lean not to your own understanding; in all your ways acknowledge him, and he will direct your paths.

"I want to trust you, Lord. I'm floundering. Help me to find the path back to you."

Faith is not fate. Cordelia felt the hair on the back of her neck stand up. She'd heard Pastor Grant say that once or twice before. She couldn't look at her situation anymore—she had to look beyond it. She had to keep her eyes on God. On his faithfulness.

"I will never understand why things happened the way they did, but I place my trust in you, dear Lord. I repent of all my sins and I want to come back to you."

Gerald entered the room. She gestured for him to join her.

"Today is the anniversary of my stroke. I will never forget how I lay in that bed unable to do anything but cry. Because of God's grace, I am able to walk at times without the cane. I've gained enough strength in my arm to hold my grandbaby. There's something I'd like for us to do—something we didn't do together as a family."

"You want to pray?"

"Yes. Do you mind?"

"No. Besides, you're going to need me to help you get off your knees," Gerald teased.

Cordelia broke into laughter.

They got down on the floor and turned facing the sofa, hands clasped together and heads bent in prayer. Cordelia began. "Dear God, open my eyes that I may see You more clearly. Help me not to blame bad things on You but trust that Your gracious hand strengthens me in and through all things. Open my eyes more each day to Your steadfast and unfailing love through Your son, Jesus Christ."

She gave Gerald a slight nudge.

"Most gracious Father, I thank You for my family and for allowing me this chance to spend time with them again. Help us remember that You are eternal and cannot be overcome. Neither will You fail nor forsake us in our darkest hours. Help us remember the we should cling to You in all times, but especially in sorrow. Let us be still and know that You are with us always. Amen."

"Amen," Cordelia murmured.

68

Everyone navigated out of the conference room. Bonnie noted the way Tangie and Sabrina glared at each other throughout the entire unit meeting. She'd never seen them look so angry with each other.

Pulling Tangie aside, she asked in a low whisper, "My goodness, what is going on between you and Sabrina?"

Frowning, Tangie said, "She doesn't know how to keep her mouth shut. I've been a good friend to her and she stabs me in the back. She was miserable because Maxwell tricked her and she couldn't stand my being happy."

"I kept telling Sabrina that her mouth is going to get her in serious trouble."

"I've had it with her. I'm done."

"You two have been friends for much too long. Don't let this break you up."

"Bonnie, not even you can fix this. Sabrina will not get another chance to screw me over again."

"I'm so sorry."

Shrugging, Tangie uttered, "It's okay. I'm glad that it happened this way."

"I hope you two can work it out."

"It's not likely, Bonnie. I hope you won't be offended if I don't do lunch with you all anymore. I just don't want to be around Sabrina any more than I have to be."

Cordelia called just as she'd sat down at her desk.

"Bonnie, remember when you asked me about going to church this evening with you? Well, I'd like that. We're going to have to bring Christina with us. Devon has a lot of studying to do."

"That's wonderful news. I can't wait to see my goddaughter. I'll be there to pick you up around eight. What made you change your mind?"

"Today is the anniversary of the stroke. I started thinking about the way my life was before it happened. The only thing I've missed was my relationship with God. I want to get it back. I want to open my heart again to him."

"God is so good," Bonnie murmured.

"Yes, he is."

Cordelia told Bonnie about praying with Gerald for the first time in their lives.

"He really cares for you, Dee."

"I know," she admitted. "Gerald's changed a lot since our divorce. I guess I was too angry to notice it before."

"Think there's a chance you two will get back together? I have a feeling you care for him as well."

"Only God knows the answer to that. However, I wouldn't exactly be opposed to it."

They shared a laugh.

"How have things been going at the office?" Cordelia asked "I'm thinking about talking to Human Resources to see if I have a chance at getting my job back—part-time, at first."

"You'll have no problem, Dee. I'm sure of that. Oh, it'll be so good to have you back. Things are getting crazy. Sabrina and Tangie aren't getting along. They had a huge fight."

"What's going on with them?"

Bonnie repeated what Tangie had told her.

69

Sabrina hadn't missed the way Bonnie and Tangie were huddled together in the conference room after the meeting. She had a strong feeling they had been discussing her, and she was on the verge of tears because of it. Tangie had no right going to Bonnie with this situation. It had nothing to do with her.

She wiped away a tear with a trembling hand. For some reason her nerves seemed really bad today. Maybe it was working right beside Tangie and not being able to talk to her.

The phone rang, startling her. Sabrina glanced at the caller ID. It was her mother.

She picked up. "Hey, Mama. How're you doing?"

"I just left the bank," Mamie announced coldly. "They tell me all I have in the account is two thousand dollars. I got a statement yesterday but I was sure they'd made a big mistake."

Her stomach churned with anxiety. "Mama, I can explain—"

"How can you do this to me, Sabrina?" Mamie interrupted. "After all I've done for you."

Sabrina didn't want to be overheard by one of her coworkers, so she said, "I'll come over when I get off work."

"There's no need. I know what happened. You gave my money to Maxwell."

"Mama, I'll pay you back every penny. I promise."

"I never thought . . ." Her mother started to cry.

Sabrina's heart broke. She couldn't stop her own tears from flowing. "I'm so sorry."

Mamie hung up the phone.

She sat at her desk staring at the monitor for almost an hour. Sabrina wiped her face with a tissue. Maxwell had stolen from her, Elwood was suing her, Tangie wasn't talking to her, and now her own mother hated her. This was not the life she'd envisioned for herself.

Maybe there was a way she could fix this mess. She picked up the phone.

"Hello. This is Sabrina."

"I'm surprised to get your call," Elwood confessed. "I figured you'd be married by now. By the way, I'm not sure we should be talking. Have your attorney call mine."

"I don't have an attorney. And I didn't get married. Things didn't work out between Maxwell and me."

He laughed. "I wonder why . . ."

His sarcasm hurt, but Sabrina tried to ignore it. "Elwood, the reason I called is because I treated you terribly and I'm very sorry."

He didn't say a word. He was not going to make it easy on her.

"You have always been good to me."

"Why did you call, Sabrina? What is it that you want? For me to drop the lawsuit? Well, it's not going to happen. I want my money."

She picked at the buttons on her blouse. "I don't want anything, Elwood. I've . . . I've just been doing a lot of thinking about what happened between us."

"What happened is that I was a fool."

"No, you weren't. I was the fool."

Elwood was quiet, prompting her to ask, "Did you hear what I said?"

"I don't think this is a good idea."

"Excuse me?"

"Sabrina, I don't think you should call me anymore. See, I know what this is about. I heard about how your little rich boy ran away with all your mama's money. You think you can call me and shed a few tears, and I'll drop the lawsuit. I'm not falling for it. Tell me something. Was your mother ever really sick?"

"No."

"I don't know what kind of woman you are. . . ." Elwood lapsed into a long list of vile names.

"I deserve all of that. All I can do is apologize. I can't undo the past. I am sorry, Elwood. I'm going to find a way to pay you back."

"What did you say?"

"I'm going to pay you back. The reason I called was to see if we could work out some kind of payment plan. I've got some stock I'm going to try to sell—"

"You're serious?"

"Yes, I am."

Elwood was quiet. After a moment he said, "Look, Sabrina. If you can come up with five thousand dollars I'll write off the other five. But if this is another ploy of yours—"

"It's not. I'll call you in a day or two."

"Good luck, Sabrina."

"Mama, please say you'll forgive me," Sabrina pleaded. "I really thought Maxwell would double the money. I never thought he'd run off with it."

"That's not the point. I told you to leave it alone in the first place. Chile, you don't have any idea how I had to humiliate myself in front of that high and mighty Mayhew family for you."

"What are you talking about?"

"Those people had written your father off long before he met me. When he died he had no insurance, and we were in so much debt. I was scared, so I went to them. I was counting on his parents' love for their son. Sabrina, they looked at me like I was dirt. They didn't even care that their son was dead. Do you know what they said?"

She shook her head.

"They told me he'd died a long time ago as far as they were concerned. He was an embarrassment to them." Tears rolled down Mamie's face. "They wrote a check for fifty thousand dollars and said it was mine, but only if I signed a document giving up any rights to their estate and saying I would never bother them again."

"You signed the agreement?"

"I did it for you. I needed the money and I wanted to give you a good life—a decent life. That's why I married that jerk. I did all this for you, but you were never satisfied. You always wanted more."

"But what's so wrong with wanting a life of wealth and security?"

"It's wrong when it doesn't come with honesty and hard work. You are a greedy girl, Sabrina."

"I didn't just want these things for me—I wanted them for you, too. Mama, I just wanted to make your life easier."

"At least be honest, Sabrina. This is all about you. You want to show off. You want everyone who has wronged you to see how successful you've become. Be happy with who you are. You had to have that fancy car, all those expensive clothes that you can't afford, and that condo . . ." Mamie shook her head sadly. "Sometimes I feel like I'm supporting two households."

"I didn't know you felt that way," Sabrina muttered. "I'm sorry. And I want you to know that I'm going to sell the condo. I'll sell everything, if that's what it takes to get you your money back."

"You can start with that car," Mamie suggested.

Sabrina's eyebrows rose in surprise.

"Oh, you thought I was going to fall for that trick. Not anymore. If you have to walk around buck naked, you're gonna get my money back. My name is on your car and your condo. If you don't sell them, I will."

She nodded. Sabrina got up and made her way to the door. There really wasn't any more to be said. This time her manipulations had cost her the love of her mother.

Mamie stopped her with her next words.

"Since you're gonna be selling that condo of yours, I know you will need somewhere to live." Her voice softened. "I guess you can stay in your old room, but just until you get your life straight."

Sabrina rushed to her, embracing her. "Thank you, Mama."

"I love you, chile, but sometimes you can work a nerve."

"I love you too. I never wanted to hurt you. I swear I didn't."

"I know that, baby. I just wish you'd stop hurting yourself."

"I'm going to pay you back, I promise." Sabrina kissed her mother on the cheek. "I'll see you later." She resumed her stride to the door.

"Where are you going?"

Sabrina glanced over her shoulder. "Home. I'm kind of tired."

"Don't you want to eat?"

"I'm not hungry, Mama." She gave Mamie a wry smile. "I'll call you tomorrow."

When Sabrina made it home, she walked through her condo, going from room to room, walking like a zombie. Tomorrow she was going to have to call a realtor and put her place on the market. She was going to have to sell her stock, her car, and probably some of her artwork—if not all. Sabrina was losing everything she had schemed to get.

She showered and slipped on a pair of silk pajamas. Sabrina

didn't bother to turn on the television. She just sat on the edge of her bed staring off into space.

Taking a deep breath, Sabrina fell to the floor on her knees.

"I know I deserve all that's happened," she whispered. "I'm a bad person. Mama's right. I'm greedy, self-centered—I'm even a liar. But the truth is that I don't want to be those things." It was a moment before she continued. "I wanted to be admired and respected . . . and envied." Her eyes rolled heavenward. "I know that's wrong, God. The reason I'm coming to you is because I want to fix this stuff. I want to be a better person. A good person."

70

"Lula, I don't know if I can do this." Tangie turned on her heel. "Let's go."

"Honey, we've driven two hours to Raleigh for this meeting. Now come on. This is something we both need."

Tangie stared at the door. "I can't believe we're doing this."

Lula took her by the hand. "The meeting will be starting soon. We should go inside."

Apprehension flowed through Tangie.

Lula handed her a cup of fruit punch. "Let's find some seats," she suggested.

"Near the back. That way we can leave when we want to."

"Okay, hon. Whatever makes you comfortable."

Tangie couldn't stop her trembling. She was scared of the unknown. This was her first meeting, and she had no idea what to expect.

A young woman strolled over to the podium. "Hello, everybody. My name is Janice, and I'm a sex addict. . . ."

Tangie reached over and took Lula's hand.

*   *   *

On the way back to Bridgeport, Tangie and her mother talked about the SAA meeting.

"When that one lady talked about her going after married men, I could really see myself in her," Lula confessed.

"One thing I realized tonight is that you really don't need Sex Addicts Anonymous. You're just doing this for me."

Inclining her head, Lula asked, "What are you talking about?"

"You loved those men, didn't you?"

"I loved Ben . . . and your father. With the others it was only about what I could get from them. I need these meetings for me, too. Remember, that Janice lady was saying that most of us have the same characteristics in common. One of those is that we're drawn to people who are unavailable to us." Lula grinned. "I'd say that's me in a nutshell."

"For me, sex was a way to escape reality, a way to be in control. I saw you being controlled by these men—you were at their beck and call for sex. That's all you really got from them. Sex and maybe a few trinkets here and there."

Lula stared straight ahead. "I didn't see it that way when I was younger."

"I felt like they took you away from me. I hated them, but I hated you more."

"Because you thought I chose them over you," Lula finished for her.

Tangie nodded.

"I guess in a way I did. Honey, I'm so sorry. I just wanted to be loved."

She glanced at her mother. "But why married men? You only went after married men."

"I thought they would do for me what they did for their families."

"You really believed that?"

Lula nodded. "Your father was the love of my life."

"But look how he treated you. He left you high and dry."

"Yes, he did," Lula admitted. "He didn't love me in return. He was out to satisfy his lusts. I believed his lies. . . . I don't regret it though."

"You don't?"

"If I hadn't met your father, I wouldn't have had you. I always wanted you, Tangie."

"But you let MeMa raise me." Shaking her head, Tangie continued, "I was never able to understand my grandmother. Why'd she have to be so mean?"

"I think that's just the way she was born. MeMa had been quick-tempered all her life."

"Don't get me wrong, Lula. MeMa did the best she could for me, but there were times she'd get in one of her moods . . . she would just go off on me and start calling me a whore."

"What?"

"MeMa was always doing that. She would always tell me that I was going to turn out just like you—only she was going to try and beat it out of me."

"MeMa beat you?"

Tangie shook her head. "No. She never got physical with me unless I really deserved it. She just threatened me all the time."

"I'm sorry."

"It's not something you could have prevented, Lula. MeMa was just mean and verbally abusive. No family is perfect."

"I should have taken care of you myself."

"Lula, it's okay. We can't change the past. We can only work on the present and look to the future."

"Did you notice back at the meeting how God kept coming up?"

Tangie nodded.

"It gave me an understanding why I've always felt like I've been missing something in my life. You ever feel that way?"

"Sometimes."

"I've been thinking about joining a church. Step three says that we have to make a decision to turn our will and our lives over to the care of God. I'm going to do that."

"You?"

"Yeah. If God is as wonderful as all these people are saying, then I want to get to know Him. I need to get to know Him." Lula gave a short laugh. "You don't think He'll nail the doors shut if I come?"

"You're really serious about this, huh?"

"I'm getting older. I want things in my life to change."

"Have you picked out a church already?"

"What about the one Brandon goes to? Don't you like that one?"

"Lula, I can't go back there. Brandon will probably think I'm stalking him."

"You don't have to hide from him, Tangie. Besides, step nine says that we have to make direct amends to people we've harmed."

"We just went to our first meeting and we're already on step nine," Tangie complained. "Lula, I don't know if I can do this. I just want to crawl into a hole and hide from the rest of the world."

"I'm not going to let you quit, hon. Now you know what a pest I can be."

Tangie couldn't help but laugh. "Lula, there are hundreds of churches we can go to—"

"I know," she interjected. "But this church is special to you. Your heart is there."

Tangie was dressed and ready by the time Lula arrived. She'd even purchased a study Bible to carry with her. Shopping for the Bible had been quite an adventure for Tangie. She'd had no earthly idea that so many styles, translations, and colors existed. After two solid hours in the bookstore, she selected a black leather-bound study Bible with large print and an NIV translation.

She and her mother slid into the very last pew at the start of the praise-and-worship portion of the service. Tangie caught a glimpse of Brandon in one of the rows near the front. She swallowed her heartache, intending to focus completely on the morning's sermon.

Tangie broke into a smile when her mother started to clap to the music. Neither one of them knew the words to any of the songs.

The pastor got up when the choir ended their song. He began his talk with Charlie Brown and Snoopy. He ended the tale with Charlie Brown moaning about not being right for the part in a play.

She had no idea where he was going with this story. What did it have to do with God? she wondered. Tangie didn't have to wait long for the answer.

"How many of us, like Charlie Brown, have looked in the mirror and felt like we were not right for the part?"

Tangie shifted in her seat.

"It's that feeling that turns into the attitude of rejection and inadequacy. This is a lie. A lie whispered to us by the devil. If this lie is not checked, it could lead to depression or worse. . . ."

The pastor had Tangie's full attention. When he asked the congregation to turn to Psalms, she had some trouble finding it. The spelling of the word threw her off. Finally she located it. Tangie read what the pastor called the eternal truth.

Psalms 51:5 stated, "For I was born a sinner—yes, from the moment my mother conceived me." This was a revelation to Tangie. *I was born into sin. Even if my mother had been married, I would have been born a sinner. Everybody in this church, including Brandon, started life this way. A sinner.*

The pastor was now explaining how sin separated a person from God.

That's why I never felt a bond with God, Tangie surmised.

No amount of washing can cleanse me. The thought brought her profound sadness. She yearned to know more about the Lord everyone spoke so lovingly about. This forgiving and gracious God.

"King David was honest with himself and recognized that he was a sinner. He called out to God to cleanse him and give him a pure heart. Psalms 51:2 says, 'Wash me, clean my guilt. Purify me from my sin.' "

Tangie repeated the scripture over and over in her mind. She didn't want to forget it.

After church, Brandon spotted her and came over.

"Hello, Tangie. How are you?"

"I'm fine. Brandon, this is my mother, Lula Thompson."

He shook her hand. "It's nice to meet you, finally."

"We enjoyed the service this morning."

"I'm glad to hear it." Brandon glanced over at Tangie. "It's really good to see you here."

"I enjoyed coming. I believe it's what I need right now."

Lula cleared her throat. "Hon, I'm going to the car."

"I can take you home," Brandon offered. "I'd like to talk to you."

"Lula, I'll meet you at your house."

She waved and was gone.

When they were alone, Brandon asked, "How are you doing, health-wise, Tangie?"

"I'm doing great." Walking toward his car, Tangie explained, "I'm going to have to have another HIV test in about four months, but since I had been tested over a year ago and then again recently, things are looking pretty good."

"I'm glad to hear it. I've been praying for you, Tangie."

"I destroyed that tape too. It was the best thing I could have ever done for myself."

Brandon held the car door open for her. "I miss you, Tangie."

"I miss you too."

He got in on the driver's side and closed the door. "I'm sorry about the way I treated you. I was in shock and I—"

"I hurt you, Brandon," Tangie interrupted. "I hurt you deeply, and I feel terrible about it. I didn't even realize how much I loved you until you walked out of my life. The one good thing that's come out of it is that I now know what my problem is."

"Come again?"

"I have a problem—an addiction, actually." Recalling step one of SAA, Tangie took a deep breath and said, "I'm a sex addict."

Brandon's eyes rose in surprise.

"I've joined SAA for support. I'm in the twelve-step program and I'm going to join the church, now that I know God loves me in spite of all I've done." A tear rolled down her cheek and she wiped it away. "It's still hard for me to believe that He would want anything to do with someone like me."

"God is awesome, Tangie. He loves us no matter what."

"I'm going to make Him proud." Tangie gave Brandon a tiny smile. "I want you to know something. I really meant it when I said that I loved you. No man has even made me feel the way you do. But you put me on a pedestal. You made me out to be this perfect woman, and deep down I was so unworthy."

"Sweetheart, I still think you're wonderful. I admire you for taking such an important step in your life."

"Lula deserves the credit—not me. She's in the program too. We're doing this together."

Brandon took Tangie's hand. "I want you to know that I'm here if you need a friend. Right now that's all I can offer you."

She nodded. "I need time as well. I have a lot of stuff I need to work out. Lots of layers to peel off until I find the real me." Tangie's voice broke. "Thank you, though. Thank you, for loving me."

71

Gerald packed up the last of his things. "You forgot this," Cordelia said. She handed him a shirt. "You sure you don't want to stay a little longer?"

"I need to get back to work. I'll try to come back on the weekends."

"Gerald, I want to say thanks for everything. We've been through a lot, but you've always come through for me in your own way. I'm sorry I didn't see it a whole lot sooner."

He met her gaze. "I still care for you, Dee. That won't ever change."

"I never thought I would say this, but you are not a bad guy. I once told you that I regretted marrying you. Gerald, I lied. I never should have said that."

"It hurt, Dee."

"I know. I would've felt the same way if you'd said that to me."

"What happened to us?" Gerald asked. "When Christina died, we didn't turn to each other."

"No, we didn't," Cordelia admitted. "I turned to God in my

pain, and nothing else mattered. Not even my family. I think that's why the stroke happened. It was my wake-up call."

"I know that God comes before all else, but family should be second in the scheme of things. With everything that happened to us, I resented God. He'd taken my child and then my wife."

"You're right. It actually took Bonnie to remind me of that." Sighing, Cordelia said, "I treated you and Devon unfairly. Can you ever forgive me?"

Gerald smiled and embraced her. "I've missed talking to you. We were such good friends once. Do you think that we'll ever get that back?"

"I want that too," Cordelia admitted. "It's been comforting having you back in the house. Although in the beginning . . ."

He burst into laughter.

Cordelia joined in. When the laughter died, she said, "Thank you. I will never forget the sacrifice you made. We wouldn't have made it without you."

"Yes, you would have. Dee, you would have found a way. Remember, I know you."

"Gerald, can I ask you something?"

"What is it?"

"Are you moving to Florida with your brother?"

"Been thinking about it. Why?"

"I don't want you to go," Cordelia admitted. "I'd feel better knowing you were only a couple of hours away."

Gerald smiled. "That admission was hard for you, wasn't it?"

Cordelia threw a pillow at him in response.

Cordelia and Devon stood in the doorway waving Gerald off.

"I feel like he's leaving us again."

Slipping an arm around her daughter, Cordelia said, "He's not really, honey. This time it's not in anger."

Devon glanced over at her mother. "Does this mean you've forgiven him?"

Cordelia nodded and closed the front door, locking it. "It's something I should have done a long time ago."

As they walked toward the den, Devon announced, "Mama, I think I've found an apartment. It's near the campus, and so is the day care. Daddy's offered to pay for Christina's day care while I'm in school."

Cordelia wasn't surprised. He was a doting grandfather.

"I'm going to miss you."

"Sweetie, I'm going to miss you and the baby. It really has been nice having her here. Christina's a good little girl."

Devon smiled. "I love my baby. I never thought I could love anybody as much as I love her."

"That's how I felt when you were born."

"How do you feel now?"

"The same way. Every time I look at you, it's like falling in love all over again. You are my pride and joy, Devon. I want all good things for you."

"I understand that now. Having Christina has given me a whole new perspective in life. I don't want anything bad to happen to her. I don't want anyone hurting my baby. I know I wasn't ready to be a mom, but this is the life I created. Now that Christina's here, I intend to be a good mother—just like you."

Cordelia was surprised.

"Mama, I'm sorry over the way I treated you. I felt like you were against my being happy. You were only trying to protect me. I see that now."

"You are going to be a good mother. She'll be angry with you and rebel just like you did, but you never give up. Do the best for your daughter—she'll thank you in the future."

"I hope so, Mama. I hope she won't put me through all the things I put you through."

Cordelia laughed. "Oh, honey, you're going to get that and more. A mother's revenge is grandchildren."

72

One year later

"I can't believe I'm getting married tomorrow," Tangie gushed.

"You are going to be a beautiful bride." Cordelia held up a glass of sparking cider. "I wish you much happiness."

Bonnie handed Tangie a plate laden with freshly baked chocolate chip cookies. "Just what you need—cookies."

Laughing, Tangie passed the plate to Devon. "No, thank you. Here, you have some."

"I'll pass. I'm still trying to get off the weight I gained from the baby."

"What weight?" Cordelia questioned. "Women would kill to look so good after having a child."

Devon embraced her mother. "You can have one cookie, Mama. Just one."

"Well, I'll just have a cookie myself," Bonnie said. "I'll go back on my diet after the wedding."

"Bonnie, I'll join you," Lula offered. "I'm not going to worry about a few more pounds."

The knock on the door drew a silence in the room.

"Who can that be?" asked Lula.

Tangie shrugged. "I wasn't expecting anybody." She broke into a wide grin. "I bet its Brandon."

Rising to her feet, Lula announced, "I'll get it. I'm going to let your future hubby know that he only has five minutes with you."

She came back to the family room and said, "It isn't Brandon."

"Then who is it?" Tangie asked.

Sabrina entered the room. "Hey, everyone. I hope I'm not intruding. I was going to leave this outside the door, but then . . . then I figured that the worst thing you could do was slam that same door in my face."

Cordelia and Bonnie glanced over at Tangie. None of them had seen Sabrina since her job transfer to another county thirteen months ago.

Tangie rose up on her knees. "No. You're not intruding, Sabrina." She gestured to an empty club chair. "Have a seat."

"I brought you a wedding present." She held out the gift to Tangie.

"Thank you, Sabrina. It's very thoughtful of you."

Earlier the room had been filled with laughter and light banter. Now there was only uncomfortable silence.

Bonnie spoke up. "You know, this last year has really been something, don't you think?"

"I'm sorry," Sabrina said quickly. "I was wrong and I'm sorry for everything."

"We've all made mistakes," Cordelia interjected quietly.

Sabrina continued. "I never meant to hurt you, Tangie, or any of you, by the things I said."

"Yes, you did," Tangie countered. "You were jealous and angry because your life wasn't going the way you wanted it to—you struck out at us." Tangie met Sabrina's gaze. "At least be a woman and admit it."

Sabrina swallowed hard. "You're right."

"Thank you for finally being honest."

"I regret it. All of it. Y'all were my friends . . . my only friends."

"I believe that much," Tangie uttered.

"I want y'all back in my life. I will be a much better friend this time around. I promise. Just please . . ." Sabrina's voice broke. "Please give me another chance."

Tangie wasn't moved by her plea. "You went through my things, Sabrina. You invaded my privacy."

"I was wrong for all of that. Tangie, I'm so sorry, and I'll do anything to earn your forgiveness."

"I forgive you, Sabrina. However, it's going to take time before I'll trust you again."

"I respect that." Sabrina looked at Bonnie expectantly. "Can you forgive me for the way I've treated you?"

Bonnie nodded and said, "I already have."

Sabrina shocked them all by bursting into heartrending sobs. Devon tried to console her.

Tangie jumped up and went to the bathroom to wet a washcloth. She returned and handed it to Devon.

Sabrina's crying came to an end. She accepted the washcloth and wiped her face.

"Are you okay, Sabrina?" Cordelia asked.

She nodded. "All the mistakes I've made came back all at once. I guess I was overwhelmed. I was a horrible person."

"It's painful to admit it, though, isn't it?" Cordelia placed a reassuring hand on Sabrina's arm. "I'm guilty of making terrible mistakes myself. I lorded my faith over everyone and sat in judgment of everyone—including my family."

Sabrina remained silent. Her eyes had become bright with unshed tears.

"I wasn't that great a person either." Tangie dropped down into a nearby chair. "I guess none of us are perfect." She held out her hand to Sabrina. "It takes courage to face up to our

344   *Jacquelin Thomas*

wrongdoings and try to correct them. I applaud you for selling all your stuff to give your mother the money back."

"Tomorrow is a day of new beginnings, so tonight we're going to leave our past behind," Bonnie announced. "We will renew our friendships and strive to be even better. A friend is someone who knows all the bad stuff about you and still loves you no matter what."

"That's the truth," Lula intoned. "You guys have been through so much separately. You made it through, but just think . . . think how much better it would be if you'd had a friend to share it with." She placed a hand on Bonnie's shoulder.

Bonnie agreed. Taking Sabrina by the hand, she said, "Love and laughter bring you friends, but it's the heartache and tears that build your friendship."

"Forgiveness is the ingredient that seals the friendship." Taking Tangie's hand, Cordelia continued, "And makes it everlasting."